THE ABSOLUTION OF AIDAN

KATHY COOPMANS

Granette

Absolution

Kathy Coopmans

Copyright

@Copyright
Kathy Coopmans

Editor: Julia Goda Editing Services
https://www.facebook.com/juliagodaeditingservices/?fref=ts

Formatting: Affordable Formatting
https://www.facebook.com/AffordableFormatting74135

Dedication

**This book is dedicated to my dad, James Richardson.
I will always be your little girl, and you will always be the man who taught me to do the right thing.**

PROLOGUE

DEIDRE

"Please dad. Get me out of here. I... You know I hate hospitals." I'm so tired. All I want to do is sleep for days, weeks even. I'm forced to lie on my stomach, for at least two weeks the doctor said, while these wounds on my back heal.

I have twenty-six cuts across my back and shoulders, two of them deep enough to require stitches. The majority of them will disappear; they're minor, they say. Minor to whom? Them? It's the scars on the inside I'm more concerned about. Who's going to nurse them back to health? Make them evaporate into thin air? No one. They will be there for the rest of my life.

"Honey. This is the best place for you to be. You need to heal." My mom tries her best to settle me down. Heal! Heal! Heal! That word has become my most hated word; if I ever hear it again, I may kill the person who says it.

Beth La Russo, the best mother a woman could ask for, takes hold of my limp arm, running her hand up and down in what I assume is supposed to be a soothing gesture. *Don't say the 'H' word anymore, mom.* Of course, I don't say that to her. I really would never do anything to purposely hurt my mom or my dad, but god, can't they see I'm losing it here?

My body is entirely numb. Drugged up on morphine to ease the pain of the scars that Royal Diamond left behind, permanently reminding me of his legacy of maiming people with a knife.

My wrists are raw, black, and blue, covered in cuts and scrapes from where I was frantically trying to escape the chains I was hanging down from like a slaughtered animal.

My body may be free of pain at the moment. However, there isn't a damn thing anyone can do to erase the plague of shit that's running through my head. I desperately want to sleep. But I'm fighting it with every ounce of strength I have left. If I sleep, he will be there. He will kill me and he will beat Aidan more. Or force him to watch while he does vile, repulsive things to my body. Things I will never forget. Things that will haunt me if I sleep. Even though he didn't touch me sexually or rape me like he threatened to. That doesn't mean I can forget. I still feel his hands on me. The knife scraping across my skin. My name rolling off his tongue like a sudden high tide.

I know he's dead. I've been reminded repeatedly by my dad over and over while I lay here on my stomach begging them to get me out of here. I can't be here. I feel trapped. This tiny hospital room is closing in on me by the second. I can't breathe. I can't move my arms. I need to move them. I need to walk to see with my own two eyes that Alina, Aidan, and everyone I care about are safe. Hell, my chest feels so tight I can barely breathe. Maybe if I succumb to this sleepiness sensation my inner awareness is commanding I need, I will forget. Concentrate on the good. The only problem is, there isn't anything good about any of this. I'm mutilated, scarred for life. Again, it's all on the inside. I cannot stop my brain from wheeling around like a giant tornado. It keeps spinning and spinning.

"Sweetheart, you need to rest. Close your eyes and sleep. We will both be here when you wake up." Stefano La Russo, my father, the only man I will ever trust, will ever let touch me again, squeezes my leg through the blankets that feel like they are suffocating me everywhere.

"No," I scream loudly. My mom jumps from the side of the bed I'm facing at the tone of my voice. "He's here. I know he is. He... he said he'll kill me. Drug me and rape me. He will, too. That evil man is capable of doing anything. Why won't you listen to me? Why won't you help me? HELP.ME!" I scream.

Soft muffles escape my mom's mouth, her hands flying up to cover her face.

"He can't hurt you, baby. He's dead. You're safe now," my dad says, trying to soothe me.

"He's not really dead," I choke out. Royal Diamond may not be alive on this earth anymore but by god, he is in my head. He's there. All I can see is his face. His bloodshot angry eyes. His filthy hands on my body. His fingers stroking my skin. That knife digging into my back. He's surrounding me. Cutting off my air supply. Taking away my sanity. My will to survive.

"Son of a bitch," eases out of my dad's mouth.

"Stefano, we have to do something." I crane my neck the best I can to see my dad's reaction to what my mom said.

His nostrils are flaring. He's gripping the steel frame at the edge of the bed. The man who never loses control, unless he's in the courtroom, looks as if he's ready to unhinge.

He says nothing as he exits my room, disappearing from my sight. *Please bring the doctor back, dad, persuade them to get me out of here.* I want to lie in my small twin bed in the home I grew up in. That's where I feel safe. No one will touch me there. My dad won't allow it.

"I swear to god, mom, if he doesn't convince the doctor to get me out of here, I'm going to lose it." Tears fall down my face. I try to reach up and wipe them away. I can't. My arms are too weak to move. Either that or I simply don't give a shit if they fall. I don't care about anything except getting out of this hospital, getting away from his voice that's taunting me in my head. One minute he's speaking low, the next he's screaming. Voices, so many variations of Royal's voice. His laugh is the worse. Devious. Deathly. Destructive.

I sag into the bed, defeated, trying helplessly to focus on something or someone else.

Aidan Hughes. I can focus on him. No, not him. Images of his bruised and battered face invade my mind, mixing with those voices.

Aidan can never see me like this. He's lodged in my head too. I should hate him after the things he said to me, the way he treated me after we gave in to the carnal desire we felt for each other. I know I treated the man poorly, but he just kept getting under my skin. His deep voice. His bright blue eyes. His muscular body. His six-foot-something frame. I hate him.

Oh, I heard him, all right, demanding for me to hang on while I felt like I was going to die every time Royal pierced me with his knife. He even called me baby a few times. He's a callous asshole. A user. A fucking tool of a man, and I don't want to see him. I've gone insane. I don't want or need anybody. They can let me die. Yes. The only way to get rid of any and all of these voices in my head is to die.

"Deidre." An older woman comes into my room, followed by my dad. The look of concern on their faces stops me in the tracks of plotting ways to kill myself.

"I'm Doctor Jenkins. Your father here has told me you want to leave. I cannot discharge you. This is the best place for you to be. You have to heal. Now, are you in any pain, sweetheart? Would you like the nurse to give you—"

"Noooooooooooooo! Quit saying I have to heal! You don't know what I need or have to do! None of you do!" I scream. Her body jolts back.

I've fucking had it with these people not listening to me. I start to thrash in the small bed. Kick the covers off. My body is so weak I have no idea what the hell I'm doing. All I know is if they won't help me, then I will help myself. I will get out of here. I will. Then I will die. The howling laughter, the slimy deep tones, their faces, they will all be gone.

"Deidre. My god. Stop." I feel my dad gripping my legs to try and calm me down.

"Fuck all of you. Get off of me." Somehow I manage to get up on my knees. Out of the corner of my eye I see two men run into my room. I move like lighting and rip the IV out of my arm. I feel my stitches tearing open in my back. I don't care. I need to get the fuck away, get him out of my head. Get everyone away from me. Life is too much for me right now. I'm completely depleted, both internally and externally. My limit has been reached. The tether has snapped. My nerves are shattered.

Suddenly, it happens. I drift away. And just like that, I feel nothing at all.

When I finally wake up, my eyes are blinking rapidly to the blinding sunlight coming from the one and only window in a cheerily bright room. I see pale yellow walls, smell fresh flowers. *Where in the hell am I?* This is definitely not my old room. My old room is green. I have Justin Timberlake plastered all over my walls, not pictures of a spectacular sunset or a photo of a woman walking through a field of wildflowers.

I close my eyes for a few moments, my head groggy. My throat is incredibly dry. Maybe I'm dead, and this is my cheery, little room in heaven. I must be dead. I feel no pain.

Recollection hits me like a freight train, the memoires smashing into me, taking my breath away. I have no idea where the hell I am. I'm exhausted, mentally weak. And I sure as crap am not dead.

A throat clears in the corner. Lifting my head from the comfort of my pillow, I beam at the sight of my mom sitting on a floral print couch. Her beautiful appearance stares at me with a smile spreading clear across her face.

"Mom." My ability to speak is strained.

"Oh god, sweetie." She stands. Her small frame is so much smaller than I remember. She looks terrible, for lack of a better word. Older even. I have no clue how long I have been out. I remember everything, except for where I am or how I got here. So many questions are running a long distance marathon in my head. I need answers.

"Where am I?" I rasp out.

"Let me get the nurse, honey." She steps up beside me, picks up a cord, and presses a button.

Her delicate fingers then slide through my hair, brushing it back from my face.

"You look so rested, sweet girl." Tears stream down her face when she talks. There's something in the way she's looking at me that sets me on edge. Don't ask me how I know when my head doesn't even feel like it's attached to my body. I know my mom though, and something is wrong.

I wiggle my toes, my fingers. Lift my arms just to make sure all my limbs are still there.

Before I can ask her what's troubling her, a young, tall woman walks in. Her skin is flawless, her smile contagious.

"Good morning, Deidre. My name is Karrie and I'm your nurse during the day. It's a pleasure to finally meet you," she speaks cheerily.

"Mom." I look at her for answers.

"It's okay, honey. Let her do what she needs to do, and we will talk when she is done." She looks to Karrie and nods her head. I watch Karrie skitter from monitor to monitor, hitting buttons, adjusting the drip in my IV. She doesn't say a word as she takes my blood pressure, my temperature, and my pulse.

"Are you thirsty?" Her smile is warm, her touch feather light on my arm.

"Yes," I say.

"I'll give it to her," Mom says, the two of them exchanging a familiar glance. I'm quickly becoming agitated. Both of them are keeping something from me. Something monumental. I can sense it.

"Sure. I'll let Dr. Brown knows she's awake." *Who the hell is Dr. Brown?*

"Mom. What the hell is going on?" I ask the minute Karrie is out of sight.

She exhales. Tears swell in her eyes.

"I think we need to wait for your dad." Turning her back on me, she slumps her shoulders forward.

"Where is he?"

"He went to make a call. He should be back here… here he is. She's awake." Her slender frame twists toward him.

Dad comes into my sight. Jesus, he looks worse than my mom. *What in the ever-loving hell is going on?*

"Damn it," I say to the both of them. I cough afterward. Mom reaches for the water, bringing it up to my mouth. I sip as much as I can. The cool, crisp tingle feels like heaven soaking into my cotton-dry mouth.

"I know everything that happened before I came to wherever the hell I am, but what I don't know is, what are you keeping from me? Am I dying? Is my back not healing right? What is it?" One of the monitors beside me starts beeping faster and louder, the sound driving me even crazier than I know I already am.

"Deidre. Calm down. It's nothing like that at all." Dad glides to the other side of my bed, then bends down and peppers my face with kisses. "We've missed you so much, sweet girl." He brushes my hair back just like Mom did.

"You've been out for three weeks, honey." His manner is light.

"Three weeks?" I look between the two of them. Christ, I had no idea I was out that long. No wonder I'm lying on my back. The pain from being cut is barely there anymore.

"We're in Maryland at a woman's health care retreat facility. You had a nervous breakdown, Deidre. Your mind completely shut down." I shake my head at my dad's words. *Is this his nice way of saying I'm crazy? That I've lost my mind?* Because if it is, that's what I was trying to convey to them all along.

There's more though than what he's telling me. I know my parents.

7

My mom isn't looking at me. She's caught up in her own head, looking out the window. My dad is looking at her. It's as if they are both waiting to see who will speak first.

My mom does, and the words that tumble out of her mouth have me gasping, shaking, and screaming one loud "WHAT?"

"You're pregnant, Deidre," she repeats.

To say I'm conscious now would mean I have woken from nothingness, neither seeing nor hearing a damned thing. My view of my surroundings goes off into forgetfulness. For the past few weeks, my entire existence has been scattered off into the universe of the unknown. Living in lala land. Those weeks are gone. Poof. Vanished.

But this. Those three words coming from my mom's mouth I heard loud and clear. How could this be? I've always been safe when I had sex, was never unprotected.

"Oh, god." My brain shoots to my stomach. Immediately, my hands span across there too. "The baby." Those are the only words I can seem to get out. I clutch my stomach, pain ratcheting to my heart. I've been drugged by a madman, then drugged again at the hospital, and now I still have drugs dripping into my arm. I panic, my hand sailing to tear the IV out.

"Deidre, what the hell are you doing?" Strong hands grip me by my shoulders, pressing me back into the bed. My dad's face is hovering over me.

"Drugs. I've been pumped full of them." I panic.

"And your unborn child will be fine." A woman steps into my room, wearing black jeans and a white-pink, loose t-shirt. Her gray hair is styled into a sleek bob.

"Good morning, Dr. Brown. As you can see, we've just told her." Mom pulls up a chair beside the bed and sits down, folding her hands in her lap, her sternness screaming at me to stay composed.

Glancing up to this Dr. Brown, who is not dressed like a doctor at all, I sense the same tranquility of peace from her as I did from nurse

Karrie. On the inside, I start to laugh uncontrollably. I'm in a god-forsaken nut house, so of course they are all going to act peaceful, quiet, and collected. God forbid they should upset the crazy lady, who somehow got herself pregnant by a man who hates her fucking guts.

And so it begins.

Eight months of therapy. Confined to a place I learned to love. A place where I coped with being kidnapped, tortured, and learning I was pregnant. Followed by every test imaginable to make sure the health of my unborn child was not jeopardized in any way from the events that brought me here.

I've been hiding out for the past few months, building the courage to face reality.

Now, a year later, with so much more to tell, I'm heading to tell my best friend I have a baby. Not just my baby.

Aidan's baby.

CHAPTER ONE

AIDAN

"You Bastard," What's-her-name hollers while gathering her clothes off my living room floor. I hate this shit. Do these chicks think it's only men who get all decked out, head out for a night on the town, looking for a piece of ass for the night? I mean, what in the ever-loving fuck? Seriously, though? This chick wanted me the minute I walked through the damn door of Jim Bob's.

That's right. There's a bar in New York called Jim Bob's. Best damn bar around. That man and his staff can mix a mean straight up double shot of Jim Beam. On the rocks. Neat. Dirty. Shit, they'd even leave a drink out for Santa if you asked them to.

"You really have problems, dude!" she squeals louder than a mouse when you step on its tail. While I conspire to steal guns, I bet this bitch conspires with other women on how to set fire to a man's ears. "You're a dick. An asshole. Trash." Jesus, I love a pissed off woman, sassy and a mouth made to fuck, but not from her.

She needs to tell me something I don't already know. Like how the hell to make her understand I want her gone?

If a guy screws around, fucks anything that walks, he's a man-whore, or a bastard in this chick's case, as she calls me the word once again. But if a woman does it and we call her a bitch or a slut, then holy war breaks out. They become irrational, insensitive, and irate. Fucking women.

"You got the name right, sweetheart, now please leave." I lift my brows, standing there with the door to my apartment wide open. "I hope your dick rots off. It shouldn't take very long as small as it is." She storms past me, her blond hair hitting me in the face, the scent of her cheap-ass perfume filling my nostrils. *Christ, Aidan, you can pick them, man. Classy.*

Slamming the door shut with my bare foot, I burst out fucking laughing at her comment about my dick. She wasn't screaming that half an hour ago when she actually saw how big he is. The bitch actually started gagging. Hence why she suggested Viagra. I mean, good lord, what man's dick wouldn't deflate once a woman starts to gag, then looks up to you shaking her head no. And this is my fault? No damn joke.

The only thing she got right all night is that I am a bastard. Hell, that plus worthless or piece of fucking shit. Take your pick. Those words right there stop my laughing in an instant.

My entire life, my own mother has called me every name except the name she gave me at birth. Now you talk about a fucking bitch. She's the queen bee of them all. Fucking rich bitch with an even richer husband and my fucking punk of a half-brother. Fuckers. I hate them all.

I have no clue who my biological father is. In reality, I am a bastard. So fuck that bitch right along with my worthless mother.

I haven't spoken to any of them in five years. Even then it was only in passing at my grandfather's funeral. God, I miss that old man. He was the only one in my entire family who made me feel like I was worth something. Always picking me up from the mansion that seemed to stretch a mile fucking wide in the middle of the Pocono Mountains. I hated that place about as much as I hated the people who lived in it.

My grandfather and I never talked about why he wouldn't come inside of his only child's home. I know it had everything to do with my step-dad and my envious half-brother. But what did they all expect when every time he did come around all they would ask about was his land? They even stooped as low as having little Ryan Junior start questioning him about it. The kid had no idea what the heck he was even talking about. I have no doubt that's why he cut his ties completely from them all. Including Junior.

Every single letter I've received from either my mother or her power-hungry attorney have gone in the trash, every phone call to voice mail. I have nothing to say to her. She wants the hundreds of acres of land my grandfather willed to me. Fuck her. I know all she wants to do is sell it. Pad her wallet even more. The bitch can die with all her money. She sure as shit won't ever get her hands on that land. I have no idea what I will do with it, if anything, but it's mine. I may just leave it the hell alone. Why not? My grandfather did. I loved walking that land with him. He was the only one who I could release everything bottled up inside of me to. Got me started my love for Jim Beam. "I love ya, old man," I mumble.

I flick the lock on my door and make my way into my kitchen, grabbing my bottle of Jim beam off the counter, taking a long slow gulp. The burn feels priceless as it smoothly flows down my throat. Thanks to my two good buddies Cain and Roan, I have this thirty-seven hundred square foot apartment overlooking the skyline of New York, on the same floor, right around the corner of the hall where Roan and his now live -in girlfriend Alina Solokov live. Lucky fuckers. Both of them. I never in a million years thought I could settle down with one woman, but hell, I hate being single. I want it all. The woman who only has eyes for me. Someone to talk to. To hold at night. To fuck when I want to. To tell me she loves me and that I'm worth something.

"You're so fucked up, dude." I take another swig. This one is even longer. It burns. It burns so damn good.

Twisting the cap back on, I sit it back on the black marble counter. I stare at the deep blue-black of the counter, flashes of the same color running through my mind. A color so rich and dark, it's the prettiest color I have ever seen. Until in a flash, it was fucking gone.

Deidre La Russo. "FUCK!" I shout. I've tried to forget every damn thing about her. I brace my hands on the edge of the counter and tilt my head down, taking a deep breath, waiting for the guilt to flow quicker into my veins than any amount of Jim Beam can do. I'd give anything for her to storm through my door with her attitude. Any damn thing at all.

After everything that happened to her, she up and disappeared. Guilt ate me up worse than the brutal beating and the drugs Roan's brother inflicted on me. The unmentionable things he did to that woman while I was forced to watch. I cringe when the sound of her screams ring out in my ears. I can still hear them from time to time after a nightmare, when I wake up in a cold sweat, only to realize that motherfucker is dead. But her...I will never be able to forget her, nor the things we said to each other. The names I called her. Christ. The moment I could get out of that hospital bed, I did. The first thing I did was check on her. Make sure she was going to be ok, only to my surprise she was gone. Fucking gone and for a year, her parents have kept her whereabouts a damn secret.

Why I'm all of a sudden thinking of her now beats the hell out of me. *You're always thinking of her, you asshole. Always.*

Maybe it's because I've never had a woman rile my ass up the way she did, with her sassy attitude. Her sweet, yet tart mouth. And her ass. What man in their right mind doesn't love a nice ass? The moment I walked into her apartment over a year ago and I saw her with her back to me, my instincts shot straight for her ass, and hell, the first thing that ran through my mind was how round it was. I hadn't even seen her face yet and I wanted to grab that ass and grip it tight like a damn bowling ball, squeeze for firmness and flexibility.

And then she turned around. I had nearly came undone, was void of speaking. I've seen some beautiful women in my twenty-nine years, but Christ, not a damn one of them compared to her.

Those hazel eyes blinked in astonishment at me. Most women do when they get their first look. I'm not one to brag, and shit, but I'm a big guy. I can only imagine the first thing that ran through her mind was 'Holy shit, this dude is big.' I'm six foot seven. I do my best to keep myself in shape, working out as much as I can with Cain and Roan. Most people fear me, claim I intimidate them, but not her. She stood tall, even though she can't be much over five foot five or so. When those first words tumbled out her sexy as fuck mouth, I knew right there I was imperially screwed.

"Who the hell are you?" she said, her hands firmly planted on her curvy hips.

"Don't act like you have no clue who I am," I dropped my bag on the floor. My long legs carried me straight to her. I was there to protect her. She didn't realize it, but she was about to get her first lesson; either that or I wanted to shove my tongue down her throat.

"We all know there's a dangerous man out there. One who will kill anyone who gets in his way of getting what he wants. He wants your best friend, and what do you do the minute I knock on your door?" I leaned into her, my face close enough to see the gold flecks in her eyes. She didn't budge, flinch, not a damn thing except tilt her head up to look right at me. Those long raven-colored locks of hers touched the tip of her apple-shaped ass.

"What? Are you pissed off because I didn't greet you at the door? Say 'Oh hey, badass guy, thanks for invading my privacy? And double thanks for making sure I stay cooped up in my apartment until psycho man is found?'" Her brows lifted, waiting for me to answer. My answer was in the palm of my hand. Literally. I wanted to bend her over my knee right there and spank her ass.

"You never holler 'Come in,'" I quote. "You go to the door and you check the peep hole. That's what it's made for. You get me?" I glared down at her.

"You're a dick," she retorted.

"Don't get me started on my dick, sweet-tart, little thing. You can't handle my dick."

From there it was game on. The two of us couldn't say jack shit to the other without it turning into a full-fledged yelling match.

I stand here and shake my head, thinking about that woman and her damned mouth. Christ almighty, she has a mouth on her.

And could she ever suck cock with that mouth. Fuck. Now I'm hard. I'm always so damn hard to the point I realistically ache everywhere whenever I think of her. My chest. My mind. God.

My way of thinking goes right to that night we hooked up. The things she did with her mouth. The way her ass felt in my hands. It felt exactly the way I knew it would. God knows I've had my eyes glued to the way it moved the entire time. I wanted her more than I've ever wanted anything in my life, and when those words "Fuck you" tumbled out of her mouth, I snapped like a rubber fucking band. Swung her sexy ass around, shoved her against the wall, and did just what she said. I fucked her. Hard. Fast. She took all of me in her tight pussy. Her stunning eyes turned damn near as black as her hair when I dropped my pants and she got her first glimpse of my pierced cock. Four bars underneath the shaft that was angry and ready to stroke her walls, to give her the best fuck of her life.

She looked back up to me, her mouth opening then closing again. Then I sheathed myself, hoisted her up, those toned legs wrapping around my waist, shoved her panties to the side, and slid my dick in her. She screamed my name. My real name. Aidan. No woman has called me by my real name in years. I got lost in that woman. Five times to be exact. And now, fuck. I'd give anything to hear her call me by my name again.

I shake my head. She's gone. I need to clear my thoughts of her.

I take a quick glance at the clock on my stove. Nine o'clock. "Shit, it's still early," I say once again to all these walls in this place.

Shoving my sorry ass away from the counter, I grab my keys out of my pocket, then shove them right back in. I've been drinking. I can't fucking go anywhere. "Goddamn it." I run my hands through my hair in frustration and head toward the tall windows overlooking New York.

Again I wonder if Deidre is out there somewhere. What the hell she's doing. If she's all right.

"Open up, asshole." A loud bang on my door along with the boisterous sound of Roan fill the hallway and the silence in this place.

"Fuck off," I say when I swing the door open. I'm agitated as hell. Grateful now that his pompous ass has stopped by. Well, maybe not, once I really get a good look at what a disheveled mess he is.

"What the hell, dude. You look worse than I do." His hair is all over the place, his brows wrinkled. Ever since the earth has been free of Roan's wacked out brother, he's been laid back. The stunned expression on his face tells me he's anything but laid back right now.

"I'm cool." He saunters in, heads right for my favorite black recliner, and sits his ass down.

"You just got back. What the hell are you doing here?" I shut the door behind him.

He just sits there and stares at me.

I'm dumbfounded as hell. It isn't like him to show up at my place out of the blue, especially when he just got home. His dick is bound and fucking gagged to Alina, so what the hell?

"Alina has some shit to do. I'm bored out of my mind. Can't a guy have a drink with his friend?" He chuckles. Lying ass. Something is up.

"All I have is my Beam, man. You hate that shit." He pulls his ass up a few inches out of the chair, smiling in a way to annoy the hell out of me, slides his hand behind him, and then starts waving a silver flask in the air. "Fucking hilarious," I mumble.

"You want some?" he asks after downing probably half of his expensive shit.

"No. What I want is for you to tell me why you're really here." I raise

16

my brow in question.

"I told you. She's busy. Now, sit your ass down. Let's watch the game."

The little prick snatches up my remote and turns on the ball game. I eyeball the man I know all too well for the rest of the night, suspicious of his actions. He's hiding something from me. Why is it that I have a sinking feeling deep in my gut that whatever it is has something to do with me?

CHAPTER TWO

DEIDRE

My nerves are tingling, like I'm being tickled all over with a silk-like feather when I pull into a parking lot next to the building where Alina is now living.

Thanks to my parents, I know that she moved in with Roan after Royal was finally killed. I couldn't be happier for her. She was always the first person I asked about whenever they came to visit me. I've missed her more than anything.

Her reaction to seeing me is the only thing I've thought about the entire drive over here. My whereabouts for the past year have been tightly sealed. It hasn't been easy for my mom and dad. They stuck true to their word by not telling anyone until I was ready to tell people myself. They've also told me Alina calls them regularly just to check up on me. I can only hope her reaction to seeing me after all this time is the welcoming reply I'm hoping for.

Sitting in my parking spot, my palms are sweaty and the words I've wanted to say to her choke me half to death as they claw their way up my throat, only to plummet right back down to the acid building in my stomach. Will she even want to see me? Will she be disappointed in me for up and running? What will she say when she finds out about Diesel?

Anxiety smashes into me, my every thought filled with how any of these people I left behind will react when they find out about my sweet, little baby boy. Especially his father. But I cannot think about Aidan right now. One person and one step at a time.

Surely none of them can deny Diesel isn't Aidan's. He looks just like him. Dark hair. Blue eyes. And he's big for only being three months old.

"You can do this, Deidre. You have to," I say to myself. I tug the keys out of the ignition after shutting it off. My shaky hands reach for the door handle. With one last deep breath, I open the door and step out, closing it behind me. I smile when I retrieve my sleeping son out of his car seat, sling his diaper bag over my shoulder, and kick the door shut.

"You're a chunky, little thing," I'm speaking to his sleeping form, inhaling his sweet baby scent. Call me crazy, but the minute my mom told me I was pregnant, I've been completely consumed by his heath as well as my own and the ability to nurture him. For the two of us to adapt to one another. To be the best mom I can be. Love him, soothe him, and be there for him like my parents have always been there for me.

Even though he doesn't understand a word I say to him, I've told him every day how he needs both his parents. Aidan and I aren't together and we never will be, but that doesn't mean our child shouldn't know the both of us. Both Diesel and Aidan deserve to know each other.

Aidan is going to shit a brick, for lack of a better term, but the truth is this little boy is his.

I can hear him now. His mouth denying it. Yes, we used a condom, every time we had sex. Doesn't mean one didn't break. Especially with a man the size of him. Oh, and lets not forget those piercings. God, my pussy clenches remembering the way his dick felt the first time he entered me. My mouth nearly hit the floor when I saw those bars. God, I've never felt anything like it. The way they scraped against my walls, not in a painful way, but giving me the most pleasurable orgasmic feeling I have ever had.

"You're losing it, Deidre." Yes. I chat with myself a lot. Par for the course when you're lost in your own head for a year. The only things consuming you are your inner demons. Your ability to go from one day to the next. I conquered it for my little man and myself. I'm stronger than I was before I was taken, proud of it too. Most importantly, I'm happy.

"Here we go, bud." I step into the building, the bright lights stirring my little man in my arms. It's early evening, the dark clouds in the sky indicating a storm is brewing. I pray to god there won't be a storm inside this building when Alina sees me.

I stroll across the tiled floor, the heels of my wedge sandals digging into the bottom of my feet. "Mommy needs to wear better shoes when I carry you, Mr. Chunky Man." I drop my gaze to one of the only men I need in my life, and he's zonked out again. Figures. All he does is eat, poop, and sleep. I suppose most babies do. I cannot wait until I hear him speak. I tell him every day his first word better be momma or his butt's in big trouble.

I kiss him once again. Having him near me seems to shove some of my nervousness aside. It's funny how my big bundle of joy can calm me without saying a word.

I head straight for the security guard sitting behind his stand next to the elevator. I've been here a few times before well over a year ago. This man is new. Distinguished looking. I swear I see some sort of appreciation flicker across his face when I approach. Then he glances to the big bundle I'm holding in my arms, and the flicker disappears. I internally roll my eyes at the cute but now a total douche man. I'm a smart enough woman to know most men want nothing to do with a woman who has a child. I say fuck them all, beginning with this asshole. I don't need him or any man.

"Hi. I'm Deidre La Russo," I say politely, even though I want to smack his face off his body.

"Yes. I received a call from Salvatore Diamond that you're here to surprise Roan and Alina. I just need to see your ID and I can let you go up?" the dickhead guard requests. I'm thankful my dad works for the Diamond family. His call earlier to Salvatore, Roan's dad, must have gone well. He had to call someone in order for me to get upstairs without them knowing I was down here waiting for them. This needs to be done my way. And my way is to just get this all out in the open at once. Salvatore promised his discreetness. I appreciate him for it.

I reach into the diaper bag, which is also my purse, pull out my wallet, and hand him my ID. He scans it over then hands it back to me while his eyes travel up and down my body. Fuck off, dickface. You just turned your nose down on my baby and now you have the nerve to pop your eyeballs out of your head and gawk at my boobs.

"Thank you," I say casually. My urgency to get upstairs and get this over with outweighing the fact I like being ogled, even if he is a twat. Wait? Isn't that what all men want? Until they see a woman holding a baby, that is. Jerk.

Diesel decides to fully awaken at this time. He grunts and stretches, his eyes blinking to the light. Lifting his head, he looks at me with his sleepy, little eyes, then lays his head right back down on my shoulder.

I shrug at the guard then walk to the elevator. One thing I haven't forgotten is how to swing my ass. And it's a swinging. I know he's staring too. I can feel it.

I may have a baby, but every part of my body still functions properly. Including my fingers, which would love to flip the fuckface off. Nope, I remind myself again. I definitely do not need a man.

The elevator dings and opens right after I push the button.

Stepping inside with a deep breath, I kiss my boy on the side of his chubby, little face. The doors click shut behind me. My stomach hits the floor the minute we start to climb.

Diesel reaches forward and grabs a chunk of my hair. "Ouch. You decided to wake up, huh?" I wrinkle my nose at him. He lets out a little snort. By the time we come to a stop, I think he's pulled out half of my hair and shoved it into his mouth.

One step off of the elevator has me coming to a complete halt when I hear a voice I'm not prepared to hear yet.

"You got the name right, sweetheart, now please leave," I hear him say. I scurry around the corner, my heart playing as fast as a fiddle in my chest. "Christ," I whisper as I rest my head against the wall. For the first time since Diesel started chewing on my hair, I'm thankful he has his mouth full right now or he'd be babbling away. God, this is so not how I wanted this to happen.

I wait until I hear the ding of the elevator and the slamming of a door. Does he live here? If he does, I have not been informed of that, and I will definitely be asking my parents why the hell they did not tell me.

Curiosity does get the better of me, though. I need to see what she looks like. I peak around the corner. Her back is to me. My examination of her is quick when she steps in and starts to turn around.

Tall, blond. Shortest damn skirt I've ever seen. God. Is she a hooker?

I look back to the now closed elevator door, then down to my boy. "If he's messed up with hookers, then maybe I don't want you around him at all." He tilts his head to the side. His little, chubby hand comes up and smacks me in the face. "Ha," I whisper to him. "You're never going to date, buddy."

A few seconds later, I'm standing in front of Alina's apartment. "You got this." I reach up with clammy hands, press the doorbell, and wait.

"Oh, my god, Deidre!" Alina exclaims, pleased to see me. At that juncture, she goes silent. She shifts her gaze down to Diesel, then back to me. Her expression turns to shock, then wonder.

"Deidre. I... he's—"

"Mine. Yes," I say with excitement.

"Come in." She moves out of the way so we can step inside.

"You have got to be shitting me?" Roan smirks, glimpsing down at the baby.

"Well, hello to you too, Roan. And no, I'm not shitting you. However, this one," I point to Diesel, "shit's a lot."

"Wow. I'm not sure what to say," he stresses, then laughs lightly. I'm assuming he finally got my 'shit' joke.

"That's exactly what I said when I first found out I was pregnant." I move to the couch. My feet are killing me. Not to mention Diesel is now starting to fuss.

"Is this why you disappeared?" Roan points down to Diesel where I've laid him down on the couch. I drop the diaper bag on the floor. *Well, let's get right to the point here, Roan.*

"No." I begin to pull out all the items I need to change his diaper. I've pined away for days now about the right way to approach everyone, not only about the baby, about everything. Why I really left. What took me so long to come back. All of it. Now, here I sit, changing my son's diaper, and my speech is gone, as if it's floating down the Hudson River. I sigh and fold up the dirty diaper, stuffing it back inside the bag along with everything else.

"May I hold him?" I pause mid-stride from setting him on my lap.

"Of course." I smile as Alina holds out her arms and slips her hands under his armpits, taking him from me. Silence falls all around us, the only noise coming from Diesel's baby gibberish.

I swallow and sit further back on the couch, my hands folded on my lap.

"Please listen to everything I have to say before you ask me questions," I release blatantly, then swipe a wayward tear from my face.

"All right," they both say simultaneously. Roan moves to sit next to Deidre. I tell myself this has to be done. It's the only way I can move forward.

"I had a nervous breakdown at the hospital. I wanted to die when I finally woke up. It all hit me at once. Everything that he—" I glance up to Roan. God, I don't want to hurt him or bring back the memories of that horrid night to either one of them. "I'm sorry," I say, looking him dead set in his eyes. He shows no pain, only remorse, maybe guilt. I don't know.

"Deidre. It's me who should apologize to you. I'm sorry for the things he did." Roan says, the good man he is, the guilt, regret, and the pain now clearly visible across his handsome features.

"I don't blame you. The man to blame is dead. He can't hurt us anymore." My tone is light. It's true. At first I didn't believe it. Now I know it's true. He can never harm anyone again.

"No, he can't," Alina chimes in. The two of them look at one another. More tears seem to swell up, only they're happy tears. The way Roan looks at Alina like his next breath depends on her happiness is enough to let those tears go. I'm so damn happy for the both of them.

Alina and I have all the time in the world for her to catch me up on the past year. I can't wait to hear everything. Right now, though, I need to get this all out. I'm so close to the final stretch of ending my therapy, starting with these two and crossing the finish line with Aidan.

"My parents told me he was dead. At the time, I couldn't believe it. I kept waiting for him to come and get me. To make his promise of killing me come true. I lost my mind over that fear." My lips start to tremble. I dig deep, close my eyes, and continue.

"I woke up three weeks later in Maryland at a facility for women. A retreat I was referred to by the doctor at the hospital. I was disoriented, had no idea where I was or what was happening. Once I calmed down, well, that's when I found out I was pregnant. I panicked all over again. Worried to death about the drugs I had been given would do my baby harm."

The two of them look down to Diesel. "He's fine. Perfect, really," I say with a shine in my eyes when I take him in.

"I needed the time. Needed to be healthy. To deal with it all before I came back. I'm sorry if I caused you worry. I really am." Roan stands, walks over, and takes the seat next to me. He reaches over, taking my stress-relieved hands into his.

"Neither one of us are ever going to judge you. We all handle things differently. The shit you went through, I can't even begin to imagine. What I do know is what it feels like to be out of control, scared for yourself and the people you love." Hearing those words lifts the heavy feeling off my shoulders. I know this is only the beginning of many conversations I need to have. The easiest one actually.

"Thank you," I say truthfully.

"What's his name?" Roan asks.

"Diesel."

"I love it. That's a badass name for a badass little dude," he says with glee.

"I also need a really good pediatrician for him. The two of you wouldn't happen to know of anyone, would you?"

"There she is. Her smartass mouth is back. Damn, I missed you." Roan pulls me into his arms for a hug. The three of us chat for another hour or so. Everything seems to be back to normal. I tell them all about the doctor who treated me. All about the delivery, which was a bitch. Delivering a nine-pound baby naturally feels like you're being ripped in two. I promised myself then and there I would never have another one. Not unless some promise from god would drop down on me, telling me there is no way I will have a baby that size again. I'm kidding, really. I would have ten more if they all turned out to be exactly like Diesel.

"I'm going to skip out for a bit. Let you two have some time alone." Roan comes back from the kitchen, stuffing a small flask into his back pocket. My nerves instantly go on edge, wondering if he's going to Aidan's. I scowl confused. Begging him to not say a word with my eyes.

"I'm not telling him, Deidre. That's your call. Not mine. But don't keep it from him for very long. He has a right to know."

He is going to Aidan's? I trust Roan. He's never given me a reason not to. I swallow the little bit of jealousy I have in my gut that he's going to see him, and tell him what I need to say. "I know you won't. And I couldn't agree with you more. I would never keep either one of them from knowing one another." He simply nods. Nothing more needs to be said, not now anyway.

With his parting words to me, he bends down, kisses Alina, winks at me, and rubs the baby's head. I trust Roan. I've known him most of my life. It's Aidan and the reaction he's going to have when he finds out about Diesel I don't trust.

CHAPTER THREE

AIDAN

Silence met me once again the minute Roan left. The thing about silence is it has the power to make you think. The energy from complete muteness can slow down the mind. In this case, it has mine reeling. I mean, what in the hell was tonight all about?

The way he sunk into his chair, one leg crossed over the other, tapping his fingers nervously on his leg. The minute I looked away from him, he was looking at me. I felt like he was studying my profile, searching for something.

I've known him for a long time. He's never been one to keep secrets, unless he's asked to. If he has something to say, he says it. Roan was off tonight. Something big is going down, and for the life of me, I have no idea what the hell it could be.

I'm a member of this family. Been through the ritual of the ceremony, swore to put it first. Keep my mouth shut by pledging an oath of silence. I've stuck my neck out many times over the course of this past year. Running errands. Beating the shit out of men who try to pull one over on us.

I'm a bodyguard to his woman. Even though their families have made peace with one another, not to mention the red scum of the earth, Royal, is fucking rotting in his hole of death somewhere, the families still have enemies. Especially Alina's, with her dad and his dealing with drugs.

I push away from the locked door, the only light on in my apartment coming from the half bath in the hallway giving me enough to make my way to my bedroom, still not understanding why the hell the Solokov family still deals those fucked up drugs. After everything these two families have dealt with over the past few years, you would think people would say 'Fuck this shit, we don't need it anymore,' especially the goddamn money. I've seen first-hand what money can turn a person into. That shit is not for me. I'm not complaining by any means. I have one hell of a roof over my head. Food in my belly. But fuck me, there's some crazy ass shit out there. I really don't have room to talk or to judge, though. Hell, I help steal guns when I'm not watching out for Alina.

Shaking that shit out of my mind, I flip off the light in the bathroom as I go by and walk in the dark to my room, not even turning on my bedroom light. I strip down to my boxers and climb into bed with the covers draping low on my waist. The minute I close my eyes, all I see are the massive waves of black hair and the hazel eyes of Deidre La Russo. *She's gone, man. Get her out of your head. Sleep, asshole.* Who knows how long I lie there thinking about her. But I do, until I slight my head a little and see what time it is.

With Alina demanding to walk to work every morning, means I'm up early making sure she arrives at the hospital safe. Once she's there, I hightail my ass to one of the club houses to deal with whatever Roan or Cain need me to do. Which is usually rough some asshole up or steal guns.

I actually laugh out loud at that shit. If my head-up-her-own-ass mother of mine knew what I did, she would be embarrassed to claim me as her son even more than she is now. Which means nothing, because the dumb bitch hasn't paid me any attention my entire life.

Fuck it. Enough dwelling on shit I have no control over. Whatever the hell is eating away at Roan, if he needs to bring me in on something, then I'm there. If it has to do with him and his woman, then that's between them. Most importantly, enough about my mother and Deidre.

With my mind finally shutting down, I sleep. And goddamn it, now I'm dwelling in my sleep, because when I wake from a dream that felt so fucking real, I question where in the world that fiery, foul mouthed, jet black-haired woman with those hazel eyes is in this fucked up world we live in.

Alina greets me at their door at the butt ass crack of dawn, handing me my usual to-go mug of coffee. Her expression is much like Roan's from last night. Somberly she says good morning after shutting the door behind her. I escort her from the hall to the elevator in silence. This silence bullshit will be the damned death of me, I swear to Christ it will be.

By the time we exit the elevator and step out into the warm morning mid-summer air, I've had enough of this shit.

"What the hell is going on?" I demand from her when we start to walk down the street.

"What are you talking about?" Her words are coming out almost apologetically.

"Cut the shit, Alina. First Roan shows up last night, acting way the hell off, like he's keeping something big from me, and now you're as quiet as an old lady listening intently to the preacher's sermon on a Sunday morning. What the hell gives?" She stops and stares at me for a moment, her eyes flitting back and forth between mine.

She turns and darts across the street without saying a word, leaving me no choice but to follow her.

"Goddamn it, Alina. Is something wrong? Trouble between you and Roan? I mean, seriously, fucking hell?" I sound like a prick, but at this point, I don't fucking care anymore. I know these two, the three of us are tight. On top of that, being cautious my entire life, tip-toeing around my mother my entire life whenever I knew she had some kind of poisonous snake up her ass, I know when something is wrong. And something is definitely not right here.

Her feet continue to move at a much faster pace than normal, her gaze cast down to the cement on the sidewalk.

"Hell, I may get myself in trouble for telling you this." She sighs deeply. "Deidre came over last night." She continues to walk. I stop dead in my tracks.

The moment she realizes I am no longer beside her, she stops too and swings around with a look on her face that is unrecognizable to me.

Her words finally sink in. "Is she okay?" I ask quietly.

"She's great." Tears fill her eyes.

"Bull fucking shit. You're lying." I make my way to her in three long strides. I knew Roan was off last night, and now I know why. He knows how fucked up my head was when I was tied down, left to watch an innocent woman get tortured. And then she disappeared, fucking my mind up even more. The guilt clawing away inside of me because I couldn't fucking save her.

"Where has she been?" I demand to know.

"Oh, no." She spins around and starts walking at a rapid pace again.

"I shouldn't have said anything to you at all. I promised her I wouldn't."

"What the fuck?" My words come out sharp.

"Look, Aidan. This is her story to tell. I've told you enough. When she's ready to come see you, she will. Believe me when I tell you she's fine. Now, you can walk me to work or you can turn your ass right back around. I'm not telling you anything else." She waves her outstretched hand in the air.

I'm far from done though. I will find her, goddamn it. And I will find her today.

I beat Cain and Roan to the gym in our building. We all have gyms in our apartments, but they never get used. We tend to hit the gym that consumes half of the third floor of our apartment building. The three of us work out together as much as we can. Me, I'm constantly needed as a spotter. I push myself to the limit when pumping iron. The rip, the ache in my muscles ready to give away. It's who I am. I push as hard as I can in every damn thing I do. Today, I'm pushing harder, my blood pumping like a caged beast's, the treadmill I'm running on at full speed daring to steal my breath as sweat drips down my face, chest, and abs. I'm soaked, and I'm fucking pissed off at the whole damned world. I knew he was off last night. And fucking hell, he kept that shit from me. "Son of a bitch." I reach up and pull the tiny red plug, shutting the treadmill off. Hoping off, I bend, retrieving my water bottle, and walk around the large room filled with men and women working out before they head to work. I pace around the room a few times, cooling down and guzzling the water.

Then I spot them both strolling in with smiles plastered on their smug faces. Does Cain know, too? Am I the last one to know she's back?

I weave in and out of the machines until I come face-to-face with the two of them. Even though she isn't here, all I can see is Deidre's face by the time I come to a stop.

"The hell?" Cain holds his hands up in the air.

"Fuck," Roan says.

"You got that shit right. Why the hell didn't you tell me she was back, you fucker?" I point at his chest.

"She asked us not to, asshole. And get that finger out of my space." He sidesteps me, heading straight for the weights.

"Where has she been?" I ask the same question I asked Alina, knowing damn well he isn't going to tell me either.

"Wait? Are you guys talking about Deidre?" Cain throws his towel on a bench and starts to adjust his weights.

"Yeah. She showed up at our place last night." Roan rubs the back of his neck.

"Wow. I'd like to know where she's been, too." Both of us look at Roan. Waiting.

"She's here in New York," he states calmly.

"I fucking know that, but where?" I abruptly shout, stammering backward, my head smacking against the wall.

"Come on, man. I'm telling you she looks good." Roan comes and stands in front of me.

"You know the shit I went through. It's not that I don't believe you, but damn it, man, it's something I need to see for myself. You of all people should get that shit." I close my eyes, shaking my head. I never should have thrown what he's been through in his face. FUCK. "I didn't mean that. Shit, I'm sorry." He shrugs it off like it's no big deal. I know better. He went through the exact same thing I did, only worse. Time can never erase the helplessness a man feels when he's ceased and forced to watch a woman get tortured.

"I do get it, brother. Doesn't mean I'm going to betray her. Betrayal isn't what I'm about. I stick true to my word no matter whom I give it to or whom I have to hurt in the process. But I fucking swear she's good. Hell, she's seems better than she was before." He pats my shoulder. I know I'm not getting any more out of him. I respect him for his loyalty. Doesn't do my bleeding brain any damned good, though. I will still look for her.

Leaving the two of them to finish their workout, I stretch my t-shirt over my head, grab all my shit, and bust my ass to get to my apartment to shower. The first place I'm going is straight to her and Alina's old apartment. Opening the door to my place, I'm instantly assaulted with that damn silence again. I fucking hate it. Toeing off my shoes by the front door, I head right to my old stereo, lift up the lid, and place the old needle across the album. The deep smoky rumble of Bob Segar echoes throughout the built-in surround system I had installed. This stereo is older than dirt, one of the very few things I kept for myself after my grandfather passed. His record collection, too. They don't make albums like this anymore. Everything's all digital, computerized shit, which comes in handy when you're driving around, but not when I'm home.

I let the music sink in. Bob talking about how guys love watching Her Strut. God, how I would watch Deidre strut her fine ass across her apartment with those tight jeans or her yoga pants, hell, even those short little pajama bottoms she used to wear.

Get that shit out of your mind, man. The woman hates you!

With Bob playing, I make my way down the hall to my bathroom, take a much-needed piss, turn the spray on in the shower, and drop my sweaty clothes to the floor. I clean and shampoo my hair in record time, have clean jeans and a light gray t-shirt and my boots on in fifteen minutes.

Digging my key to my bike out of my old Sinners leather vest, I reach for the door to leave just when the buzzer alerts me from downstairs.

"What's up, Nerd Boy?" I chuckle at the nickname I call one of the security guards downstairs. He's the opposite of a damn nerd. People think I'm huge, but I'm a goddamn chipmunk compared to him. He's seven feet tall, burly as hell. In reality, though, they don't come any nicer than him. The dude has been married for twenty years. Has five daughters who are all tall; every single one them has him wrapped around their finger. The oldest one plays basketball at NYU. He's always riding Roan, Cain, and my ass to come watch her play. We can't get away from him when he starts going on about any of his children. Can't blame the dude. Who knows how I would be if I ever had kids of my own.

"Fuck off, dickface. You have visitors. Want me to send them up?"

Them? I think to myself.

Maybe it's Deidre and her parents. She's afraid to be alone with me. I have no damn clue, all I hope is it has to be her. "Yeah, send them up." I disconnect. Hell, I'm getting all sweaty again just thinking about seeing her.

A few minutes later, I'm standing in front of my door, gripping the handle when the doorbell rings, my nerves bouncing all over the place.

I swing the door open, expecting to see a dark-haired beauty, but instead I'm face-to-face with a blond-haired bitch, her finely coifed hair piled on top of her head, and her psychotic son.

"What the fuck are you doing here? And how the hell did you find me?" I go to slam the door in her face when my mother shoves me aside, walking in like she owns the place.

"Get out," I yell to the both of them. Fuckwad strolls in with a self-righteous smirk on his face. I ought to beat him until he begs me stop, then turn around and cut his balls off.

"It's been five years, son. I need to speak with you. You don't return my calls or my letters, therefore you left me with no other choice than to track you down." Her shady little eyes scan my entire living room. It's boring, just like this conversation is.

"Well, you didn't have to bring a pile of fucking dog shit with you." I curl my lip and lift a brow, daring my so-called half-brother to say one goddamned word.

"Aidan, enough. I did not come here to argue," she carries on.

"If this is about the land, you've wasted a trip. You know damn well I'm not selling it, so take your fancy ass and leave. I've got way more important people to see than the two of you."

"Looking around this place, I'd say you're the fancy one now." Fuckface has the nerve to speak.

I walk casually to him until we're near chest-to-chest. He's bulked up over the years, but still stands a good couple of inches or so shorter than me. I have no qualms about taking this pussy down, right the fuck here.

While the two of us stare each other down, my mother starts to speak.

"Ryan's dead." I crane my neck to look at her, the urge to laugh about my step-dad's death scratching at my throat.

"And how is this my problem? Let him rot." I may sound unsympathetic. For good reason. I hated that bastard about as much as I hate his son standing here, stinking up my apartment.

"I... I need you to come home," she stutters.

"I am home." Knowing damn well what she means, the notion to rile these two up kicks into high gear.

"We need your help." She reaches up to place her arm on my shoulder, and I swat her away. I will never hit a woman, but this person in front of me is the description of the female devil. She's as dark, calculating, and manipulating as they come.

"Fuck you. And fuck you, too," I point to Ryan Drexler Junior. "You two are nothing to me. I don't care if you need my help. Figure it out on your own. Call your lawyers. Call Freddy motherfucking Krueger. I will never step foot in your house again. Now, I would appreciate it if you got the hell out of mine." I don't want to hear any more of their shit. Whatever kind of help they need, they can find it from someone else. I move to open my door, but before my hand even reaches for the doorknob, the words barely fall from Junior's lips, yet I hear them.

"What did you say?" My back is to the two of them. I heard the little prick, but I need him to repeat it; as self-centered as he is, it has to make his skin crawl to say those words. To pull them straight out of his ass, knowing his dad wasn't as perfect as he made himself out to be.

"I said, my dad has another family." The vibration in my shoulders caused by my laughing must not sit well with Alexis Drexler, because she gasps loudly.

"That is the funniest thing I have heard in a long time." I flip my body around to look at the two of them.

"You think this is fucking funny?" Ryan seethes at me.

"I think it's very fucking funny. Especially when our mother here used to fuck around on your dad all the time. Isn't that right, Alexis? Do you know if Junior here is really Ryan's or is he a bastard, too?" Fake tears start strolling down her face.

"Fuck you. I have a half-sister, who's twenty-three years old. She wants some of dad's money. She doesn't deserve a dime," Junior sneers.

"What does this have to do with me? I couldn't care less about the fact he had another family or if she even gets it all. I hope she does. Christ, what's wrong with you people?" I knew they were money hungry animals. Ryan's glaring at me like the world owes him everything. And Alexis has her head cast down. Then suddenly she straightens herself out and looks me up and down, her aspect bitter.

"I want you to kill them," she finally says. This time I heard her loud and very fucking clear.

CHAPTER FOUR

DEIDRE

"Alina, no. I... I'm not ready yet." Startling the both of us, she sighs into the phone while I fidget in my chair. And damn it, I do not fidget.

I'm sitting at my kitchen table, drinking coffee and applying makeup. Why I'm attempting to apply makeup is beyond me. It's not like I was planning on going anywhere or expecting any visitors.

Now, I'm listening to my friend warn me that Aidan knows I'm back.

I contemplated for days on whether I should go see them first or him. I chose them. Alina is one of the strongest women I know. I needed her strength, her guidance to get me through telling Aidan about Diesel.

Once I knew she respected my decision for the way I choose to handle my life, she listened. I'm scared and nervous of his reaction. The sooner I tell him, the better it will be for all of us. But there are a few factors that concern me now that I have a baby. I don't know, maybe I should talk to Calla first. Surely, she must know by now, too. Shit. My theory on the outcome of the conversation I'm stalling to have is inevitable. It's who we are. Nothing will change it.

However, my child comes before anyone or anything, and for the first time in my life, I can honestly say being connected to the mafia in a roundabout way scares the fuck out of me.

I'm the daughter to one of the Diamond family's top lawyers, which technically means I'm not connected to them at all. I know things, though. I grew up with them. Went to school with Roan until he moved. There are lots of things I know and wish I didn't.

One of the things I know is Aidan works for them. What he does exactly, I'm not sure. All I do know is that no way in hell do I want to put my child in danger. This is why I needed to dredge up the courage to go see him. If he's going to be a part of Diesel's life, which he has every right to be, then I need to make it perfectly clear I want him kept far away from this life, that I want him to have nothing to do with it at all. I'm smart enough to realize there are a hell of a lot more enemies out there. Ones that kill innocent people to pay back those that have crossed them.

Digging into my purse, I retrieve my Xanax and take my two daily pills out of the bottle, swallowing them down with my now lukewarm coffee. I'm right where I want to be in life, and this medication helps me stay calm. Not worry or panic. I'll take it as long as I need it, even if it's for the rest of my life.

"I'm sorry, Deidre. He knew something was up with Roan last night. Then this morning he asked me. I couldn't lie to the man. I didn't tell him where you were living." Her voice is full of apology. It's not him knowing I'm back I'm afraid of. She knows this as well as I do. We discussed it in great lengths when I showed up unannounced at her doorstep.

Alina also told me how much of a change she's seen in Aidan over the past year. He's calmer, more subdued and laid back. Maybe that night changed his outlook on life as well as it did mine. I don't know. I'll have to see for myself.

"I know. It has to be done. It's best to get it done. This way the two of them can get to know each other. All I want is for my son to have a relationship with his father." I think back to when I was six months pregnant. How I knew absolutely nothing about my baby's father. But with my dad being an attorney, having resources in abundance, I was able to find out so much about Aidan.

He has a mother, a step-dad, and a half-brother, who live in Pennsylvania. To my dad's knowledge, they haven't spoken to one another for years. Aidan comes from a wealthy family. It's obvious he doesn't care about the money.

His step-father Ryan Drexler of Drex Enterprises owns several car dealerships all over the state of Pennsylvania. He is a very shrewd yet successful man, while his mother comes from old money—bankers, investors, you name it—they dipped in it. She must be a real bitch for a man like him to not want anything to do with her. I hate bitches, plain and simply hate them. It doesn't matter what your child has done. Not that I'm saying Aidan is to blame, he doesn't strike me as the kind of man to hurt his own mother. A parent should always be the one to step up, makes things right or at least attempt to.

I will admit I'm curious to know why he doesn't speak to his mother. Something dreadful must have happened in order for Aidan to leave his family.

The only thing my father wasn't able to find out was who Aidan's biological father was. No name was put on his birth certificate, just the name of his mother, Alexis Hughes, which was her maiden name. I was relieved to know he didn't come from a family of crime.

"I need to get to work, but I felt like you needed to know. Knowing him, he won't give up until he sees for himself that you really are ok. Like I said last night, your disappearance did a number on him. For a long time, he withdrew from everyone," she articulates sincerely. The man must have gone through his own private hell, which does nothing but make me feel worse.

"I appreciate it. Will talk soon. I love you, Alina. Your support mean everything to me."

"I love you, too. And I'm so incredibly proud of you." Hearing those words of encouragement mean more to me than anything.

We hang up, with me promising to call her any time, day or night, if

I have concerns regarding Diesel. I have many concerns, but none of them have to do with his health.

With my phone still in my hand, I rub my temples, thinking about how I want this all to play out. I need to do what's best for the baby. My gut is telling me I need to speak to Aidan first before he sees Diesel, but what if he rejects him? Starts yelling, demanding why I waited this long to tell him?

The pills are taking effect. My head is clearer now. No matter his reaction, I can and will handle this.

I need to go to him before he comes here, which I know he will.

I dial my mom, the only other person I trust right now to leave Diesel with. When she says she can be here within the hour, I hustle to finish getting ready. This isn't a date or an I'm-here-to-impress-you kind of thing, yet I still want to look good. If anything, I'm doing it to reassure Aidan that I'm doing great, that I'm fully capable of raising our son.

Most people may not truly understand the after effects of having a breakdown. I'm better, so much better than I was a year ago, but that doesn't mean I don't still have a long way to go to get my life back. The dreams still come and go, leaving me fearful to fall back to sleep. The small dosage of Xanax helps me and millions of other people in this world face days when it seems our plate is piled so high we don't know what to do. It helps us climb it. Conquer it. Some of us need a little extra shove to get to the top.

There's absolutely nothing wrong with taking medication to help us get through the day, to deal with the shit we have to live through.

Stuffing my makeup back into my bag, I make my way down the hall to the baby's room. The sun is shining in through the windows. He's sleeping on his stomach, clutching his favorite blue blanket in his tiny little hand, peaceful after his morning bottle feeding. The one thing I didn't get to experience with him was breast-feeding. Medication passes through the breast milk, Xanax especially. It can cause serious issues, such as drowsiness, weight loss, and other complications. No way was I taking my chances when it comes to my sweet gift. I never want harm or danger to cross his path. Not as long as I'm around to defend him, which will be for the rest of his life. That's what parenting is all about. It doesn't matter how old your child is, a good parent will do everything to make sure their child's life is healthy and happy and full of love. That's all I want for him.

Bending over the railing of his crib, I kiss him lightly on his head before I leave him to his sweet dreams.

By the time my mother gets there, I'm dressed in a light yellow sundress, my long, black hair pulled into a high pony tail. I slip my feet into a pair of brown flip-flops, greeting her at the door.

"You look lovely, honey," she says, pulling me into her arms.

"Are you sure you're ready to do this?" she asks.

"Well, no, but it has to be done," I say with a fake smile. She's been through so much with me this past year. It won't matter what I say to try and convince her to not worry, she will anyway.

"Thanks for staying with him. I need to go before Aidan decides to show up here first." I tell her in a rush how Alina told him I was back before I hesitate to get out the door.

"Go. We'll be fine." She shoves me out the door. *So much for stalling.*

I waver. "Deidre, go. You can do this." *I can,* I think to myself.

Forty-five minutes later, I'm sitting in the same parking lot I sat in last night, only this time my stomach is rolling. My entire body is sweating, I'm shaking so bad.

"Get out," I tell myself. I grab my wallet, phone, and keys, then step out into the humid air. My feet feel like they're full of some sort of heavy lead by the time I enter the lobby. Glancing up to security, I see that there's a different man sitting at the podium. *Shit, will he let me up without notifying him?*

I stop and dial Roan, praying he's still here. When it goes to voicemail, I turn around, wondering what the hell I'm going to do.

A soft hand grazes my shoulder. I jump, then turn around to the soft voice of Calla Bexley, and see her holding the cutest little baby girl I have ever seen.

"Deidre. It's so good to see you. You look great." She smiles.

"You do, too. Congrats on the little one. My parents told me all about her. She's beautiful. I love her name, too. Hello there, Justice," I say softly. She grins toothlessly. Adorable.

We stand there for a few minutes while she explains the meaning behind her daughter's name. I get it, especially after the shit she's been through. Royal did a number on both of us. I will not bring either one of our experiences with that man up, though. Justice was served when he died.

"She's a handful. Teething right now." *I know the feeling*, I want to say. I don't. I have no clue if Roan has told her or Cain anything. Instead, I focus on her baby. She has two dimples, blond, curly hair, and eyes that twinkle.

"Are you here to see Alina?" she asks politely.

I sigh and forge a smile. "No. Aidan, actually. I wanted to surprise him. I tried to call Roan to see if he could get me past security." She cuts me off by reaching for my hand.

"You don't have to say any more. Come on." She guides me past the guard. We both say good morning.

"Thank you," I say when we get to the elevators.

"You're welcome. And Deidre," she calls out as I step into lift. "Believe me when I say he'll be happy to see you. We all are. I'm running late for work, we'll talk soon." With that, she turns and leaves.

I press the button for his floor. The second the doors close, I pace two steps one way, then two steps the other in the tiny compartment. The blood drains from my face the closer I get. I take a deep breath when it stops at his floor. The minute the doors shut behind me, I take one step toward his apartment and halt when I hear his loud voice from where I'm standing.

Damn it. I hope it's not the same woman from last night. Alina assured me he wasn't dating anyone. She was also very confident that he doesn't do hookers. Yes, I went there with her last night. I couldn't help it. Curiosity got the best of me, I guess.

Whomever he's having a conversation with has him enraged. In fact, the more I hear him shouting, the more concerned I become.

I walk closer, pressing my ear to the door. The disagreement he's having   surprises   me. I hear everything. "Oh, my god. It's his mother," I whisper softly.

I take a step back, ready to press the button on his doorbell, when I hear declarations that instantly put me in protection mode.

I lose my shit when she says his step-father is dead and the voice of a man I assume is his brother starts talking about a young woman who wants money. The last thing I hear before I grasp for the door handle to see if it's unlocked are the viscous words, "I want you to kill her," coming out of his mother's vile mouth.

"Honey, I'm home." Three pairs of eyes turn my way. The only one I'm focused on is the man's whose eyes look exactly like our son's. They grow wide with shock, then travel slowly down from my face to my chest and then to my tanned legs. When they meet my eyes again, his brows furrow. I'm hoping he can read my expression trying to tell him to play along.

"Who are you?" His mother looks me over with contempt. Asking me like it's her business of who I am.

"I'm his fiancée. Who the fuck are you?" I'm still spinning out of control from hearing her say the word 'kill'. And fiancée? Good lord almighty, I've lost my mind again. I'm pissed. But it's obvious he doesn't want them here, from what I overheard, so it's for a good reason.

My hands clench at my sides. I'm ready to lurch at her, to take her ass out, when Aidan strides to me, bringing me into his strong arms.

My insides melt, filling up with this indescribable feeling. His warm, strong body pressed up against mine. His strong arms holding me close. Squeezing. My heart embraces him too, doing this little flip in my chest.

"What in the every loving fuck?" he whispers in my ear. I look up into his handsome face. His hair is darker than I remember, his eyes brighter than the sun glistening down on the ocean. I need to step back. My body feels all tingly from his simple embrace.

"Aww, baby, I missed you too," I coo loudly enough for them to hear. "Now shut your big fat trap and play along. What's going on here?" I demand quietly. Looking right at his mother, I try to escape the hold he has on me, to step around him. He resists. I think of those big hands more often than I should, and damn it, right now they have me all flustered.

"Nothing I can't handle. These two were just leaving. Weren't you?" He slings his arm around my shoulder casually. I tuck closer to him, because, well, he feels good. Too damn good. Like I-could-lick-him-up-and-down-and-all-around kind of good.

"You have a fiancée?" the man I know to be Ryan asks. Good thing this dip-shit spoke. I was beginning to visualize licking Aidan like you do with the extra batter on a wooden spoon.

"He does. Not that it's any business of yours. Now, I believe he asked you to leave." His mother's eyes go wide. The bitch's undertake on what I said does not go unnoticed by me at all. She stands there gawking at me like she cannot believe I've spoken to her the way I did. *Screw you, you uptight, good for nothing Botox face bimbo with the 1980s hairdo.*

"I came all this way to see my son. We have unfinished business that does not concern you." She looks me over as if she were better than me. *Oh, no way, Bitch. You have no damn idea who the hell I am or the things I will do or say to get you the hell out of here.*

"Anything that has to do with the man I love is my business. Now, if

44

you don't leave, I will personally make you." Aidan chuckles beside me. Yeah, love, right? I'm sure he's thinking more like hate. Which is far from the way I truly feel about him.

"I'd like to see you try," Ryan says.

"Oh, please. The two of you show up here after not speaking to him for years. Demanding he kill someone. That's a crime. You and your last year's Louis Vuitton bag could spend a long time in prison for plotting a murder. Just in case your brain is lodged in that beehive of a hairdo you have, I thought I would mention that. Now, get the fuck out of my apartment." I unlodge myself from Aidan's arm, move to the door, and open it.

"Get out now. And don't you dare come back. And one more thing. Aidan doesn't kill people, but I sure as hell do." Which is a lie. But hey, if it gets them out of here, then I really don't care.

"Why, you little bitch. Do you have any idea who I am? I can destroy you both." I take a step closer to this dickface Ryan. He thinks he can threaten me? Oh hell, no.

"I know exactly who the two or you are. She's an ugly nit-witted troll who has no idea how to be a good mother and you're the male version of her. He's your family. Your brother. The two of you come here, unwelcome I might add, and ask him to kill someone?" The part of my brain that triggers angry emotions has gone crazy. Aidan and I may never have truly liked each other, well that's not entirely true, but that's not what's in question right now. What is, is how these two people are his family. One being his mother, and how dare she treat him like shit.

Diesel flashes through my mind, which causes one part of my body to catch fire and the other part to flood like a tsunami.

"This isn't over by a long shot." Ryan glares at me with steely eyes.

"It's definitely over. If either of you step foot in this building or even in New York ever again, you won't have to worry about the money you're trying so hard to keep. I will have you both killed." My rage of fire starts to gradually put out the flood inside of me. I feel my face turning red. My entire body starts to heat up. These assholes don't get it. They're still standing here.

Aidan doesn't give either one of them time to respond to my threat. He grabs Ryan by his throat with one hand and backs him up, slamming him hard against the wall.

"Don't ever come here again. If you do, the first person I will kill will be you." He slams his head hard against the wall, releases him, and turns to the bitch troll.

"And you. Get the fuck out of here. I never want to see you again. Do I make myself clear?" he asks, pointing his finger at her.

"Aidan. I knew the moment you were born that you were going to cause me nothing but grief and heartache. That you would desert me just like your father did. You're exactly like him." Oh, my god. She is horrible. Like I-want-to-jump-her-and-pull-her-eyeballs-out horrible. Does she not see what a decent man she has in her own son? I hate her.

"I wouldn't know that, now would I? Being that I don't even know who my father is? I will say this though, I'd much rather be like him than be like you. And one more thing. If I find out anything happens to this woman you're talking about, you're both dead. Now, get out."

I stand there while Ryan adjusts his clothes and his mother pulls her purse straps over her shoulder, the two of them saying nothing else. They walk right out the door, slamming it shut behind them.

Then there's the deafening, eerie soundlessness of silence for several seconds, minutes. I'm not sure how long exactly. I do know that now that they are gone, my thoughts are back on why I came here. I'm scared, not just because of how Aidan will react to knowing he has a son. It's the fact that I know with every ounce of breath I have left that this is the beginning of trouble.

"You're back?" Aidan's low words feather lightly across my neck. He's standing close to me. His warm breath scatters across the back of my neck.

My breath escapes my lips when he touches the long scar across the top of my back, lightly tracing his finger from one end to the other. The dark, hollow places I have buried deep inside of me cease to exist as his smooth lips trace behind his finger. The floor beneath me vanishes. I'm left floating.

"Aidan," I whisper. His reaction to me barging in here as if I owned the place baffles me. I came prepared for an argument. Which undoubtedly I received, just not in the way I was expecting. And after I tell him what he deserves to know, we will be talking about his obvious shocking visitors. I snap out of my trance his simple touch has put me in. I step forward a few feet, my heated skin suddenly cold.

"I... we need to talk." Staggering on unsteady feet to his gray leather couch, I sit. There is so much to say. The first two being me telling him about his son and why I left. Then I need to know exactly what is going on with the two people who left here. It's not just Aidan and I who we need to worry about anymore. It's our child. I will live in hell for the rest of my life to protect my son. From what I witnessed a few moments ago, I believe Aidan will, too. The horrible things she said to him weigh heavily on my heart. God. How could a mother say those things to her child? She may think she's some high classed woman. She isn't a woman at all. Hell, she's a cunt. A worthless piece of shit.

Our son may have been conceived by one night of passion between two people who can hardly stand each other, whose last words to each other before the worst night of my life happened were hateful. Words I did not mean.

By the way he's seeking out my teary eyes, the look of guilt and remorse coming from his, he's sorry too. He doesn't even have to say it.

I take a deep breath and lean forward, those conversations I had with myself over and over on how I planned on telling him meaning nothing now.

47

"Aidan. We have a three-month-old son."

CHAPTER FIVE

AIDAN

I sit, stunned. I'm a father? Jesus Christ. This is why she left?

I don't know whether to be pissed that this has been kept from me or to snag her sexy, little ass in her tight, little yellow dress, that has my dick throbbing painfully, off from the couch and kiss her until she's numb.

My brain has shut down. I'm trying to suck in air. My body is starving for it. It all seems to have left this apartment. Fucking hell, a father?

"Aidan." My name falls softly from her mouth. Jesus. It's been a year since I've seen her beauty, smelled her sweet scent. Heard her tart mouth. And fuck me if the sound of my name coming from her doesn't sound like the sweetest thing I've ever heard. *Focus, you asshole. She just told you you're a father.*

I scratch my head, deep in thought. What the hell do I even say? We study each other for the longest time. Me wondering what to do, how to hold on to what she told me; her more likely freaking the hell out, wondering the very same damn thing.

"I'm not sure what to say to this, Deidre. I don't want to sound like a jerk, but woman, you have some explaining to do before I can even comprehend this," I state truthfully. She has to tell me everything.

Her mouth curves into a tight-lipped smile. One I don't like at all. I'm about to ask her what is wrong when her question sears through my heart.

"I'm surprised you're not denying he's yours." What in the ever-loving fuck?

"I'm not denying shit. I'm confused as fuck. I won't lie to you about that. We used a condom, every time." Obviously, she knows we did. She was there. Hot and incredibly perfect.

"I hate to be the one to tell you this, big boy." She looks down at my dick, then back to my face. "Condoms do break, especially when a man has sexy as hell piercings." Her perfect brows lift as if she's challenging me to say something smartass right back to her. If this feisty little minx wants to go at it, then game on.

"Are you saying you loved my piercings, Deidre?" Her tanned skin turns a light shade of pink, starting from that sensual neck of hers all the way up to those rosy, little cheeks.

"I..." She pauses.

"You're what? Tongue-tied? Thinking about my cock? How good it felt brushing up against your tight, little pussy? How my piercings made you come over and over? Is that what you're trying to say?" I'm trying like hell to keep my voice steady. My dick is straining like a motherfucker to get out, to have her wrap that pouty little mouth around him. Fuck me. How in the hell did we go from us discussing having a son to talking about sex?

"You have got to be the biggest asshole I have ever met." Ah... here we go. Here comes the spitfire woman I missed. I need to change the subject before I bend her over my couch and remind her exactly what my cock and my piercings can do to her. On top of that, I want to know where she's been this entire time, and if she knew she was pregnant, why the hell she kept it from me.

"I may be an asshole, Deidre. I've said terrible, hurtful, and unforgiveable things to you in the past. One thing I'm not is a man who will accuse a woman like you. Accuse a woman I know to be loyal, confident, and as honest as they come to walk into my home and lie to me." I'm serious and she knows it. I incline my body toward her. "Now, talk." I grin at her. She looks so goddamn tense and worried. That pretty little shade of pink is gone. When this conversation is over, I'll be doing everything I can to make her blush again.

"Thank you," she says shyly. This woman went from almost killing my mother and fuckhead of a brother to sitting on my couch like a good girl. Which I know firsthand she is not. I don't mean that in a bad way, either. I mean it in a very good way. She is or was a naughty little thing. I'm glad she still has her mouth and feistiness in her. God, her mouth. My gaze drops down to it, and she sucks in a sharp breath. Yeah, the sexual pull is still very much present between the two of us. Even after all this time. We can talk about her being under me later, because by god, she will be under me. On top of me. Filled with me. And most undeniably begging for me.

"I didn't know I was pregnant when I left here," she says quietly. I train my attention to listening to her speak. I don't understand. Then why? Why would she take off? Was this her way of punishing me for the way I treated her? No fucking way. She's not the type of woman to run away. She's tough, controlling, and a pain in my ass. Never would she take off, leaving those she cares about behind. There's more to this story. A hell of a lot more.

"Why did you leave?" May as well get right to the point. I want to know about our son. I'm still spinning that we have a baby. This is one hell of a day already and it's not even half over.

"I had a nervous breakdown when I woke up in the hospital." I can hear the trepidation in her voice. Every word that she speaks next soaks up my aching gut like a dry sponge soaking up water. They strip me. Wreck me and consume me.

Fuck. It hurts when you listen to someone tell you a heartbreaking story. One of strength and determination to fight. To gain control of the shit life throws at you unexpectedly. My chest is splitting in half, hearing Deidre tell me how she broke down. Freaked out and spent months dealing with her attack by a man who is burning in an inferno. I pray to god he burns to ashes every day, the process repeating itself continuously. That man deserves nothing more or nothing less than to suffer eternally. Jesus, if only I could have stopped him from destroying her. From breaking her. God, I will never forgive myself.

As I listen more intently, the darkness pulls me under even further when she brings up how she woke up disoriented, not knowing where she was, her surroundings unfamiliar to her. How the first thing she thought about when she found out she was pregnant was the health of our child.

"Stop." My one word command makes her jump. I'm so full of fucking guilt, unworthiness, and shame. This woman suffered so much.

"Aidan. What the hell?" I scrub my hands down my face, the overwhelming urge to fucking explode crawling into my skin like fucking poison. I know the situation she's been through isn't my fault. But the way I feel can't be helped.

Contempt. That's a better word to describe how I feel. For god's sake.

"I'm so damn sorry, Deidre." I lean forward even more, hoisting my ass out of the chair. What I need to say to her has to be said where she can see me. I mean really see me up close. It's the only way I can move forward.

I drop to my knees in front of her. Her hazel eyes go wide. "What on earth?" she says questionably. This knee-jerk reaction to what she told me has me questioning my own sanity at the moment. We study each other. Her most likely freaking out as to why I'm kneeling on the floor in front of her; me, lost in her natural beauty. Her bravery.

Damn, there are no words to define how beautiful she is. Christ. I cannot take my eyes off of her. Deidre La Russo has brought me to my goddamn knees. Her power to possess me with the most prestigious word known to man has rendered me speechless. Beautiful. She is fucking beautiful.

"My god, you are stunning." I lay my hands on her legs. She tenses underneath my touch. "Are you trying to seduce me?" Well, shit. She sure didn't lose her snarly, little attitude.

"No," I shake my head. I carry on with what I now remember I wanted to say. "I'm sorry I couldn't help you that night. I've kept it here the entire time." I lift a hand and point to the center of my chest. "I've dreamt about it. Destroyed my self-worth over it. Tried to think what I could have done differently to protect you. I failed and I'm sorry. And the things I said to you the last time we spoke...I have no excuse for it."

Bringing her hand up to the one on my chest, she places it over the top of mine, our hands now connected over my heart. Her face is within an inch of mine. She throws me one hell of a perfect curled-up smile with those light pink lips of hers.

"I've never blamed you. Not once. I felt you. As silly as this may sound, I felt you that night, and I heard you telling me to hang on. To be strong. If you hadn't been there, I would have given up. I wanted to give up so many times, but I kept repeating the words I heard you say. "Don't give up, Deidre. Stay strong, baby." Don't apologize anymore to me, you've done nothing for me to have to forgive you for."

"God, you're just as beautiful on the inside as you are on the outside," I stress. She is so undoubtedly unselfish. Never in my lifetime would I have guessed there could possibly be a woman out there for me. Not with how my own mother ran my self-esteem into the ground. This lively, mouthy woman and mother of my son could be that woman. Who the hell knows? A son. We have a son. It hits me finally. Rocks my world in a good way. I have a child.

I sit back on my legs. Her hand falls from my chest. "We have a son?" I speak like I'm finally catching on and I am. Deidre has more to tell me. I sense it. I see it in the way she looks at me. She's frightened, nervous. I swallow hard. Our internal battles match. Those same sensations are surging through my veins. Hitting every live cell like a wake-up call. I don't know if there's more to the past year of her life she wants to tell me. As long as she's healed, freed from the chains that tore her apart in the first place, I don't need to know more. If in time she wants to share more factors that took her away, generated her mind to collapse, she can, but right now, my heart is full. I want to know about this little boy. I need to meet him. Be a good parent. Give him love and support. Something I never had and always wanted. Just to be loved. I love him already and I don't even know him, yet.

This day reminds me of trying to dodge a storm and then fuck out of nowhere, the winds pick up, sending you head first into the side of a brick building, knocking you unconscious. And when you wake, the sky is clear, there are no dark clouds lurking around like my mother and Junior, full of darkness and hatred, ready to strike you like a damn rod of lightning. No worries twisting your insides into a goddamn knot because the woman you saw hurting vanished. Fuck no. I just woke up at the end of the rainbow.

"We do. He's three months old. His name is Diesel."

"Diesel?" I let the name roll off of my tongue.

"Yeah," she replies shyly. "Do you like it?" she requests softly.

"I do. It's kind of manly and shit. Like my badass Harley or a kick ass engine." It's hard for this to sink in. Me being a dad. I vow right then and there before even knowing anything about this young man I helped create, before I even know what he looks like or what kind of man he will grow up to be, I promise him I will always protect him, love him, and make damn sure he is one, if not the greatest accomplishment of my life. I will never walk out on him; not like my mother claims my biological father did once he found out she was pregnant. I will never call him a name, other than the name his beautiful mother gave him. He's mine to protect. Mine to cherish and mine to make damn sure he grows up to know he was and always will be loved.

"When was he born?" I straighten my body up from the floor and move to sit next to her on the couch. Her floral smell inebriates my

54

senses. She has no idea what kind of gift she has given me. For the first time in my life, I feel needed and wanted. And Christ, he's too small to know a damn thing, but hell, I even feel loved.

Gliding her dainty hand over the top of her wallet lying next to her, she stills then unzips the small leather compartment, pulling out several pictures.

"He was born on April 3rd. Nine pounds even. He's a big boy." Her face softens. She then places a few pictures of him in the palm of my hand. I glimpse down quickly, then close my eyes. These tiny photos are a part of me. A part of her.

When I open them, my hands are shaking. My eyes tear up. I'm staring at the most precious little man with dark hair. At eyes that twinkle. He has his thumb in his mouth in one photo, is propped up on Deidre's lap; he is naked and on his belly in another, rolls of baby fat or whatever the hell it's called on display. He looks to be trying as hard as he can to hold his head up. I want to jump in this photo and urge him on. Tell him he can do it. He can do anything if he puts his heart and mind to it.

"I've never been a godly man. My childhood was so messed up, but Deidre," I look up into her wet eyes and see a woman who has given me a blessing, and I speak the god's honest truth to her. If I sound like a pussy or a man whose raw emotions have surfaced, then so be it. "I believe there is a god up there somewhere. Someone brought this boy into our lives for a reason." She sniffles, finally giving in to those tears that have glassed over her beautiful eyes, making them look greener than the mixture of multiple colors.

"We created this little guy. He's perfect," I say happily. Then she surprises me by reaching up and wiping the single tear that has fallen from my eye with her thumb.

"He's everything, Aidan. Who knows, maybe someday we'll know why he was gifted to us. Maybe we'll never know. All I know is I'm going to be the best mother I can be. Diesel deserves to be loved, by both his parents. I don't know much about the way you were raised. What I do know is I've seen firsthand how you stepped right into the role of protector when you came here to guard me. To me that shows what kind of man you truly are. You're loyal, faithful, and even though you're a pain in my ass, you're going to be a wonderful father." Her words are full of intense passion. She now has my emotions bouncing all over the place. I'm happy, nervous, excited, scared, and proud all rolled into one chunky little bundle of a baby boy.

"Would you like to meet him?" My eyes widen. My heart leaps somewhere between my chest and my throat. My breathing increases. With eyes misting with water, I train my gaze back down to my son and run my finger across his face in the picture. "I would love to meet him," I whisper.

CHAPTER SIX

DEIDRE

For the first few months of this past year, I lived in a world of depression, overcome by reoccurring nightmares that tormented my mind. The shadows of nightfall would cocoon me in my own little surroundings of the small room I lived in. The walls always caving in, squeezing tightly to the point I could hardly breathe.

All of that changed the very first time I felt my son move inside of me. Even though my doctors tried to reassure me I was getting better every day, proven by the fact that I was no longer afraid to go outside for fear I would be taken, that my mood was no longer somber, my panic and anxiety were no longer overtaking me. All of that may have been true. However, I owe my healing to my son and to this man sitting next to me, trying so hard not to burst out of his skin with the same excitement I did when I first held my newborn son.

Unlike me, Aidan was raised without love. I knew he was estranged from his family, and now, after walking in here and hearing the way his mother talked to him, I know why. She's a fucking bitch. A selfish woman. How she's lived this long without a heart baffles the shit out of me.

What really surprises me is Aidan. I mean, I knew he wouldn't turn his back on his responsibility. He's proven his loyalty by coming here and protecting me. Standing by his friends' sides. Roan and Cain are his family. Blood doesn't mean a damn thing when it comes to choosing whom you consider family. Your heart chooses for you.

Aidan's mother deserves none of the credit for the man he is today. There's someone in his life who does, someone who showed him how to love. One thing is for damn certain, that fucking cow and her low-life son will have nothing to do with my child. It's obvious they somehow know Aidan's involvement with the mafia. I know firsthand that there is a lot of bloodshed. People die or disappear to never be heard from again. But Aidan's not one of the ones who kills. He's a thief, which I'm not particularly fond of, either. But this is my life. I am the daughter of one of the mafia's attorneys. Diesel will be loved and protected. There's danger all over this world. As much as I wish I could shield my son from it all, I can't deny either one of them to bond like a father and his son should.

I realize now that when we first met and I kept telling myself how I hated him, that it wasn't true. In fact, it's so far from the truth, it scares me. I took my anger and frustration out on him the same way he took his out on me. The two of us couldn't leave for fear of the consequences that lingered right outside my apartment door, which would even make a married couple want to claw each other's eyeballs out.

He blames himself for not being able to help me. But I've never blamed him. I pray with everything I have he believed me when I told him he's the one who saved me. He did. Even when I gave birth, I could still hear his deep voice, his words of reinforcement telling me to hang on. To not give up when all I wanted to do was scream and tell the doctors to get the baby out of me now. To stop pushing with every hard, painful contraction that ripped through my stomach. Every bit of pain I've been through this past year was worth it, not only because I've been blessed by becoming a mother, but also because of this moment right here, where I'm watching my son's father fall in love with the greatest gift god can give to a person.

"Let's go." Aidan's words snap me out of my little daydream bubble. He stands, holding his hand out for me to take.

"I hope you have more photos of him, because these are mine." Letting go of my hand, he pulls his wallet out of his back pocket, sticking the photos inside. Instinctively, I want to snarl at him, tell him to give them back. I have plenty of photos of Diesel, that's not the point. But those few photos are my favorites. I bite my tongue though, which is hard for me to do. He deserves to have them. He's his son too.

"Are you all right?" Aidan shoves his wallet back in his pocket, a look of concern on his handsome face.

"I'm great. Why?" I frown, confused. Shoot, I don't want him to think I'm upset about anything. This is a happy time, for all of us. I'm being selfish, so unlike the man standing in front of me. He doesn't have a selfish bone in his god-blessed, candy-coated, rippling, muscled body. And there I go again, thinking about his body. I'm worse than those men who cannot seem to hold back their drool when they hit you up with those cheesy pick-up lines. Only I'm not lying or trying to pick him up. His body *is* like freshly made cotton candy. Hot, sweet, and sticky. Fuck. I need my bob-ette. Or my finger, my thumb. Right now, any extremity of my hand will do.

He scoffs. "You were very convincing a while ago when you barged in here and claimed to be my fiancée." He lifts his brows. "But, my little sweet-tart girl, I'm very good at reading people, and I can tell that right now, you're lying." He looks down at me. *Sweet-tart girl? Where did that come from?*

"No. I'm not," I lie.

"Woman, you are," he groans.

"Fine," I may as well tell him one other thing that's bothering me, too. I place my hands on my hips. It's the truth, but it's not what's running through my mind right now. He doesn't need to know that, though.

"I don't want the baby anywhere near your mother." Oh shit.

Maybe I shouldn't have said that. His face is turning red. He's angry. Surely not about what I said. He can't stand her.

"If that cunt comes back here again, I meant what I said. I won't think twice about having her and her little pawn vanish." He tilts his head to the side, studying me. He's a hard one to read at the moment. Hot then cold.

"Don't bring her up again, Deidre. That topic is off subject. They don't exist to me. Which reminds me, how did you know who she was?" A loud laugh escapes me. Why, I'm not sure. Maybe it's because our conversation is playing a game of ping-pong. Back and forth we go. By the time we get to my place, we will have weeded out the entire year I was gone.

"Now, come on, big fella. I just told you I spent the better part of the last year in a treatment facility. I had a lot of time on my hands. I also needed to know more about my baby daddy." His eyes flutter, his manner changing from mild anger to pure amusement.

"You investigated me?" He cages me in with his stare. His observation flashes down to my lips. I swallow hard. The room goes quiet. Why he chooses this precise conversation to look at me like he wants to kiss me, I have no idea. All I know is my nipples are striving like hell to have him wrap his mouth around them. My pussy tightens. Oh, no. I will never give in to this man again. He may have given me our son, and we may bond through him, but he will never fuck me with his big, pierced, beautiful cock again. Nope, no freaking way. My pussy can tuck her herself right back up. My nipples can stay flat. Neither one of them are getting what they want. All my little bitch-ette of a pussy is getting is bob-ette, the vibrator. No man is touching her again.

"Kind of," I squeak out.

"Did you find out anything interesting in your baby daddy research?" His tone is comical. He thinks this is funny. I do not.

I place my hands on my hips, angry now. "It's not funny. Your mother is a bitch."

"That she is. You're still avoiding my question, Deidre."

"Fine," I lift my hands in frustration. I don't want to argue with him. "I found out where you grew up. I know you haven't seen your family in years. When I walked up to your door, I heard everything, and I came apart. I don't know the woman and I don't want to. But when I heard her ask you to kill some innocent woman, I lost my shit. What kind of mother would ask her son to do such a thing?"

He shocks me completely when he lifts his hand and cups the side of my face. His touch sends a zip threw my body. I become immobile. "Very few people would have done what you did today. You stood up for me. And," he draws out that singular word, "you seeking out about the man I am proves to me how great of a mother you are. I promise you right here, right now, Deidre, I won't let that conniving bitch or her son anywhere near our boy. They're long forgotten. I have a son I want to meet. She's always hated me. When I was younger, it would tear me up. Now, I don't care anymore. She's harmless. All she has are her words. It's Ryan I'm more concerned about. But I'll handle him and make sure this woman they're talking about is protected as well. Now, can we please go?" With that he drops his hand and my damn body misses his touch already.

***

My stomach alters restlessly. I notice my hands are gripping my steering wheel strongly. My pulse is pounding at my temples. Aidan followed me to my apartment, and now he's walking toward my car. I'm afraid to step out for fear I may trip and fall flat on my face from how bad my legs are shaking.

Why I'm nervous about the two of them meeting beats the shit out of me. I just am. Maybe it's because I haven't shared Diesel with anyone else except my parents since he was born. And now, I'm not going to be the center of this little boy's universe anymore.

"Get a damn grip, Deidre, he's his father, for Christ sake. They need each other." I reach over, grabbing my phone and wallet off of the passenger seat, and twist back to open my door when Aidan beats me to it, opens it, and guids me out, slipping his hand into mine.

"Hell, I'm nervous," he blurts out. I chuckle at the irony of both of us feeling the same way.

"Don't be. He's a baby." I hold back my own nerves the second I see his face when I look up and see his descending, slanting eyebrows, his downward-turned lips giving him an unnatural-looking frown.

"Would you stop?" I let go of his hand and thread my arm through his. "He's going to love you," I say truthfully.

I almost want to laugh at this big man who's scared to meet his son. Aidan is dark, mysterious, and sexy as hell. God, is he sexy. I would love to be able to start licking from the tips of his toes up those muscular, meaty legs, stop and lick his big, thick cock. *Oh, for god's sake. I might have to go see a sex therapist next. Nah. Do they make medication to tame down a woman's aching pussy? Like a reverse Viagra pill? Get your head straight, Deidre.*

I toss my tainted desires aside, pushing forward the reason why we're here.

Maybe, just maybe, the two of us can come to an agreement of some sorts. We took our sexual frustrations out on each other but we don't have to live together anymore, grating down on each other's last nerve. We're going to be fine raising a child separately yet together as parents. There, with every step further we take, I feel better.

He's changed over the past year. He's still hot-tempered, well, maybe not. I don't know. He had every right to blow his fucking gasket with his family today.

The way he handled the news I told him today, though, is solid proof he's changed the way he feels towards me. The dickhead of a man I remember would have accused me of trapping his ass or some shit. I was expecting him to deny it. To be pissed the hell off when he saw me. Not that it was any of his business where I went or what I did with my life. But he was the exact opposite.

The ride up the elevator is quiet. Out of the corner of my eye, I can see he's starting to sweat. There's nothing more I can say to him. This is something he has to deal with on his own terms.

The closer we get to my floor, the more anxious I become, all nerves demolished. Happiness floats through me like a fast current. I'm happy for my boy, happy for his father, and happy for myself. If anyone would have told me a little over a year ago that I was going to be a mom, or that a one-night stand destined to happen from the moment Aidan and I set eyes on each other would be the reason for this happiness I'm feeling now, I may have either cunt-punched or dick-kicked them, sending them flying. Your life can change quickly. You blink one second, and the next someone is telling you you're pregnant. Your life doesn't belong to you anymore. You become a parent. Your life revolves around them and their needs. It's the greatest feeling in the world. One you can never explain to another person unless they're parents themselves. Which is why I don't get the way Aidan's mom can be so hateful to him but kiss her other son's ass. The man gives me the fucking creeps. There's something about the way he looks at you that has you crawling out of your skin.

"Fuck." Aidan runs his hands through his hair, then down his face when we step off the elevator. I should be sympathetic with him, but that's not in my nature right now. I want the memory of the two of them meeting for the first time forever etched into my mind.

I am usually quick-witted and known for having a smart mouth, but our proximity in the elevator has me steaming in between my legs, and his scent is doing me in.

I do something I never thought I would do. Something my naughty, little body has been craving since I first saw him again, and I kept resisting, smacking her upside her head. I hadn't realized until this very moment, standing outside my door, that I'm not only physically attracted to this man, but that he's also about to own my heart. I don't mean in that I love him kind of way. I mean that our hearts are going to be filled to capacity by the same little person, by the bond that will never be broken between the two of us.

I swing his powerful frame around to face me. With every scrap of muscle I have, I shove him back against the wall, then get up on my tip-toes and kiss him, my hands cupping his face, my body pressing level with his.

My act of kissing coming from some unknown, uncontrollable act to calm him and myself.

Our kiss is awkward at first. Both of our eyes are open. I'm telling him with mine to give in, while he's asking me what the fuck I am doing. When my tongue sweeps across his bottom lip, the danger spikes through his gaze and the kiss becomes inevitable. His controlling ways snap to attention.

He spins us around, his large frame trapping me against the wall. Every large part of his body smothers me in a way both shocking and desirable. Longing makes its own path into my body from his simple touch. A desire to be touched by him slices through the web of lies I've been telling myself for a long time. I missed him. I can't explain why. Not now, maybe never, but I did. My body is speaking my mind for me. The depression that dampened my life while I was gone slowly dissolves as Aidan coats over my body, mind, and soul at this moment with a fire that smolders that dampness, burning me to a much-needed and wanted crisp.

My heart starts pounding, and my mouth is dry and thirsty as all hell for him. He nudges my mouth open with his tongue. I moan into his mouth. Those shaking legs are now quivering. My hands flow down to his ass. I squeeze the hard flesh into my hands. He grinds his hard dick against me. I may regret doing all this later, right now though, I'm enjoying every damn moment of the way he sucks my tongue into his mouth, releasing it, then swirling, tasting greedily. I'm left panting. My chest is heaving up and down when he steps back from me. My god, he's a beautiful man. My hands fall stiffly to my sides.

"Fuck me. If that was your way of drawing my nervousness out of me, it worked. But what the hell do I do about this?" He points down to his dick.

I start to laugh. "I'm sorry," I say through my laughter.

"I wouldn't laugh too long if I were you." His expression is determined and his phrasing strained. This has affected him as much as it has me. *Well, obviously, Deidre. He is sporting a very nice erection.*

"Why not?" I say. Sarcastically.

"Those nipples of yours are pointing straight at my mouth." I look down, and shit, they are. They're so damn hard, they're protruding like a semi's blinding high beam headlights.

"Not so funny now, is it?" He steps back into me, his hands gripping firmly at my waist.

"My cock has been dying to get inside of you again for a very long time. Don't think I won't take you raw, hard, and deep right here. And one more thing, the next time I take you, and there will be a next time, I will take you bare, no barrier. By the way I look at the situation, we've already made a baby. I'm clean. I have no doubt in my mind you haven't been with anyone else since me. So when I do fuck you, your ass will be full of everything my cock has to offer. That one kiss just put all kinds of dirty thoughts into my head. Now, I have a boy to meet. Do you think you can handle introducing me to him?"

He pulls away from me. Every single part of my body wants him back up against me. Raw, hard, and deep? Oh, geez. And bare? *I'm not sure about that one, buddy.*

I fight it and fake it. This is what we do to each other. This is what we will always do. The one thing I know for a fact is, those words spoken about having me again are going to wage heavily on my scattered brain. It was only a few hours ago I told myself I would be fine with my bob-ette. After that kiss, bob-ette is going in the trash. I'm human. I rotate with the revolution of the earth like everyone else.

Today, my world has been tilted off its damn axis.

When daylight crested, I was fine. When early morning crept upon us, I was nervous. When noon hit me, I was livid. Now that's its early afternoon, I'm happy. Good lord, what I really am is an emotional glob of wet confusion.

CHAPTER SEVEN

AIDAN

"Mom?" Deidre calls out when she opens the door. My fucking nerves have my hands shaking. Realization is sinking in. I'm about to meet my son. Hours ago, I had no clue he even existed.

"How did it go?" Deidre's mom's eyes grow wide the moment she stands up from the chair she was sitting in and notices the both of us standing there. The book she has in her hands falls to the floor.

"Hello Aidan." The expression on her face is easy to read. She's gone into protection mode. Her gaze is shifting straight to her daughter, her eyes pleading for her to say everything is all right.

Deidre picks up on her mother's tension quickly. "Everything's great, mom."

Relief flashes through Beth's features. I'm no fucking idiot. I watch her mother go from a woman who more than likely has been by her child's side for the past year to a woman whose entire demeanor fills with relief and gratitude.

"Diesel is sleeping." Her voice trails off quietly.

I clear my throat. The way her mom is looking at me, I feel as if she needs to hear from me that everything is and will be all right. I'm not abandoning my child. No damn way.

"I'm not going anywhere, Beth. I give you my word. This may not have completely sunk in yet, and I have no clue what the hell I'm doing, but I promise you I'm not leaving your daughter or our son."

"Thank you, Aidan." Her voice is trembling with either thankfulness, or the woman just lost all of her pent-up worry she more than likely has been carrying around for a long time. I suppose all of it.

I watch tentatively as Deidre gives me a keen smile, tosses her wallet on the couch, then takes hold of my hand, pulling me behind her down the hall.

Standing outside of the room I slept in when I stayed here has me feeling emotions I cannot begin to explain, knowing my boy is sleeping right behind this door.

I look down at Deidre, who has excitement seeping out of her, while me, I'm a damn mess.

And then I hear him. The sweet sound of a tiny, little voice making noises. My hand instantly grabs the handle of the door, pushing it open.

"Aidan," I hear Deidre say my name. I keep moving like a madman. I need to see him. To know he's real. This boy of mine.

And fuck me. When I approach the side of his bed, his head turns my way. Big, blue eyes stare at me. I'm unable to move.

There are no words to describe this incomprehensible feeling. This little man and I stare at each other. Me with great intensity, him, well hell, I have no clue what's running through his little brain right now.

"Shit, he's…" Deidre comes up beside me. "Perfect," she whispers. In that moment, he takes his eyes off of mine and swings them to his mom. I cannot wait for the day when he recognizes the sound of my voice like he does hers.

"Hi, buddy." Reaching in, she picks him up with ease. His chubby hands go right to her hair. I stand here having trouble fucking breathing in the fact that this little guy is my creation.

He was unquestionably not planned, but my god, hearing Deidre's next words nearly bring me to my damn knees again. I'm a father.

"Look, Diesel. I want you to meet your daddy." She turns him around so he's facing me. If I open the floodgates and let my tears go, that would be twice in one damn day I've lost it. Only these are tears of joy. Right now, I'm holding them back. Son of a bitch. This little boy is a miracle. How you can immediately fall in love with someone you don't even know, want to do everything to protect them, to show them you will live up to the word dad, pop, or whatever name he decides to call me, is beyond me, but Christ, I'm here. I will always be here for this kid.

"I'm going to go home," Beth speaks from the doorway. Her eyes are full of tears, but unlike me, she lets them flow freely down her face, exposing her happiness for her daughter when her lips angle upward into a smile.

"Thank you, mom," Deidre says without turning away from me. Her own eyes are wet. Hell man, this joyous emotional shit is all new to me.

I go back to looking at my boy. He's looking at me again. It's like a bond has already been formed between the two of us, and I haven't even touched him yet.

"Go sit over there, Aidan. For god's sake, you look scared to death." Deidre tips her head toward a rocking chair in the corner. This is when I gather my first glimpse of my boy's room. Fucking hell, this woman has some badass taste. I've never given a thought to decorating a room before, let alone a kid's. My apartment is plain. Black, white, and gray are the only colors throughout the entire space I live in. Now, the divine colors in this room seep into my skin, making me feel colorful, not bleak and dreary. Fucking hell, this is real.

"Damn." I let out a puff of breath and take in my surroundings. The walls are painted orange and black with a strip of chrome down the middle. A few Harley Davison photos are hung on one wall, and in big black letters above his kickass black-framed crib with Harley sheets and a blanket is his name. I suck in a breath. Close my eyes and move to the rocking chair, my long legs stretching out before me when I sit.

"Here." Leaning forward, she places him in my clumsy arms,

69

adjusting my hands to hold him how I'm supposed to, I guess. Fuck if I know.

"He won't hurt you, Aidan. Loosen up. I'm going to just," she points her finger behind her, "let you have some time with him, then I'll come back and change him." Then she leaves me with no choice and all kinds of shit running through my head, like what if I drop him or what the hell do I even say to a three month old?

Right here, right now, I finally understand what the word love means as I scan this little boy's face. His body is stretching in my lap. Love is this magical little boy, who a man like me does not deserve. I've done some fucked up shit in my life. I will continue to do the same every day, but one thing I will never do is fail him. Not fucking ever.

"Hey, dude." I try my hardest not to cry. Jesus, I cannot help it, the tears drift down my face. What the hell did I ever do in my life to be holding a miracle in my hands? To see him looking up at me as if he knows who the hell I am? I see so much in his eyes. A life full of memories. Good ones. Not the shit life I've lived, not knowing what kind of mood my mother would be in when I came home from school. Or if one morning I would be called a bastard, and the next the person who ruined her life. Screw that. He's going to have the best childhood memories any child can have.

"You have a kick ass room here, boy." His tiny hand reaches upward, and when I place my finger in his, he grips it tight. Badass right there. Strong.

"Are you a tough little man?" He mumbles and grips my finger tighter. This is the purest love can get. I'm pulled to this little boy. My heart is aching to promise him I will never let him down, never make him feel less than the true person he is. Never leave him with a void in his heart so deep that he looks in all the wrong places just to be able to feel.

He will never have to try and earn my love, because he already has it. My unconditional, irreplaceable love.

"You doing all right?" Deidre walks in. I cannot help but travel my eyes over her body. She's changed into a pair of those tight yoga pants and a loose tank top that's hanging off one of her shoulders. Her tanned skin is exposed. Am I an asshole for wanting to bite her shoulder? Then turn around and lick her exposed neck all the way up to her mouth? No, I'm not. I've always been drawn to her. Knowing she gave birth to my son out of her sensual body makes me crave her all the more.

I temper my shit down. We have so much to talk about before I have her under me, but I will have her. She's mine. Both of them are.

"I'm not ready to give him back if that's what you mean," I shrug.

"Well, I need him so I can change his diaper. Unless you want to do it?" She starts laughing wildly.

"What? You don't think I can change him?" I joke.

"No, I don't. But hey," she holds up her hands in defeat, "have at it." She walks toward a small table and pulls out a diaper and what looks like some cream and a bunch of other shit. Fuck, I should have just handed him to her.

"Come on, big daddy. Let me give you your first lesson." She twists that cute, little body of hers around, her eyes beckoning me to come to her. I look from her to the baby. How the hell do I stand up?

"Put your hand under his bottom and the other under the back of his head, Aidan, and just stand." Her arms move in a dramatic upward motion.

I do as she says, wondering if this women's retreat she stayed at taught her how to read minds too? I stalk over to her with steady hands. She reaches out, taking him from me, then lays him down and steps back.

"What?" she mocks. Her hands go to her hips. Little Miss Sass is back, and she finds this shit funnier than I sure as heck do.

"Get the hell over here." I grab her gently by the arm and tug her to my side.

"Oh, no. You need to learn just like I did. Undo those little tabs right there, then lift his butt up and take the diaper off." Demanding little witch.

"I'm doing this shit," I say. And I do. I got this shit down the first try. Powdered his little ass, cleaned around his junk, and put the diaper back on.

"Oh, my god," she belts out in a humorous laughter. Her hands go to her thighs. Tears start to form down her face as she cackles away.

"What the hell?" I say, baffled at this crazy ass woman, who cannot seem to get herself under control.

"You dip shit. You don't put the dirty diaper back on. You grab a new one. Oh, my god!" She keeps on with her laughter. Fuck. I thought I had this shit.

"I'm sorry, Aidan, but this is funny." *Yeah, what the fuck ever*, I want to say to her. Her goddamn facial expression does not show any remorse whatsoever.

"There's a bottle on the kitchen counter. Will you grab it? Let me do this. We'll be right out." She's wiping her tears off her face.

I watch her pull the diaper off of him, grab another wipe, and clean him up again.

"Didn't I clean up his junk right?" I mimic her stance from a minute ago, my hands on my hips.

"Junk? You do not call a baby boy's tally wacker his junk." I laugh. Then stop. Then internally laugh. God. She's totally serious right now. Well, so am I, damn it.

"Junk sounds better than tally wacker. I mean, what kind of name is that? I know he's a baby, but hell, can't you come up with a better name for his manhood than that?" I point my finger in his direction.

"Fine. Penis. Don't call his P.E.N.I.S. junk." I debate what my response to her little outburst should be, running my hand across my chin.

Taking a few steps back, debating how to respond to her ridiculous remark, I see her fine ass in my line of view. Fuck this, I'm not saying anything. I go to her. My arms wrap around her tiny waist. She flinches then relaxes when I lay my head on her shoulder and watch.

"He's perfect, Deidre," I whisper in her ear.

"Yeah," she answers. God damn, I want nothing more than to kiss her senseless right now. To dominate her. To fuck her. It has nothing to do with the fact she's the mother of my child, not this time. It has everything to do with the fact I have never gotten her out of my mind. Not one damn day went by that somehow, someway she crept into it.

She squirms away from my embrace, which pisses me off. She felt too damn good in my arms.

"Um. The bottle," she says as she lifts the baby up, shifts her way around me, and stalks out the door. That cloud of fucking smoke that just crawled up her ass is about to explode when I tell her what I have on my mind. It may turn into a burning fire, one I'm not afraid to put out. I'm staking my claim right the fuck here and now.

I stand in the hallway that separates the living room from the kitchen, barely out of sight, listening to Deidre talk to our son as she feeds him. Her tone is light, nurturing.

The shadow of the side view of her face is all I can see. The way she looks at him, speaks softly, telling him how much she loves him. I was never a man to get into this sentimental shit, yet right now, I feel what I can only describe as warmth spreading throughout my entire body that my child has a mother who loves him, who will help teach him right from wrong, who will show him what it's like to let someone into your heart.

I become more alert and creep forward when she brings him up onto her shoulder. His little head lies down, but his eyes, those eyes that look just like mine have now found me. He lifts his head to the best of his ability, which causes Deidre to glance my way.

I may as well get this shit over with. Let her know I'm not budging one goddamn inch on what I'm about to say.

"You're good with him, Deidre," I announce. She smiles but makes no attempt to reply.

Her guard is back up. I get it. We haven't seen each other for a year and the last time we did, we were both going through hell. Before that, extremely harsh words were exchanged between the two of us. Our bodies may respond to each other in such a way that we want to rip each other's clothes off and fuck until we can no longer fuck, but our minds need to catch up. Be on the same level. This is why what I'm going to say to her next is going to piss her the hell off. Make her go out of her ever-loving mind.

I move across the living room and sit in a chair opposite of her. I remember this chair very well. Big, overstuffed beige leather with a matching ottoman. The only chair big enough to fit my huge frame.

"Do you want to hold him?" Something in the way she says *him* has me sitting up straighter, ready to spit my words out.

"I'm moving in here." Her stare becomes wild. While mine stays calm, sincere, and ready to throw down with her if I have to.

"Like hell you are." Her words are clipped, angry, and full of that smart fucking mouth I'd give anything to stick something into, preferably my cock, just to get her to shut up and listen to what I have to say.

"It's not up for discussion. I want, no, I need to get to know him, and I'm not doing the visitation shit. Hell, I can't take care of him by myself." I arch my brow in challenge to her.

"You can come and see him whenever you want to, Aidan, but you and I both know we cannot live under the same roof together." She glares at me. I glare back with a devilish smirk.

"That's bullshit and you know it. Things are different now. We have him." I jerk my chin in her direction.

"All we do is fight. Plus, you're a pig. You leave shit everywhere." She stands then lays Diesel on a blanket on the floor. I watch in adoration as he lifts his head with every bit of strength he has and peaks up in my direction. Screw it, I'll use him as bait to lure her ass in, to make her see I'm right. I lower myself to the floor, position my body on my side next to him, and run my hand through his dark hair.

"I'll clean up after myself and I'll stay out of your way, but I need this and so does he." I know she's killing me with those eyes. Plotting away my murder. I can feel it. I say no more. Instead, I play with my boy. Talk to him. Tell him all the things we're going to do together. Make him promises I vow not to break. After what seems like fucking forever, I finally look her way. She's watching our interaction with intensity. I can tell right away I have her right where I want her. At this particular moment, it has nothing to do with me and her, and everything to do with me being with my son.

"You're right. He's yours as much as he is mine, but... I have a few stipulations." Her jaw juts out and her eyes grow large. My cock twitches. The big boy loves her sass as much as I do.

"Name them." I remove my hand from my son, who now has the corner of his blanket shoved into his mouth, and stand, placing my feet firmly in front of her, leaving her no choice but to look up at me.

Her breath catching does not go unnoticed due to my proximity. Nor does the fact that my cock is practically level with that fucking mouth of hers. I smirk. She puffs out a steaming breath of air.

"That kiss in the hallway will not happen again. You're here to get to know him. And this is definitely not permanent." I chuckle, which I can tell pisses her off by the way those once large eyes turn into small slits. Christ, every expression on her face is so damn beautiful.

I do the first thing that comes to my mind. I bend down, placing my hands on each side of her head, caging her in, placing my mouth an inch or so from hers.

"That is where you're wrong, Deidre. That kiss wasn't a mistake. You wanted it as much as I did. You're the one who initiated that kiss. You want me to kiss you now, and I know for a damn fact that if I touched your sweet pussy, it would be drenched." I reach down and grab her

75

hand, placing it on my rock hard dick.

"What are you doing?" she hisses.

"Showing you what you do to me. You make me so fucking hard." I then dive in for the kill. Taking hold of a handful of her hair, tilting her head back, I lick her neck, deliberately slowly and teasingly light. Once I reach her chin, I begin to kiss her, stopping shy of the corner of her mouth. Lord help me, those sweet to my ear noises escaping her mouth mixed with her sweet smell send a firestorm through my body.

"I'll be back in a few hours," I whisper in her ear. I know with certainty I have her. She never once took her hand off my cock until I stepped away from her. She can lie, disagree, and deny us all she wants. I will have her and I won't stop until she is mine.

CHAPTER EIGHT

DEIDRE

"What in the hell?" I lay my head back against the couch. "Shit." This sudden turn of events has my head floating around somewhere in orbit. Out of control.

My faithless body is deceiving me. Just hearing Aidan's voice turns me the hell on. Now he's moving in here? Christ, if I could lift my leg up and kick my own ass for agreeing to let him stay here, I would.

He knows his way around a woman's body, that's for damn sure. And his tongue...Good lord, it's like a lizard's. I remember all too well the way he flicked, licked, and then sucked up every bit of my orgasm, making me scream and beg for him to stop his relentless assault on my pussy.

I'm so screwed, in more ways than the pleasurable one. I know damn well I shouldn't be thinking of sex with Aidan at all, yet here I sit with my arousal soaking through my panties.

We have a child together, a beautiful little boy, and that's it. Well, I don't mean it quite like that. Diesel is my entire world. He's everything to me.

"Oh, my god," I all but screech when I lift my head and see my boy has flipped himself over onto his back. Tears instantly form in my eyes. For one, this is the first time he's done that. For two, Aidan missed this monumental moment.

My hands fly over my mouth. "Look at you, big man," I say, flopping down on the floor next to him. He looks up to me with his sappy, cute little smile. And in this moment right here, I truly understand that Aidan is right. These precious moments in our son's life should be shared by the two of us. He has every right to experience all of this as much as I do. I need to shove my sexual frustrations aside. Not let the fact the man has abs chiseled to perfection influence me, or the way his biceps pop out when he flexes just so, or even the way his ass looks in his jeans. Nope, not going to pay any homage to any of that at all. I'm going to let him get to know our child, and once he feels comfortable with taking him on his own, he can move out again.

Right now though, I need to praise my little boy. I pick him up, running pepper kisses all over his chubby, little cheeks, all the while telling him how proud I am of him. I can't wait to tell Aidan. He's going to be bummed he missed it. Well, I technically did too, because I had my mind in the dirtiest part of the damn gutter, but I was here and he wasn't.

"I wonder who that could be." I push up from the floor when the doorbell rings and cradle Diesel in my arms, my legs cramping the minute I stand up straight. We must have been playing on the floor for two hours. They say time slips away from you when it comes to your children. Hell, I'm realizing this to be true.

"Geez, is there a party here I forgot about?" I open the door to Roan, Alina, Calla, and Cain.

"Welcome home." Calla pulls me in for a hug and immediately takes the baby from my arms.

"Come on in." I gesture with my hands, but hell, they're already making themselves at home by the time I have the door shut.

"She's beautiful, you guys," I say, not taking my eyes off of Cain and Calla's little girl, who I saw earlier.

"We came to welcome you back as well as let these two get to know each other." Calla points down to the floor where both of the babies are now on their stomachs just staring at each other.

"Holy shit, he's a mini Aidan," Cain barks out.

"He sure is." We all turn around to Aidan walking in the door like he owns the place. Christ almighty. He's changed his clothes. First thing on my shopping list is to buy one of those little mini spritzer fans you carry around with you, because if he's going to wear a white wife beater tank that's stretched damn tight across his solid chest, then this bitch is going to be in heat twenty-four hours of the day. Which reminds me, I will need to be buying more batteries for my bob-ette on top of some kind of gag to stick in my mouth from screaming his fucking name when I come.

For a moment I become dizzy from gawking at his massive chest right along with those abs that are defined and protruding like the incredible hulk he is. My reflexes instantly reach out to steady my weak, wobbly legs.

By the time I reach those pulse-pounding eyes of his, the prick has a smirk on his face. He knows I'm clenching my damn thighs together. I scrunch up my nose, which causes the jerkface to chuckle. Damn it and damn him. Why couldn't my baby daddy be some loser? Like a deadbeat dad, who has twenty kids scattered around and doesn't give a shit. UGH.

"Would anyone like a drink?" I smile tightly at Aidan, then spin to greet my now unwelcome guests. They're unwelcome because I need to rush my ass to the bathroom and change my god darn panties. I may as well never wear a pair of them again.

There went my plan from a few hours ago about keeping my head on straight and only wanting to parent with Aidan. That shit is never going to happen.

"Nah. Alina and I have to get going. Dude, you moving in or what?" Roan approaches Aidan while I think, *To hell with these guys, I'm having a drink*. Walking the long way around the couch to avoid the hot male scent of Aidan, I approach the kitchen, place my hands on the counter, and take a deep, well-needed breath.

"Hey. What's wrong?" I can't help but laugh, then lift my head to look into the eyes of my best friend.

"I agreed to let him stay here. That's what's wrong." Alina lets out a deep sigh, sensing what's coming next. I brace myself for her talk.

"I'm proud of you for letting him stay here. I'm sure it won't be easy. Just keep telling yourself it's for your son." My mind knows it's for my son, but my body sure as shit doesn't, and herein lies the problem. I'm lonely, desperate to be touched by a man and not just any man, but by Aidan, and that shit scares the living hell out of me. I push back from the counter and tell her that in a quiet whisper, and what does the little bitch do? She laughs.

"This is not funny, goddamn it," I snap.

"Oh, but Deidre, it so is. I remember a conversation similar to this not so long ago… now, wait for it. It went something like 'my pussy being a bank vault and frozen.'" She waves her hand in my face then stifles her laugh with her hand over her mouth.

"Oh no, you don't. You will not throw my words in my face," I say a little too loudly.

"I would never do such a thing," she leans in as if she has to tell me a secret. "Just so you know, my pussy is like one of those twenty-four hour bank ATM machines."

"You are such a slutty, little bitch. Now, come here." I pull her in for a hug.

"I'm scared," I say into her ear.

"I know, honey, but don't be. Let things fall how they're supposed to. If the two of you get together, then let it happen; if you don't, then it doesn't, but for god's sake, Deidre, don't fight it. The two of you made a beautiful little boy. Not to mention Aidan stepped right up to the plate. There aren't many men who wouldn't demand a paternity test or go right ahead and claim that the baby is theirs. That right there should show you what kind of man he is. " Our arms stay locked around each other, confusion written on my face.

"How do you know all this?" The only one who knows anything is my mom. And she's as tight-lipped as they come.

"Aidan called Roan the minute he left here. Told him everything. He's happy about the baby. Not to mention he's here, sweetie." I stumble away from her and reach for a bottle of wine and a glass out of the wine rack.

"He'll be a great dad," I reply unsteadily as I uncork the wine and pour half a glass.

"Don't be so stubborn." Alina grabs the glass from my hand, taking her own healthy sip.

"You ready, baby?" Roan peaks into the kitchen.

"Yeah." She hands me my glass back, kisses my cheek, and squeezes my arm. God, I've missed her. She's always been the level-headed one in our friendship. I sigh once more and take another sip, contemplating her words. Aidan didn't deny our son. He never questioned me once. It's just that for once in my life, I need more than sex from a man. I want a family. Someone to take care of and for him to take care of me. I'm not sure if Aidan is the man for it.

We undoubtedly have a physical attraction to each other, which is important in any relationship. But the question is if he ever wants more than that.

By the time I make it back to the living room, everyone is gone. The room is quiet. My boy isn't on the floor anymore, either.

I place my glass on the table and walk down the hallway, stopping short of the spare bedroom when I hear Aidan talking to Diesel about the first bike he's going to buy him.

It's cute, really, listening to him carry on like he's having a conversion with someone who understands what he's saying.

I back away soundlessly, deciding it's time for dinner. It's been a long time since I've actually cooked a meal. It's what I went to school for. Cooking and baking were something my mom and I have always done together. I'm overly passionate about it. There were days when I was growing up when I would start dinner the minute I returned home from school. Other days, I would create my own recipes. I miss my job at Buttercup Bakery, which is over on 2nd Street. Thank god, my uncle owns the place and my job is there for me whenever I'm ready to return. I would give anything to be able to go back to work, but I'm not sure if I'm ready to leave Diesel, yet. I know the time is coming soon, but the idea of anyone else taking care of him all day long doesn't sit well with me.

I throw my hands up in frustration over it all. I'm not going to worry about any of it tonight. There's already too much rattling around in my scatter-brained head, tugging and pulling me in every direction. Especially the man who's entertaining our child while I'm out here pulling items out of the fridge to cook... I look down at the food in my hands. Of course it's his favorite, my raspberry chicken. Now I'm sub-consciously as well as consciously thinking about the man.

You know what? I say to myself. *Fuck it. I'm making it. He deserves it, especially after everything he's done in one day to prove to me he's going to be around to help raise our son.*

I remember all too well how Aidan would praise my cooking and baking when he stayed with me. Like with everything, I need to make the chicken and maple carrots with brown butter. I begin chopping and dicing food. The feeling of having my knife in my hands is phenomenal. The smell of the spices in the air steadies my unstable mind, and I float away. Concentrating, preparing, and setting the oven and the heat on the stove. I'm so in my element that I jump when I see Aidan standing in the doorway to the kitchen, his arms spread wide, clinging onto the jamb.

"I promise to kiss you goodnight if you tell me you're making that chicken I love." I could totally get used to this, especially if his drop-dead handsome smile and those pulse-pounding eyes land on me every single day.

"I am making the chicken, but you don't have to kiss me for it." I shrug like it's no big deal. It really isn't. He knows from while we were trapped in my apartment last year, how much I enjoy doing this. Hell, it was the only thing that kept me from losing my mind. It was the only time we weren't at each other's throats.

I turn my back to him, preparing the final touches on the chicken before placing it in the oven. The heat from his stare to my backside is fiercer than the heat coming from the oven.

"Listen to me for a minute, Deidre." He's standing directly behind me now. I take a deep breath. He's so close I can smell him over the scent of the spices that are engulfing my face.

"Okay," I manage to say weakly.

"I should have asked if I could stay here instead of demanding it. The last thing I want to do is make you feel uncomfortable, especially in your own home. I'll leave if you want me to." Oh hell, now the man is going to be sweet.

"It's fine, Aidan. I have to get used to it, is all." *If you don't move away from me though, I may spontaneously combust here on the spot.* I don't say those words out loud. No freaking way.

"You sure?" he asks.

I turn around and stare up at him. God, he's simply divine.

"I'm sure." I'm not giving him any more than that. I spin back around, pick up the dish, side-stepping around him, and place it in the oven, set the timer, then turn back to preparing the carrots.

I ignore him until I know he's left the room. Then I finally let out the air I'd been holding in my lungs, grasp hold of the glass of now warm wine, and down the rest of it.

Forty-five minutes later, the two of us are sitting down to a very tense, extremely quiet dinner, while Diesel sits on top of the table in a bouncy seat, trying his best to reach for the toys that drape across the top.

"Tell me about your pregnancy and delivery." Aidan asks those words out of the blue. I stop mid-air with my fork half-way to my mouth.

I glare at him like he's lost his ever-loving mind. "Seriously?" I say. Baffled.

"Well, yeah. I understand why you didn't come back and tell me. I really do. But I want to know everything I missed." The serious look on his face melts my heart faster than the butter melted in the pan when I made these carrots.

And this is how the rest of our first night living together goes. I tell him everything, from the first moment I woke up in my room at the retreat, to finding out I was pregnant. I even go into detail about some of my counseling, how I coped with it all. How my mom was by my side during labor. I can't help but notice his sad expression when I tell him how it felt to hold Diesel in my arms for the first time, or that as soon as he left today, Diesel flipped himself over. Guilt claws away at my chest for not having the strength to tell him earlier. I wasn't ready. Hell, I'm not ready for him being here. What I am ready for, though, is sharing the most precious moments of our son's life with him.

When I glance over to our son, who's now fast asleep, I realize none of this is or should be about me or my feelings at all. It should be about him. His needs, his life. Right then and there I know without a doubt life works in the most mysterious of ways. Sends you down a path you never thought you would go. Takes you on a remarkable journey of one day at a time. I can do this. I can let those chips fall and land where they're supposed to. That's what a parent does for their child. I will bury my fears, live with Aidan, and see where destiny and fate take me.

CHAPTER NINE

AIDAN

Staring at a woman's plump, juicy, and tempting ass bent over a bathtub while she's showing you how to bathe a baby is pure motherfucking torture. It's like heaven and hell finally joined together without Satan, leaving you stuck staring at the perfect ass for the rest of your life. Tempting you to touch it. To tug it back against your aching cock. Fuck. I'm a damn pervert.

I couldn't help myself from leaning my head from one side to the other, imagining how the symmetrical shape of her ass would feel in my hands once again. Shit, I even went as far as what her ass would feel like with my dick inside of her. I want her so damn bad.

The result of her nicely contoured lines and curves has me lying in this small bed with my dick in my hands. Right now, I'm prone to combust, and my dick is the fucking wick to ignite the goddamn flame.

The woman is incredible. I'm not thinking about just her body. It's everything about her. The way she is with our son, the way she smells, looks, and cooks. She's every man's dream. I take that back, she's *my* dream. The hard part is convincing her of that fact. I know she wants me, her body screams it. This sexual attraction between us is stronger than it was before.

I'm an asshole for demanding to stay here, interrupting her life, even though we talked for hours tonight after we both put the baby to bed. I learned more about her tonight then I did in the couple of weeks I stayed with her a year ago while I protected her.

She told me how she would love to go back to work, even if it's only part time. Whatever makes her happy, was my response. Then she dove right in about not wanting to leave our son with a day care provider, not even her mom, who I know damn well would be more than happy to help. Nope, not Deidre. She's bound and determined to work something out to where she can either work from home or take him with her.

The thought of her carrying my child turns me the fuck on. When she showed me pictures of her pregnant belly tonight, something inside of me caved, knowing she took care of him while he grew inside of her. I'm sorry I missed it. That's for me to deal with, not her. She had every reason to stay away like she did. I can never fault her for that. What I can do is make life easier for her and our son.

What I need to do right now, though, is ease this sexual tension out of me before I storm into her room.

I remove the bars from my cock and place them on the nightstand next to the bed.

Bringing my hand back to my aching dick, I rub the come dribbling out of the tip, lubing up as best as I can. Stifling back the grown that wants to escape my mouth when the image of Deidre's ass flashes in front of me, the curve of her soft hip, the soft bounce of her tits, I glide my hand up and down rigorously. The friction feels so fucking good. Deidre's tight pussy would feel better. Hell, I know how it feels, like nothing else I've felt before. It's wet, tight, and so fucking warm. And Christ, can she squeeze her muscles, draining every last drop out of me. I've never come so hard in my life as I did when I was with her.

"Fuck," I roar, louder than I want to when my come squirts out of me, all over my hand and stomach. I breathe in and out, my chest rising and falling. That took less than two damn minutes. Hell, I lasted longer when I was a teenager, jacking myself off to images of my next door snooty neighbor's older daughter.

Sitting up in the dark, I curse under my breath. I don't have a damn thing in this room to clean up with. Fuck it. She's in bed. Snagging my boxers off of the floor, I open the door gently, make my way to the bathroom across the hall, and quickly clean myself up.

I snag the washcloth and towel I used, shut off the light, and come to a complete halt when I hear moaning coming from her room.

Son of a motherfucker. Is she in there getting herself off? She sure the fuck is. I goddamn know it. I may have just jacked myself off to her image, but fuck this shit. No one touches her sweet pussy but me, not even her. If she's going to come, then by god, it's going to be me and only me who makes her.

I stalk down the hall toward her room, carelessly dropping the wash cloth and towel on the floor, including the stripped- off boxers I just put on.

Stopping outside her door, I lean my frowning forehead forward. My hand is tight on the doorknob. She's moaning all right. I can hear her muffled gasps and the light buzzing noise from what I assume is a vibrator streaming through the thin wood separating me from her. My dick is hard once again from the sighs contorting out of her mouth, zapping straight to my motherfucking balls.

Thankful for my job and the many years of breaking into buildings, stores, and even homes, stealing people's guns, I slowly twist the knob, step into the darkness, and shut the door without her even knowing I'm here.

All it takes is for my name to spill out of her mouth, and the words roll right off of my tongue. Thank you, Jesus for bringing this year-long fantasy to life.

"I love being your sexual fantasy, Deidre," I speak honestly. The room is dark, but it does nothing to shield me from the all-pervading stare of her shocked face. I can picture it from where I'm standing, which is right at the foot of her bed. She. Is. Pissed. Well then, that makes two of us, and I'm about to tell her how pissed I am.

"You seriously did not just walk into my bedroom without my permission. GET OUT!" she yells.

"I'm not going anywhere. Why the fuck would you want some plastic vibrator that does a half-ass job of getting your sweet little pussy off, when what you really want is only a few feet away?" I state with pure sarcasm. It's the truth, though. I'm all into kink. Hell, I'll do anything in the bedroom, but for Christ sakes, there is no way in hell a plastic toy with fucking batteries can make her come like I can. I can build a damn castle with my tongue alone. She's done using whatever the hell she's been using. I storm to the side of the bed, reach for the light, and turn it on. Both of our eyes adjust to the light. Mine are bulging out of my head, taking in her naked body. Hers are mimicking mine when she takes me in. Fuck me hard and ride me harder. She's more beautiful than I remember.

She shuts the vibrator off, tosses it to the other side of the bed, and then hikes her knees up to hide her pussy. One hand flies to cover her stomach, the other hand barely stretches across one of her tits. Motherfucker. Those nipples are pink and fresh, and hell, her flimsy white t-shirt does nothing to conceal her set of mouthwatering tits. I want my mouth covering them, my dick dripping my come over them after he's been sliding in between them. God, she is beautiful.

"I...my god, Aidan. I should be mad as hell at you for walking in on me. Just leave, please. You've already ruined a perfectly good orgasm." Her face is flushed red, her eyes are focused on her hand splayed wide across her stomach. I'm a little disappointed that she's not yelling and screaming at me like the Deidre I know would normally do. I truly don't think she could care less if I walked in on her mid-orgasm or not. She's hiding her body from me. She's doesn't want me to see what I've already seen. Her t-shirt is hiked up enough for me to see it all.

"What if I told you I was doing the same thing you were doing?" I cock a brow and tilt my lips in a truthful smile, those words catching her attention.

"I just came all over my hand and stomach to visions of you, Deidre. Of *you*," I emphasize. "I went to clean myself up and heard you. I won't apologize for walking in here and taking things into my own hands. *Literally,* sweet-tart, let me take every inch of your body into my hands. It may have been wrong of me, but I don't really care. What I do care about right now is the fact you're hiding those stretch marks our baby gave you from me." In all of my twenty-nine years I've never been an emotional man. I've never had a reason to, up until now. Up until today. This woman lying here has turned a crappy day into one I will always remember, and I'll be damned if she's going to be embarrassed about anything as beautiful as the marks I see on her stomach.

I do the only thing I think is right. I sit down on the edge of the bed. There are several seconds of silence between us, in the course of which I take in her body from head to toe. Then I lay my eyes upon her stunned ones.

"Do you know what I see when I look at you?" I trace a finger up her silky thigh. A smirk spreads across my face when goose bumps caress her flawless skin.

"I see a woman I want to strip naked and have my way with. I see a woman, who's the mother of my child, a woman, who when she barged into my apartment earlier and ripped into my mother to protect me after not seeing me for a year got my dick so hard I could drill a hole through concrete with it. These," I lift up her hand covering her stomach, the tips of my fingers tracing the lines of the marks across her soft skin. "Make you exclusively... you. A mother. Don't hide these from me ever again. Next to you and our boy, these are the most beautiful things I have ever seen."

I look up to her when I hear her sniffle. Pearl-shaped tears flow from her luminous eyes.

I close my eyes. Vivid memories of the last time I saw her crying flash before me, of her hanging on for dear life, of when we were both kidnapped. Her expression tonight doesn't mirror that same one from a year ago. She's not full of pain or sorrow, wondering if her next breath could possibly be her last. Neither is she embarrassed anymore. I've broken through her strong barrier this fascinating woman has shielded herself with. She screams scared, vulnerable even. And maybe a little shocked from my compassionate words.

Tonight, when we talked before we both headed to bed, we didn't argue. We learned. I know this is a new chapter in my book of life as well as hers. I need to convince her more than I need to take my next breath right now that I want this chapter and the next and many more to be all about the three of us.

"You mean that?" Her expression is somewhat hard to read.

"When it comes to you, I mean every word I say."

"Well, then you're nuts, Aidan Hughes. I mean, look at you." I glance down at my chest briefly, then back up to meet her shimmering eyes.

"You're so well defined, tall, and the most striking head turner I have ever seen. You could be with anyone. Let me ask you a question." She sits up, reaches for the sheet, and pulls it up over her body. My hand falls away from her soft skin.

"Ask away." I challenge. I know a question I'm not going to like is coming. I can hear it in the tone of her voice.

"Would you want to be with me if we didn't have Diesel?" Jesus Christ, has she lost her mind? I grip hold of her shoulders, my face within an inch of hers now, her flowery scent coating my every inhale.

"I've wanted you since the moment I set my eyes on you. We're alike, you and I. There's no denying we set each other's asses aflame, we get on each other's nerves, we yell, scream. But Christ, woman, when you get a hair up your sexy ass, and your mouth starts spewing off smartass shit, do you have any idea what that does to me? The night we fucked until neither one of us could walk, the night we made our son, was the best night of my entire life, and that was before I even knew he existed. So yes, Deidre, I wanted you then and I most definitely want you now."

I'm done talking. I want and need to taste her. A few moments ago she said I barged in here and ruined a perfectly good orgasm. I know for a fucking fact if she had or was going to have one, there is no way in hell it would have been perfect. The one I'm about to give her with my tongue will be, though.

My chest rises and falls. My cock is still achingly hard. I shift my body around, lower my hands down to her waist, and in one swift movement, I have her straddling me. Her wet pussy slides across my cock. I hiss from the glorious contact.

"What are you doing?" I glance over to the baby monitor she told me she keeps on her nightstand, silently praying the baby stays asleep. Then I tear my unanswered gaze back to her beautiful face. God, she undoes me. She makes me crazy with need for her.

"You said I ruined an orgasm. One you claimed to be perfect. I'm going to remind you what a perfect orgasm feels like." One side of her mouth twists up while her humiliation diminishes.

"Really? And what about you?" She begins to glide her pussy across the tip of my cock.

"Don't you worry, baby, with what I have in mind we'll both be coming so hard in each other's mouths we may wake up the entire State of New York." I ease us both farther back onto the bed until I'm confident we have enough room before I lower the top half of my body onto the bed.

"Turn around and sink that sweet-smelling pussy on my face, Deidre." Her mouth gapes open, giving me a glimpse of her wicked tongue. "Keep that mouth open and take my cock."

I notice her trying to camouflage her excitement. She wants this as bad as I do, she wants it so much she can't stand it. It's too extreme, whatever we had or will have between her and I. We were both just too caught up in the worry, the desire to strike out to hurt one another. Back then it was like we couldn't help ourselves. Not anymore.

And fuck me, when she shifts her weight off of me and slings her sexy figure around, and I get my preview of her pretty little pussy, I grip her hips hard and inhale her scent deeply before drilling my tongue into her silky flesh. She moans, unselfishly offering me what I've craved ever since I had my first taste of her a year ago. Pulling her down onto my face as far as I can get her, I lick my tongue straight up her center.

"Fuck," I rustle out the minute her tongue swirls around the tip of my cock. My eyes roll into the back of my damn skull the instant she pulls me into her mouth. Goddamn, she knows how to play my cock. It's hard as fuck to concentrate when she's sucking then twirling her magical tongue. I don't even want to know how she learned to speed up, stroke, and fucking tease.

Multi-tasking has never been easy for me, but right now, I solely try to focus on her. I want to hear my name come out of her mouth by me being the one to make her come. She begins to grind on my face, while my hips move up and down in tandem with her sensual mouth.

I lick every part of her pussy I can get my mouth on. She taste exactly as I remember. Sweet and fresh. A meal I want to gorge on. And I do. I eat her. I lick her. I suck her clit until I feel her start to spasm all around me, the taste of her appealing orgasm soaking into my mouth, quenching my dying thirst for her.

"Oh, my god, Aidan." She lifts her head, screams out her words, and goes right back to taking my cock in her mouth. I breathe in the scent of her pussy, bury my face up against her silky core, and take her orgasm. Conquer it. Own it. Devour it.

Then it happens, my balls tighten, my spine loosens, and without an ounce of warning even to my own damn self, I let loose a sling of cuss words and come harder than I did when I jacked off. She laps at my cock, taking every bit of my release down her throat.

"Now, that was the perfect orgasm." Taking her mouth off of my cock, I lift her pussy from my face. My vision stays locked on her wet pussy as she swings her legs around me and pushes herself up off the bed. My chest is about ready to explode with happiness hearing those words escape from her.

"Then throw that plastic motherfucker away. I have many more of those to give." I'm not teasing, either. She knows it when I sternly charm my way into her heated evaluation of my intent, as she tries to decide whether I'm serious or not.

"Where are your piercings?" Her question throws me off guard. She avoids my eyes as she bends down and snags her panties off of the floor, covering up her tasty little body.

I lick my lips, enjoying the best fucking taste ever. "I took them out when I jacked my cock to you." She pauses mid-step toward the bed. A delightful smile graces her face.

"And here I thought you were joking about getting yourself off just to make me feel better." The little fucking vixen knows damn well I'm not joking about it when I stare her ass down.

"You keep standing there with that sexy as fuck, barely there shirt on, and I'll stroke him again. Only this time, I'll let you watch," I challenge her.

"I'll do more than watch." She whips her shirt over her head and shimmies those panties right back down her legs then kicks them off. I watch them sail across the room. We exchange a look that can only be described as carnal, intense, and hungry. Getting up on my knees, I fist my cock in my hand while the one woman in this world who could completely undo me lies back on her bed, spreading herself wide, and slides two fingers inside her bare pussy. Not once do we take our eyes off of each other when we once again pleasure one another.

CHAPTER TEN

DEIDRE

My disoriented mind is yelling for me to climb out of bed, to dislodge from the warm cocoon I'm blanketed in. Aidan. His long, lean body is draped halfway across mine. My back is to his front, his muscular arms are wrapped around me, clinging, clenching me tightly as if he never wants to let me go. It's surreal, really, this feeling I have coursing through me.

It's all because of him. Our crazy banter turned serious last night. The words he spoke to me regarding my insecurities over my stretch marks will forever be lodged both in my heart and my mind.

I should have been stark raving mad last night when he walked in here and caught me, but seeing him standing there with his thick cock hard, ready, and all for me had me melting into my sheets. He wanted me as much as I wanted him.

God, he's just so…I don't know. Demanding. Irresistible. My fantasy, truly. He's captivated me in a way that should scare me. And yet, here I lie knowing I should get up, change, and feed my little man who's jabbering away. The sound of his sweet, little baby garble brings a smile to my face.

"Let me get him." Aidan's husky morning voice whispers in my ear. "You sure you can handle it?" I tease. If he thinks changing a diaper was hard last night, wait until he sees how soaked it will be this morning.

"I have to learn. Stay in bed. Get some sleep. You're going to need it for what I have planned for tonight." Instantly, I miss him when he releases his hold of me, kisses the back of my head, and hops out of bed like he's had a full night's sleep. We barely slept at all. We talked for hours again before we went to bed, then hours after his magically delicious tongue left me damn near weeping, right along with my pussy having multiple convulsions, contracting out of control from watching him stroke his cock, while my fingers played and pretended he was pounding me into oblivion.

However, I'm not cold. Whatever he has planned for later sends a divine heat wave from the top of my head to the tips of my toes, then shoots straight to my core. *Please, no more bob-ette*, I plead with the man upstairs. There is nothing like the big, thick cock of Aidan Hughes. Especially in combination with a body like his. Muscles are one of those things that are best in moderation. He's sculpted his into perfection.

Sweet baby of all things sinful. The morning light strumming through the slits in the curtains gives me a graceful view of his ass. Then he goes and covers that perfect ass up with jeans. Swearing profusely under my breath, I stalk, stare, and admire this gifted man in front of me. His dark hair is sticking up all over the place. World, eat your heart out, he's my baby daddy.

Normally, my mouth is dry in the morning, not today though. It's lip-smacking hungry. Who cares about drinking water when I have my own personal waterfall of lick-able man to quench my thirst?

Christ, the way his abs flex, making them look like a ladder you just want to climb, has me practically drooling all over myself. Instant sexual attraction.

"I've got this." Those deep, sea-blue eyes churn into mine with intensity. Expelled from lack of sleep, they show tenderness, a side I've seen from him before when he rattled off everything he wanted to teach Diesel. I feel giddy. Cherished.

He leans down and kisses my forehead. I watch him go, thanking him without dragging my tired eyes from his ass.

Should I feel like a slut for jumping into bed with him? I should. But I don't. This is our life, our business. A year changes a lot of things. One thing it did not change is how we feel about each other. I thought he hated me, he thought I hated him, when this entire time it's been the exact opposite. I sigh happily.

Rolling over on my side facing the monitor, I wait until I hear him start to talk before I close my eyes, falling not only back to sleep, but falling further for the man who is beginning to obliterate, stimulate, and heal me.

"What have you done to him?" Thank god, I'm refraining from beating Aidan's ass. Roan's too. My son is spread out on his blanket butt-ass naked. The two of them sit side by side, their attention absorbed by the computer screen on the table in front of them.

If I had known this was the scenery in my living room, I wouldn't have taken my time showering and getting ready for the day. Aidan told me last night he took a few days off work, so the three of us could just be and learn each other's routines. My child rolling around on the floor naked is definitely not part of his daily routine.

"Settle down, sweet-tart. He's fine," Aidan drones on.

"He's naked," I say loudly, bypassing the two of them and grabbing the diaper that just so happens to be right next to him on the blanket.

"He shit all over the place." Finally, Aidan lifts his head from whatever is more important than his child. My eyes bore into his like a wild beast's. I should have known better than to let him get up with him.

"Do I dare ask how you cleaned him up?" Both of them frown. Aidan's next words have my anger squandered to the point I laugh so hard that tears fall freely. I may pee my pants too.

"You did what?" I somehow manage to get a few words out.

"You heard me." His tone is more serious now.

"No, I don't think I did. I mean, I thought you said, 'I stripped him down, left the shitty clothes on the bathroom floor, and held him in the shower.'" Apparently, my laugh is contagious. Roan throws his head back and chimes in right along with me. This in return pisses Aidan off. I can feel it as his death glare almost knocks me over. I can't help it, I laugh some more.

"What the hell was I supposed to do? The boy had shit everywhere. I'm talking up his back, down the crack of his ass. Even all over his PENIS. How can someone that little shit so much?" I pay him no attention as I hunt through all the rolls of baby fat checking for shit. Literally.

"You did a very nice job." I turn to praise him. Oh, dear. Wrong thing to say.

He rolls his eyes. "That's the last time I'm nice to you," he says sarcastically.

"We'll see," I challenge him with a much-defined, lifted brow.

"No dick for you tonight?" Hmm.

"If I don't get the dick, then you don't get the pussy." My brow goes even higher. Take that, Mister Smartass.

"You'll beg for it," he counters.

"So will you," I grapple.

"How in the hell did the two of you make such a cute little kid? Jesus H. Christ. Would you like me to take him home, where two normal people live?" Roan tosses in.

"This is foreplay. I love her fucking smart mouth. It's sweet and sour." Oh, boy! I'm getting wet. If I trusted Roan with my son, I would take him up on his offer, but hell, I can't even trust him with his own father, so screw that shit.

And normal my ass!

"Are his dirty clothes still on the floor?" I desperately need to change the subject. Do I dare leave Diesel on the floor to play while I go into the kitchen to take my medication? I do, but I keep that little

97

tidbit of information to myself, hoping Aidan realizes I'm only giving him shit. Ha! Shit. Keeping that one to myself as well, I make my way into the kitchen, this time purposely walking by Aidan. I may inhale deeply when I saunter by him, too. *Could you please rub your smell all over my body? It's addictive.*

"Nope. I threw them away. I promised you I would clean up after myself." His response is exactly what I thought he would say. "One day. He's only been here one damn day," I mumble.

My phone vibrates on the counter, notifying me I have a couple of missed calls. I see both of them are from my mom when I swipe the screen. She's probably worried sick. She's been through more with me than any parent should have to go through in the past year.

Pulling a glass out of the cupboard, I fill it with water and take my Xanax along with my birth control pills, which I have so eloquently left on the counter. I'm positive Aidan has seen them. I completely forgot to tell him I've been taking them for a little over a month now. Not because I wanted to go out and have sex. I need them to get my periods regulated. Being pregnant, plus the stress I've been under for the past year, has my hormones all out of whack.

I'm startled when large hands wrap around me from behind. I twist my head to look over my shoulder at the man who has crawled back into my life, his fingers moving delicately across my lower abdomen. My breathing becomes erratic when he pushes my hair off to the side and kisses his way up the side of my neck to my ear.

"I hope you're not mad." His voice is smooth, yet abrasive at the same time. "I'm not," I say breathlessly. "Good. I was kidding about his clothes. They're in a plastic bag in the laundry room." He begins to circle the outer edge of my ear with his tongue while pressing his erection into my backside. "You're teasing me," I moan. "No. I'm letting you know that I saw your pills, which means when I get back, I'm sinking inside of you, Deidre. Deep, hard, and rough." The way he pronounces his words has me quivering everywhere. Especially

98

between my legs, the one spot I desire him to pummel into the most. Before I spin him around and devour him right here, it hits me he mentioned when he came back. Where does he have to go?

Weaving my way out of his hold, I turn to face him. Those deep baby blues of his turn dark, fill with lust, a craving he only wants me to fill.

I feel like I'm walking from shallow waters, where you can see the bottom, to deeper waters, where you have no idea when you're going to drop off into the deep end. His eyes are hungry, like a shark in those waters, circling around until he's ready to attack. My chest drags me under those waters, and yet, I still breathe. That is until he leans down and presses his lips to mine. Our kiss starts off slow, then rapidly turns passionate. Lingering, his lean body pulls me in tight. Our tongues taste, exploring one another's mouth. He feels so good. And god, the way he consumes every crevice inside my mouth leaves me breathless, panting and wanting more when we break apart. My scattered brain is lost to him.

We stare at each other for a few moments. I forgot all about him leaving until he speaks again.

"There's something I have to do. That's why Roan is here." My forehead wrinkles in confusion.

"Why do I have the feeling I'm not going to like this something you have to do?" My voice is raspy. A subtle film of sweat evolves in the middle of my chest along with a ping of hurt and worry.

"We found Ryan's sister. You know, the one they asked me to kill?" How could I forget? His mother and half-brother are pure evil. More fucked up than I can even begin to comprehend.

I think, no, I know I just fell a little more for Aidan right here in my kitchen. This right here proves it. He's a protector, like Roan, Cain, and Dilan. My god, if I could leap into his chest right now and hug his heart, I would.

"You're going to her?" I gulp out, my pulse stumbling down the worry path. I try my best not to let on how worried I really am. I hate this kind of life, especially for him. His crappy family showing up out of the blue, thinking they could get him to go and take an innocent woman's life, leaves him no choice but to tell her. It makes me even angrier than I was when I first stumbled upon the interaction between them yesterday.

"We are. She's in Philly. There's really not much information on her or her mother. I do know she's a dental hygienist and still lives with her mother." His face pinches into an expression I cannot quite put my finger on. Then it hits me. He's worried for her. Which now makes me more concerned. I keep my feelings hidden, although I wonder why he kept all of this from me during our many conversations last night. I'm not about to ask him, though. The less I know right now, the better.

"Okay then, go to her. Do what you have to do. We'll be here when you get back." I say this like it's an everyday habit. When a genuine smile spreads across his face, I can't help but smile, too. Even though mine is filled with dread, I fake it.

"That's my sweet, little tart of a girl," he says teasingly. I hope anyway.

"You do know that sweet and tart don't really mix well, don't you?" He moves in closer, shadowing over my petite frame.

"They do when it comes to you." His lips press firmly to mine, this kiss quick and simple.

"I'll call you when I'm on my way back." He's looking down at me with a roguish smile.

"You don't have my number." I bat my eyelashes then duck my head playfully.

"I do when you leave your phone on the counter." My eyes narrow. That fucker better not have drummed his way into my phone. I have a password on there.

"Spill, asshole. How did you get into my phone?" He grins like he's won this round of our devious little battle.

"First try, baby. Diesel's birthdate." His eyes flash to my mouth and back to my eyes several times. He's patiently waiting for me to strum up some smartass comment. Well, hell. He may have won this round, but the battle is far from over.

"You're a..." I start to say, but he shuts me up gladly when he captures my mouth with his once again. God, I could eat this man alive. Like lick, suck, bite, and engulf him in ways I have dreamed about. My tongue is thirsty. I drink him in, sucking his tongue into my mouth, biting gently as I do so. Aidan growls, consuming me the same way I'm attacking him. Devilishly. Deliciously. Want meets need. Starving meets fulfilling. And god, he's accomplishing those tasks in every way. I'm heating up. I'm aching for him.

"See you later. And no touching yourself until I'm here."

I ignore his words when he pulls away. My body that was on fire seconds ago is now left freezing cold, like I've been doused with an ice bucket full of freezing water. However, it has nothing to do with not having his warmth next to me. It has everything to do with the situation that his hand has been forced to play.

I absolutely hate this feeling of dread coursing through me. I know now what Alina felt like when she first started dating Roan. Fear. Dread of the unknown. Only this time, I know nothing. I know Aidan and Roan would not be leaving if they didn't take this threat seriously, but why? Why is it that for once in my life, I feel I could truly be happy, that the three of us could build on this foundation we've created, and then the senseless evil people in this world could show up and rip my world apart?

I've lived in hell for the first part of this past year, the only thing keeping me from completely losing my fucking mind was knowing a life was growing inside of me. I strived to get better, determined to make my child proud of me, to give him a happy and healthy life. Once again, I hold my distress inside of me. I need to remain strong, if not for myself, then for this man who in such a short period of time has become important to me. *Strong*, I repeat the word over and over in my rattled-up head.

"And I'll teach you how to change a shitty diaper when you return." I retort sweet-tart like, so he doesn't hear the fear in my voice. Fear stinks; you really can smell it from a mile away. I'm living proof life's fear and its unpredictability can catch you off guard and toss you straight into hell. I've been there. Nothing or no one is going to take me back there, and especially not Aidan's so-called family. The things he told me last night about his mother only fueled the poison I know reeks from her putrid soul. She's the one who belongs in hell, right along with her corrupted son, Ryan.

"Anything for you," he says sweetly. I know my fearless act worked when he winks as he rights himself, leaving me behind.

I stand in my kitchen, trembling, until I hear Roan tell me goodbye as he closes the front door. Then I glide to my ass on the floor, curl my knees up to my chest, and for the first time in almost a year, my mind travels back to the last time he walked out that door, only this time I know he'll be coming back.

I stand up, stronger, more determined than ever to not dwell on what started out to be a great day and now has turned to shit. I'm amused about the word 'shit' once again. By the time I reach the living room, my little man is sound asleep. My eyes roam down his body, taking in my son's apparel. If he weren't zonked out, I might scream, instead I whisper and shudder. "I'm going to kill that fucker." And I mean it. He had the balls to put a Detroit Tigers baseball shirt on my son, when he knows damn well I'm a Yankee's fan. "You're in deep shit when you get home, Aidan Hughes. Deep shit!"

CHAPTER ELEVEN

AIDAN

Most men keep their private lives private. I'm no exception. Today though, as I weave my way through the early afternoon traffic, I want to fucking roar. Beat my hands on my chest. Tell the entire world.

"That pussy-ass grin on your face speaks for itself, motherfucker," Roan barks out. I give him the you-have-a-lot-of-room-to-talk look, press down on the gas, and let my truck do the roaring for me as I exit onto the expressway.

"Obviously, I'm unqualified as fuck when it comes to knowing how to care for a baby, but Christ, the feeling of knowing I have a son is indescribable." I've endured more shit in my life than any one person can handle. But this, this is the greatest sensation my fucked-up life has ever felt.

Now, here I am, forced to leave my family so I can deal with saving a woman's life from my mother, whom I should be calling my family. God. The idea of her or her beloved son coming anywhere near my son or this woman I'm about to see sends me in a damn rage. Sick Fuckers.

This sinister emotion is more than a stab to the gut. I do not trust either one of them as far as I can spit. If the two of them were desperate to come to me, the person they despise as much as I do them, then I know damn well they're serious about killing her.

I can't let that happen. Especially not to an innocent woman, who more than likely knows nothing about how malicious those two can be when they want something, a something that rightfully belongs to her.

She deserves some of that prick's money. It isn't her fault her father was a grade A asshole. Or that he cheated on his wife. Hell, I can't even count the times I came home from school and caught another man exiting my mother's bedroom, only to get a, "Hey, what's up, kid?" or a chin lift when they passed me in the hallway. Bullshit no teenager should have to see. She's a conniving bitch and a slut, rolled up in plastic and Botox.

"I'm happy for you, my friend. You should be with them right now instead of having to deal with all of this." Goddamn. I love my friend. He's my true brother right here.

"Let's get this over with. Feel her out. See where her head's at. Like I said before, this woman has no idea who she's dealing with when it comes to them." I grip the steering wheel tighter, focusing on the task ahead. Roan nods his head in agreement to the truth I just spoke. He's one of the very few people who know about the situation with my blood family. How much hatred I hold inside of me towards them.

Roan's urge to protect this woman, Anna Drexler, and her mother, match my own. We've always been this way. Cain included, we protect the ones we care about then with a flip of our hand, we destroy the ones we hate.

Like I told Deidre, we know what she does for a living, where she works, and that's about it. I didn't tell her we knew her name, for reasons of my own. Deidre may have saved my ass the other day by barging in like she did, but she made one big mistake by announcing she was my fiancée. Unbeknownst to her, she has put herself in their line of sight by making them think we're getting married. She's targeted herself. Who the hell knows if they'll come after her or not?

"Look. You know I love you like a brother. Hell, you are my brother." Roan pauses for a bit. I'm wondering where the hell he's going with this sentimental shit all of a sudden. Proclaiming our brotherhood bond out of the blue.

"I talked to my dad the other day, after Deidre showed up. I'm going to assume she told you everything." I nod, keeping my eyes fixed on the road ahead. "All I'm going to say is I think she's still the same, yet stronger, man. And I don't mean that in a bad way. I mean just like Alina, she's immune to the life we lead, the shit we do, the trouble lurking around every damn corner. If the two of you are going to have any kind of relationship at all, then never lie to her. She's far from stupid. She knows some of the shit we do. But now, with a child in the picture and this bullshit we're getting into with your family, she has the right to know everything."

"Fuck." My outburst rattles off the interior of this truck like a goddamn rattlesnake ready to strike. Darting off to the side of the road, I slam on my breaks, not giving as many fucks as the fuck yous I'm sure the people in the cars blaring their horns at us are as they drive by.

"What the hell, Aidan. You going to beat my ass alongside the road? I'm only trying to help you out." Placing the truck into park, I drag my hands down my weary face, ignoring his comment about beating his ass. What he just said activated my fuck-up. If anything, I owe him a big thank you.

"Jesus Christ. I'm so fucking stupid. We need to get someone on Deidre, man. I can't believe I fucking forgot to get her protection. Fuck." I punch the dash then look to my friend, whose facial expression answers it all. He gets me.

"Calm the hell down. I'm on it." Easier said than done. A year ago, he was as panicked as I am now when he called me and all but demanded I get my ass to New York to protect Alina.

With a flip of his phone, he's on the phone with his cousin Dilan. Immediately, I calm down when I hear Dilan agree without hesitation or knowing why he's even watching her. We're all like a band of brothers. Hell, we have our own personal army, our own code of conduct. The main one being loyalty.

"Make sure she doesn't know. She will flip her goddamn shit if she finds out she's being protected. Unless she leaves. If she leaves, then tell him to stop her ass no matter what the hell he has to do." Goddamn it. I pull back into traffic once it's cleared, more eager now to get this day over with. Fuck.

My mind races back to the confrontation with my mother. I cannot for the life of me recall if Deidre told them her name or not. Son of a bitch. I need to get back to them as quickly as possible.

"Thank Christ for modern technology and computer hackers." Roan brings me out of my dark thoughts, slams the laptop down, and tosses it in the backseat, then gleams like a choir boy about ready to sing. I hope he has more information about Anna.

"What did they find out?" I crank the wheel to exit the highway.

"She has the day off today. Pretty damn convenient." My chest rises and falls quickly. Good news indeed. This means we don't have to confront her at work.

"Punch in her home address into the GPS. We'll start there." Pulling onto the street that would have taken me to where she works, I continue driving until Roan has the address punched in.

"She lives two miles away." How convenient once again. "Thank Christ for modern technology," he boasts out again, like a stupid fucker who thinks he created said technology. Makes me fucking laugh, which, with the heaviness my head and chest feel, I needed.

Three minutes later, we've pulled up to the curb alongside a small, white house with a perfectly manicured lawn. Charming would be the right adjective to use. Hell, I don't know. What does shock the ever-loving hell out of me is the new red F-Type Jaguar Sports car looking entirely out of place in this neighborhood. Don't get me wrong, the area isn't bad, but hell, every house on this entire block looks the same. They may all be different colors, but the style and shape are identical.

"Nice ride." I twist my body out of the seat and snatch up the keys,

106

locking the doors before acknowledging Roan.

"I bet Ryan bought it for one of them before he croaked." I state knowing what I feel in my gut to be true. That piece of shit more than likely bought them off in every damn direction to keep them silent. Unless Anna and her mother are a couple of money-hungry bitches like my mother. Something tells me they're not though. If they were, then they sure as hell would not be living in a house the size of my fucking bathroom.

"Cute little house." I'm about ready to agree with Roan when we're both damn near struck dead by the petite woman who barges out of the house with a goddamn rifle in her hands.

"What the fuck?" I say, pissed as fuck. "Jesus Christ, woman. Put that goddamn thing down," I hiss. Damn it.

"Get the fuck out of here," she booms in a voice louder than a little spitfire like her should be able to. She's like a wild, little pixie. A beautiful one at that. Long, blond hair. Short, but toned legs. She has badass written all over her tiny, little body. If she put that goddamn gun down, she and I might become fast friends. Not in the sexual way, but in the I-have-your-back-and-you-have-mine kind of way. I dig this chick. Junior obviously wants her out of the picture, doesn't want to claim her as family. Hell, I'll be glad to claim her as mine. Don't ask me why this shit is running through my head when she has a gun pointed at my goddamn chest. It just does. I can feel her pain from here.

Even though I see my entire life unravel before my fucking eyes. No raising my kid. No wishful thinking of having someone love me for me. Nothing. Then the little hellion cocks the hammer back. Fuck that shit. I may have changed my mind about her after all.

"Listen, I don't know who you think we are. We promise you we're not here to hurt you," I point out.

"Really? Is that why my mother is lying on the couch right now with a busted lip? Haven't you fuckers done enough? We don't want the money anymore. Leave us the fuck alone." Son of a bitch. Fucking

107

Junior must have been here.

"Does the name Aidan Hughes ring a bell to you?" Lifting a brow, she doesn't say anything at first. Then we both watch as she closes her eyes, takes a few short breaths, then lowers the gun and her head at the same time.

"I'm sorry." She lifts her head back up, and I can see in her eyes speak the truth. Sadness emits out of her, like a unique variety of storytelling. I feel sorry for her.

"I swear, Anna, we're here to help you." I recognize the minute it all registers with her who I am and what I'm really doing here. A face can tell a thousand stories, they say, and this young woman's expression tells it all.

"I'm Roan," the pansy-ass motherfucker finally speaks. "You found your voice, dickface." I nudge him in the shoulder as I stroll on past him toward Little Miss Pixie Stick.

"Mom." Anna's tone is comforting as we step over the threshold into the quaint little house.

"In the kitchen." A delicate, yet muffled and soft-spoken voice calls out. Then I see her. This woman my mother hates. Her lip is swollen, her are eyes red-rimmed, showing evidence that she's been crying.

"Oh, god." She takes a step back, those sad eyes darting from me to Roan, then back to her daughter. She's beautiful, like her daughter. Mid-forties, I guess. When we first started investigating this morning after I filled Roan in on everything, we wasted no time in finding out Ryan's daughter's name or her whereabouts. Our main concern was finding her. Our effort led us here. I know nothing about this woman standing before me. Not even her name.

Just like Anna, I see her recognition of who I am once she glances back at me. Obviously, they've seen pictures of me somewhere. I can find all that shit out later. My main goal right now is to get them to agree to leave with me. To get them the protection they need until we can figure this shit out.

"Ma'am," I say politely.

"Wh… what are you doing here? And you?" She points to Roan. "You're the freaking mob." She says, dropping her hand from where she was holding a wet cloth up to her lip.

"I am," Roan speaks truthfully.

"Great. Can this day get any worse?" She saunters over to sit on a blue, flowered couch. I glance around the room, a homely sensation passing through me. Pictures of Anna and dickface line the entire mantle above the fireplace. It's apparent to even my eye by the way she's looking up to him in several of the pictures that the woman adored her father. That look is mirrored right back at her by her father. No wonder the man was gone half the time. This was his happy place. Maybe he wasn't a dick to the two of them. Who the hell knows? Tearing myself away from the photos, I train my thoughts back to the reason we're here.

"Listen, like I told Anna, we're here to offer you our help." Her demeanor changes instantly. Her shoulders sag forward and a relieved smile spreads across her face.

"Mom. We need their help. You know we do. Plus, you know I've done my homework. I really believe we can trust them. You know what dad said if anything were to happen to him." Anna moves to sit next to her mom.

My head jerks back as if I've been punched in the damn face. "I know what he told us, sweetie, but I'm scared," her mother whispers.

I catch my buddy looking at me with a taken-aback expression written all over his face, like my own.

"Ma'am," I say once again.

"Please, call me Grace." God, she sounds and acts so differently from my own mother. I'm confused. This bizarre shit has my head lighting up with a million questions.

"It's clear you need our help, and it's blatantly obvious we all have a lot of questions. But one thing I can promise the two of you is we're

109

here to assist you in anything you need." The hard timbre of honesty in my voice is apparent to the two of them. The last thing innocent and sweet-looking Grace says before we help them pack up their personal belongings so they can follow us to New York is, "Help us kill the rotten son of a bitch who killed my daughter's father."

"You should mind your own business, fucker," a deep raspy voice calls out from the shadows. I've taken the women to their hiding place and dropped of Roan. The minute I park my truck in the garage at Deidre's building, I'm assaulted by some dickhead's words. "Who the fuck are you?" I creep toward the voice as I tug my gun out of my back pocket. It's obvious this is one of Ryan's buddies or someone he's hired to threaten me.

"I'm the one who's going to fuck you up, Aidan, then toss your ass in jail. I'm the man with the badge." I scoff. As if a crooked cop or a damn liar who thinks he can scare me off is going to make me back down.

"Jail? For what? Taking care of what's mine?" I deride this corrupt idiot.

"I doubt very much the gun you're packing even belongs to you. That's a charge right there, among other things. Resisting arrest. I can nail you with as many charges as I see fit." He stubs out his cigarette like we're in some damn movie.

"I don't have time for this shit. You want to take me on all by yourself in the middle of a parking lot, then bring it, motherfucker. I guarantee you will not be taking me anywhere. I, on the other hand, can make sure you disappear." I stand there watching this arrogant prick as he contemplates his next words. I'm not dumb. These cops have no clue what my family will do. He's not one of ours, that's for sure. If he were from New York, he sure as hell wouldn't be here alone. There would be a slew of other cops here waiting to take me in. Fucking cops. At least I'm not afraid to admit who I really am. I'm not on some fucker's payroll, who's scared to do his dirty work himself. Fuck no.

"Consider this a warning." The fucker lunges at me. I dodge him. And with the shit day I've had, with the images about a man slapping a woman around in my mind, I let this beefed-up, bald-headed slime ball have it. I pull my gun out, tossing it on the ground, kicking it a few feet away, then take him on with my bare hands. He doesn't stand a chance in hell against me. Not with the way I feel.

The lot is empty. I couldn't give two shits if security sees this shit. If they do, good. Get them down here and let them deal with this fucker. I'm going to beat his ass, act like nothing happened, and get to my family.

I punch him repeatedly. It's like I'm a wild man trapped inside of one of those cages with an enemy and only one can survive.

He tries his best to get out of the chokehold I have him in. His arms are swinging everywhere, missing me every damn time. I squeeze his neck tighter as I pummel his face. His grunts from my thrashing egg me on. He can take his bruised body back to the pussy who's to afraid to stand in front of me himself.

I release my hold on him, his body slumping to the ground. He's choking on his own blood as he tries to speak. I grab my gun and place it at his temple.

"Take this message back to Ryan, asshole. Tell him next time he sends someone after me, he should make damn sure it's either him or someone who can fight back, not some amateur who won't be able to wipe his own ass for the next month." Then I take hold of his arm just above his wrist, bending it back until I hear the bones snapping. His screaming follows. But I need more. My anger is surging, Grace's face flashing in my head. Letting go of his hand, I lift my boot the minute his limp-less arm falls. With all my strength, I crush his fingers, wincing myself at the agony he must be feeling. He's all but passed out. Fucking joke. I flip him over enough to check for identification. When I find nothing in his pockets, I leave the fucker there. Tucking my gun back in place, I make my way into the building. My hand is stinging. A few scrapes are showing. I decide right there to not give Deidre anything to worry about. What she doesn't know won't hurt her. I vowed I would do my best not to hurt her again, and when I give my word, I stick to it. I hate lying, but hey, if she sees them, I'll lie to keep her free from anymore worry. Tell her I had to hit the punching bag a few times. Technically, I did. "There's a body lying in the parking garage of Deidre's apartment. Can you take care of it?" I cut my words short before I step into the elevator. "You got it, man," Jeff clips back. There isn't a single person in this organization I'm a part of who doesn't have a job. Some are dirtier than others. Jeff is the one who disposes of bodies. This man isn't dead, but he will be. I warned the fucker.

CHAPTER TWELVE

DEIDRE

The mind does some crappy things to experience how slow time can drag. Today has been one of the longest days of my life. I swear it has.

After Aidan left late this morning, I tossed that Detroit Tigers shirt right in the trash bag with the baby's shitty clothes before I changed Diesel into an ensemble of Yankee attire. My child will never be caught in those clothes again. Then I called my mom in hopes of having lunch somewhere close by to be able to talk and ease her mind over Aidan and his direct approach toward welcoming his role as a dad. Even though she left here with his promise falling from those sensual magic lips of his, I know she's worried.

A few minutes after my mom gets here, there's a knock at my door. And bam, like a bitch sweating to death in a massive heat wave, I'm hit with another blast from my past. Fucking Dilan.

Aidan sent Dilan to watch me. Now I have a damn bodyguard again. I argued until I was damn near spitting glass at the man, determined more than ever to leave and have a nice lunch with my mom and enjoy walking through the park, pushing a stroller. Enjoy just a normal day of being a mom.

I'm no fool. I know this has everything to do with his mother and little Junior, or in my words of choice, Bitch and her little Bitch-ette.

So, with my mom and a very pissed off Dilan—and an even angrier

Deidre—we've been cooped up in my apartment all damn day waiting for Mr. Baby Daddy to return.

"He's clean, sweetheart." Mom strolls into the kitchen with her sing-song voice.

"Look at you, little man." I drop the wooden spoon I'm using to mix up my famous batch of brownies. It's late, almost nine P.M., and still no word from Aidan. I need more than these four walls to occupy my time. Mom offered to bathe Diesel, so here I am, standing in my kitchen.

"Love those little pjs by the way." She tosses an assuring wink my way. "You know me too well," I tease, then inhale the sweet scent of my son, his innocent odor instantly calming me. Aidan may not like them, but I do. "Yankees all the way." I lift one of his little hands, then tickle his tummy. He laughs. The sound is welcoming.

"I don't want to upset you any more than you have been all day, but I thought you should know. I received a text from your dad a few minutes ago. Apparently, I have a bodyguard now, too," she exclaims dryly.

"Great. When will these nightmares ever end?" I sigh.

"Fucking never," Dilan barks out from the living room.

"Dilan. If my grandson's first word is the "F" word, I'm coming after you first." I screw my face up by wrinkling my nose and wiggling it into the man's face who's captured my heart. "Grandma will do it, too." He jabbers on and grabs a handful of my hair.

"Anyway, I'm off," Mom declares. "Without your bodyguard?" I question. "Nope. He's waiting downstairs." She smiles not so cheerfully, kisses the both of us, grabs her purse from the table, and says goodnight. I watch her go, sadly I might add. Now, I'm stuck here with Dilan for god knows how long. I mean, don't get me wrong, the guy is HOT. Screams total badass with tattoos covering both his arms and a face I've seen turn many women's heads before. But he is not the man who makes my heart race, my pussy pulse, and my clit become

114

easily aroused just by sitting down in a damn chair. There's only one man who has ever done that for me, and I want him to come walking through the door and tell me how much he missed us before he helps put our boy to bed. It's getting late. He needs to sleep.

"I'm putting him to bed." My voice is trailing down the hallway as I go. I sigh for what has to be the hundredth time today, sit down in the rocking chair, and hum my child to sleep.

"I've never seen a picture so perfect in my life." My throat is dry when I boost my dreary eyes up to meet Aidan's. He's tucking his phone into his back pocket, a quirky grin on his face.

Standing carefully, I take the few steps to the crib and place the baby down on his stomach then cover him with a light blanket. Aidan steps toward me and lowers his big frame over the crib, placing a tender kiss on top of his son's cute little head. That sweet gesture, mixed with the fact he's here, sends all my thwarting fury out the window.

"I will be throwing those pajamas away," he says quietly.

"You will not. Seriously, Aidan, this is New York. Do you want your child getting beat up at school when he wears a Detroit Tigers shirt? We New Yorkers kill for that, you know?" I whisper back.

"I'd like to see some punk try to lay a hand on my kid. Not this boy. He'll be defending himself by the time he's one." I roll my eyes. This argument will go on between the two of us forever.

"Night, buddy," he says then grabs my hand and shuts off the light, closing the door halfway.

"How did it go?" He's pulling me down the hallway, bypassing the vacant living room before he turns sharply into the kitchen. I hope Dilan's gone. It's blatantly obvious I didn't hear Aidan come into the apartment, so how in the hell would I have heard Dilan go?

"Better than we expected. Can we talk about it later? Like after this?" He swoops me up into his arms, my feet lifting off the floor in a swoosh, then he places me on the countertop, centering himself between my legs.

"Well, all right then." I lean into him, placing my hands on his solid chest, my fingers itching to touch his skin as I go. He feels good here. Like he belongs. I tremble when he slinks his hands up my bare thighs. Those enthralling eyes of his swallow me whole, taking in every part of my face. It's as if he's… I don't really know what he's doing. What he's thinking.

"Aidan," I say quietly. I'm beginning to worry now. This big man seems troubled in a way I've never seen before. I sit quietly, not knowing what the hell to do as he draws lazy circles across my thighs. We've had some serious talks during the past few days, learning more about each other in such a short period of time. But we've always ended up laughing or joking with one another. Teasing. We're both alike in that strange, quirky kind of way.

"I realized one thing today." Inwardly, I cringe. My hands leave his chest to cup his face. I search his features carefully.

"What, honey? What did you learn today?" This is the first time I've called him some sort of endearment. He notices, at least I think he does when finally, a soft smile lights up his face.

"I realized how short life really is, Deidre. How you and I have so much to learn about one another. How I have yet to learn how to be a dad. I don't care how crazy this may sound or what the hell people might think. I want to know every," he leans in and kisses the tip of my nose, "single," he takes both of my hands from his face and brings them to his mouth, feathering kisses across my knuckles, "thing about you, Deidre La Russo." Oh, my freaking god. I have never heard anything sweeter or tenderer come out of his mouth.

"I want that, too." Good heavens. Do I sound stupid? I can't help but think I do. "Good. Now, enough of being all gushy and shit. I want inside of you right here." Well, that was short-lived, beautiful but short. I'm tempted to ask him why he said those heartfelt words, but my pussy is screaming even louder than my mind.

116

"Right here would be good. In fact," I say, challenging him with a raised brow, "I have just the thing for a little foreplay." Freeing my hands from his, I twist my upper body slightly back and pull my t-shirt over my head, my nipples already straining to be free of my black, lacy bra. I then lean to the side and grasp my wooden spoon out of the now thick brownie batter, my eyes gleaming with sordid delight. "Here," I say temptingly as I let the brown thickness drip from the spoon onto my cleavage. "Sweet mother of god, Deidre." He pulls me forward into him, his large erection making its presence known.

"You like?" His eyes catch mine. They're wide and wild. My tongue darts out to lick chocolate off the circular part of the spoon.

I watch his chest rise and fall and those alluring, tempting eyes alter between my mouth and my chest. Then just like that, they're gone, and his head is dipping low, handfuls of his jet black hair is all I see.

I drop the spoon from my hands, my fingers digging into all that hair before the spoon even hits the counter.

Aidan doesn't lick the chocolate off of my skin like I thought he would. No, not him. His tongue sweeps out and smears it clear across my chest. Desire swarms in. I hold in a breath when he begins to lick his way across my chest, while a hand reaches behind me and unclasps my bra. The straps falling down, my breasts are free for his hands to cup firmly.

I moan, squirm, and whimper as he tweaks, pinches, and kneads. My hungering breast is waiting eagerly for every rough callous, every flick to my nipple, every tug, pull, and squeeze he gives and I willingly take.

His mouth sucks, licks, and devours the sweet, sticky batter from my chest. I pull his hair. I arch my back. I want to scream out his name, tell the world how deviously wicked his mouth feels when he latches onto one of my nipples, drawing it into his mouth.

I'm panting. Throbbing everywhere.

"I told you, sweet and tart baby. Your skin tastes so sweet, mixing

117

that in with the biting slur of words that I know you want to release from that tart, little mouth of yours makes you the perfect piece of candy to eat. Every damn inch of you, Deidre. We have all the time in the world to play, but fuck, I need to be inside of you." The warmth of his breath across my tender nipple sends an acute rippling effect straight to my pussy.

A little squeal escapes from the back of my throat when I'm lifted and placed gently onto the kitchen floor. My bra is yanked off the rest of the way. I lie there, the lighting from the kitchen revealing his glorious handsome, well, shit, everything. There isn't a spot on his body that isn't somewhere in the description of handsome, or sexy, or controlling. He stands tall above me, his feet straddling my hips. I'm going insane in a tortuous yet enjoyable kind of way. One I welcome. Crave.

My gaze flicks to his hands where they grip and haul his t-shirt over his head. "Fucking hell," I croak out. I hold back the urgent need to stand up alongside him, to run my fingers across his broad chest, to kiss every expanded muscle so enjoyably displayed in front of me.

As soon as he discards his shirt, he moves those long fingers to his jeans and snaps them open, unzips his pants, tugging them more slowly than I would down his long legs. I stop my survey of his sexiness right when I see his massive cock make its appearance. Huge. Thick. I smile naughtily when I see those god-blessed barbells exposed and waiting to slide deep into my pussy to bring me the most eloquent satisfaction I've ever felt.

"Take off your shorts." I do, too. Undoing the drawstring, I slip out of them along with my black lace panties, tossing them both over my head. My hands reach up to him. If I don't have his body on top of mine in less than a second, I kid you not, I'm going to burn, sizzle right here on the hardwood of my kitchen floor.

"Aidan, I need you to fuck me." My tone is serious.

"Not yet. I need to make you beg a little better than that, Deidre," he taunts. I pout.

His tall body slopes forward. I inhale a sharp breath, hoping I'm finally going to have his big frame on top of me. He doesn't give it to me though. He reaches for his jeans and pulls out a small, colorful box from his pants pocket. With eyes as wide as the thickness of his cock, I liquefy on the inside when he rips open the box of sweet-tarts, shaking a few out of the box and dropping the box onto the floor.

"What are you doing?" I challenge him.

"You'll see." I'm so heated. So wrapped up in what he has planned, I can hardly stand it. My pussy is crying, literally weeping out for his bare cock.

He takes a step back, then drops himself to the floor, spreads my legs wide, and finally, his naked skin is on top of mine.

"Give me your mouth, babe." He plucks a few sweet-tarts in his mouth and takes mine with his.

My mouth explodes with the sweet and tart candy he releases into mine. Our tongues are dueling for the candy, battling against the fruity mixture. They dissolve quickly. I don't know if it's because we're both so heated up or if that's what they normally do. I don't really care, because the tangy flavor combined with the taste of Aidan in my mouth sends a rippling effect of steam throughout every cell of my body. I'm doused in desire. I'm covered in the only man I've ever truly wanted.

His hips start to roll. The barbells sliding over my stomach, where his cock glides over my sweaty skin. Our tongues are colliding, swirling, and still tasting. That deep growl I remember all too well rumbles from the back of his throat. He sucks my tongue into his mouth. Then shocks me stupid when he actually swirls his tongue delicately around the perimeter inside my mouth.

"Please," I beg into his mouth. "I want you so much."

"Not near as much as I want you," he says the minute those tasty lips leave mine.

119

He lowers his hard physique down to my body until his cock is between my legs. His head lifts so he can gaze into my eyes. His eyes are dark, full of spark, full of promises that are so easily readable.

"Fuck," he hisses the second his cock slides across my drenched pussy.

"I need you," I beg once again.

He never takes his eyes off of mine as I feel, oh god, do I feel his fingers skim down my stomach, all the way to where I need them the most. One finger slides through my center. Then the next thing I know, the tip of his cock is right where I need it the most, too. Pushing in slowly, filling me entirely. Sparks fly when those sexy as fucking hell barbells slip inside, scraping against my inner walls. Heaven.

"Yes," I thunderously yell out. My pussy is stretching, then clenching around his cock.

"You like?" He copies my words from a few minutes before.

"I more than like." He begins to thrust, deep penetrating thrusts. My back arches, my hips leave the floor, and I hold back the screaming once again.

The penetration from the piercings sliding inside of me have me coming within seconds. I compress around him. Exploding like fucking dynamite. "Oh, my." I can't stand it. The feeling is utterly indescribable. I was wrecked and ruined a year ago, but this, being skin-to-skin with Aidan, is unchangeable. Nothing will compare to the way he feels inside of me. He thrusts harder. My hips move faster, seeking more pleasure than I ever thought I wanted. Our slick bodies move. Our fucking is raw, bare, and unbelievably addictive.

"Fuck me. You feel so fucking good. So fucking good, Deidre." He grips my hips, gets up on his knees, and drives into me madly, deeply, and painfully good.

"I'm going to come. Give me one more, baby. One more orgasm around my cock." Those words alone have me gasping for air, have me milking his orgasm from him, mixing his desire with mine.

We stay connected for minutes, both of us coming down from an incredible high.

Am I crazy to hope this could be the beginning of forever? I mean, his sweet words about wanting to know everything about me must mean he wants this, too, right?

As we lie here on the kitchen floor, he pulls out of me and, of course, I immediately want him back in there. I've begged once. I'll grovel this time if I have to, but his next words stun me silent.

"This isn't what I would call the best after sex talk, but I need to tell you about today." I know for sure I've changed for the good in these past few days when I lay my head on his chest. Normally I would be angry to discuss anything except for the way he makes me feel. Safe. Cherished and wanted. Not today. I can tell this is weighing heavily on his mind. I only hope, it's not as bad as my heart tells me it is.

"Her name is Anna Drexler. Her mother's name is Grace. I'll tell you everything. But first, I need you to promise me, no matter what happens, you will not go anywhere without either me, Cain, Roan, Jackson, or Dilan. In light of what happened today, Deidre, I have no doubt in my mind that my mother and Ryan already know your name." I stiffen, unable to move. Without even him saying anything more, my brain knows. It registers, it elicits terror in my veins. A racing mind broadcasts like an over boisterous announcer at a sporting event, revealing danger. There's one tiny concern boiling over the rest. We have a child to protect.

"I promise," I say knowingly, willingly, and truthfully. I will not concede to the dangerous people in this world ever again. Not when it comes to protecting our child. I will kill for him, even if the people I have to kill are Aidan's mother and her mini-me son.

CHAPTER THIRTEEN

AIDAN

Thank god my hand wasn't fucked up too bad after beating who I now know was some worthless piece of shit who works—or should I say worked—for Ryan Senior. A fucking car dealer who thought he could take me down. The minute I gave Roan his description, he was on it. Found out who the guy was. Mark Jacobs. Single. No children. Thank Christ for that. He's gone now. No questions asked. Simple as that. I have no idea who took him out, don't give a shit either. As long as it sends a message to Ryan to let him know he's messed with the wrong people, then hell, it makes me sleep better at night.

And now I'm here wondering how the hell an entire week has gone by since Deidre literally stormed her way back into my life. It beats the shit out of me. Every day since seemed shorter than the day before. I fucking hate it.

I remember my grandfather telling me time and time again, "Jesus, boy, you get any taller and I'm going to have to put my old bottle cap glasses on just to be able to look up and see your face." At the time, I would laugh at the old man. Now, I understand exactly what he meant.

In this short time since I've known about my boy, I've mastered this shit. Again, literally. I can change his diaper. Feed him. Bathe him. And I fucking love it.

My kid is a motherfucking rock star. Decked out to the hilt in a tiny

Black Moods rock band shirt. Fucking love that band.

There's no better feeling in the world than this right here. Having him kicking his feet to the beat of the music, not a care in the world for him at all.

"We better turn that down before your mom gets back and chews my ass out." I filter my voice over the music. With a flick of my wrist on the remote, the tunes are down low enough, yet he still jams to them.

Deidre should be back anytime. The girls, meaning her, Calla, and Alina, all went to visit Anna and Grace, who are staying at another home owned on Long Island by Roan's dad Salvatore Diamond. Of course, they're not alone. Dilan seems to have taken some kind of liking to Anna, which I don't particularly care for. The woman is innocent. You can see it in the way she carries herself. She may be a feisty little thing, but this lifestyle will cut her up and spit her right back out. But I'm staying the fuck out of it. Not my business. I just hope the fucker knows what the hell he's doing.

Deidre flipped her shit the night I came back from finding Anna. I've never seen her more pissed off, not even the night when we got into a fight. Her motherly instincts have kicked in, and Christ, I love her for that. Her protectiveness over someone she barely knows shows the true woman she is.

Fuck all if I know the bullshit she went through has a part in her strength and courage. I won't re-hash that with her. Ever. We made amends. Said what we had to say and moved on, and god, have we moved on. This relationship between the two of us is growing stronger by each speedily passing day.

Hell, I'm getting hard sitting here thinking about her when I really should be thinking about the offer both Salvatore and Ivan laid at my feet the other day.

"You know with one phone call the two of them will disappear forever?" Salvatore said. I knew he meant he would have someone kill them, meaning my mother and Junior. Make their bodies dissolve into thin air, as if they never existed. I told him I needed time. I may be a bastard by birth and hate the bitch, but fuck, man, I don't have it in me to have someone off her. Him? Yes. Her? No.

I left the Salvatore Diamond's office grateful for his loyalty to me. An outsider. The world turns their noses down on the mafia. Stereotypically thinking, all we do is kill, deal drugs, and act like we own the goddamn world. In a way we do. But we do not fuck with you unless you fuck with us. Plain and simple, cut and motherfucking dry. Unless we want to steal your guns. Then we mess with you. But not in ways people think we do. We take what we want. It's wrong. But that is what we do.

"Honey, I'm home," Deidre calls out from the foyer. God, I love it when she calls me that. I've never truly felt at home, until her. Hits me square in the chest every damn time. Sure, my buddies are my family. They've never once shunned me, treated me any different than the brother I know I am. But nothing compares to the sensation so deep in my heart than being with these two. That's why when the days fly by, it pisses me the hell off.

"Shh." I shift Diesel a little higher up onto my lap. We wait in silence for her to see us. She is going to be pissed. I love putting a hair up her ass. Watch sparks go off in her stunning hazel eyes. Once she calms down, which doesn't take much, especially when she knows I let it go in one ear and out the other when her sweet little tarty mouth starts spewing out shit, I'm turned the fuck on.

The little temptress does it on purpose. I swear she does.

"What the hell have you done to his hair?" She looks at him like he's grown horns. He hasn't really grown them, but he sure looks like it.

"We're rocking out here, babe. Had to make him play the part." Her eyes flare, and I wait for it. Bring it, baby. Just like you did on the kitchen floor last week. Once I finished telling her all about my encounter with Anna and her mother, how they found out who I was and wanted to help them, we lay there discussing her day. How she was angry about me sending Dilan to her. And then she went into a raging tangent about the Detroit Tigers shirt I left on him. I knew that would spark a fire under her ass. I threw her shit with Diesel getting beat up back in her face some more.

You see, Deidre may get pissed and throw her little temper tantrums, and that night I let her, for all of about five seconds. Then I reached up and grabbed her bowl of brownie mix, which was going to be tossed away anyway. Couldn't let it go to waste. She shut her mouth the minute I swiped that chocolate across her pussy and ate her, along with her damn good mixture. When I had her begging for me to fuck her, I lifted her off the floor, bent her over the kitchen table, and fucked her until she was ready to scream. I had to stifle her screams by placing my hand over her mouth, for fear she would wake the baby. Fuck, she's sexy. How I would love to sink inside her right the fuck now.

I'll have her later when I return from my meeting with Cain and Roan. She'll still be pissed when I return. But she's going to love what I have planned for her tonight. At least I pray she does. I want inside her virginal ass, the ass she seduces me with every fucking day. The way she bends over with those tight jeans on that cover up her plump cheeks. The way they peak out of the bottom of her short shorts. Fuck, I'm stone hard. I lift up and adjust my uncomfortable cock that's straining against my jeans. It's fucking painful.

She begins to pace the floor in front of us. Her beady, little eyes stay locked on our boy as she does. He's watching her every move. I dig this kid. Every time he hears her voice, he perks up like the queen just entered the room, and she has, really. The queen of this realm. The queen who is slowly capturing my heart.

"He does kind of look cute." My jaw hits the damn floor. I pick it right back up. "Come again?" I say.

"Oh, for god's sake. You heard me. I know what kind of game you're playing here, Aidan. You want to ruffle my feathers. Get me mad. Just so you can—" she stops mid-sentence. I challenge her to continue when I quirk up the corner of my mouth. Lift my brows.

"So I can what?" My voice is low and gruff.

"Have your way with me," she squeaks out. I see the wind storm brewing in her hazel orbs. They're whipping back and forth between me and my little chick magnet, like the tops of the trees thrashing about, anticipating a downpour ready to approach. There's only one chick for me, though, and she knows it. There hasn't been one day that's gone by when I haven't told her, tried in some way to show her exactly what she means to me. Like I've said, I'm no romantic, but Christ, when you sense you've found the one person you want to be with, you'll do anything to make them happy. To feel cherished and loved. Christ. Maybe I better run to the fucking bathroom and see if my cock has shriveled up inside of me. I sound like a woman. Internally, I shrug. Who gives a fuck? I feel what I goddamn feel.

"You don't seem to mind when I have my way with you. In fact, you love it."

"I do. And the more I look at him, the more I adore his hair all spiked up. And his outfit, too. It screams badass." Yeah, I got her right where I want her. I smirk.

"Don't think for one second your fine ass is changing the subject." My enquiring eyes take in her tight, pale green tank top. Her breasts are splendidly perfect. Her nipples harden under my stare, leaving me smirking.

"You're staring," she says.

"So," I shrug, bringing my eyes up to her. "I love what I see. Your breasts don't seem to mind." I raise my free hand to tweak one of her nipples.

"Aidan. You're unbelievable."

"So you've said. Many times," I add in. "Are you wet?" I ask, then cross my leg over my knee to conceal my hard-on.

"Nope. I'm drier than that crap you drink," she says sarcastically.

"Woman. Don't even start on my Jim Beam. That's some good shit right there."

"You know…" She bends down over me. Her god for sakes tits are right there. I could reach out and bite one, that's how close my little cock tease vixen has them to my face. "We both better watch what we say. Quit swearing. My mom will kick both our butts if his first word really is a swear word." I hear her. I just pretend I don't. I snatch ahold of the scooped collar of her tank and pull that bitch down so I can get a better look at those tasty tits. Goddamn, she's fucking hot with her tits spilling out over the top of the pink, satiny bra.

"You are an animal." Laughing, she brings her face to mine. Her lips graze my mouth. I devour her. Mark her with my tongue on hers, slipping it deep inside of her glorious mouth. Her lips open wide. She consumes my mouth right back. Tasting me, tempting me with her succulent, little tongue. She pulls away too quickly for my liking. My cock is harder than he was moments before.

"Can I have him now?" Sitting down next to us, she holds out her arms to take him.

I should tease her more. Tell her no. Unfortunately, I don't have the time. My ass needs to get going. The minute she takes him from my lap and starts talking to him, the doorbell rings.

"Got it." I stand and make my way to the door, adjusting my cock as I go. Fuck, he's in pain.

"Hey, you two." Or more like three. Deidre's parents have arrived along with their bodyguard. We haven't had a need to find someone to take over being Deidre's bodyguard since I've taken some time off of work. This is one thing we need to talk about today. Roan suggested his buddy Jackson, who is one big man. I'm up for it. I want to talk to him first, though, make sure the man knows that under no circumstances is he to let these two out of his sight, which I'm sure he won't, but this is my family we're protecting. When it comes to them, I need to make sure whoever spends time with them understands that this is my entire life here.

"There's our handsome boy." Deidre's dad stalks over and plucks him right out from her arms.

"I hate to run, guys, but I've got shit to do." Closing the door, I roam back over to my woman, kiss her chastely on the lips, and place another one on top of my boy's spiky hair, dismissing myself.

"Be safe. And this time, please call me so I don't worry." Deidre's eyes plead with mine.

I wink at her. "You got it." Then for the first time in a week, I leave my family to prepare to take down another.

***

Veering my bike into the parking lot of one of the warehouses where we hold meetings, strategize, and package up the guns to ship, I'm not surprised to see Cain and Roan's bikes parked behind back, along with Salvatore's black Escalade.

These motherfuckers breathe, eat, and shit this lifestyle. I'm quickly becoming accustomed to it. There's a hell of a lot to learn. Hell, I thought I knew how to slip in, steal what I needed, and get my ass out. Back in Michigan, the items I stole, the buildings I broke into, are like stealing a pack of fucking gum, walking out the front door unnoticed versus trying to stuff a giant television into your back pocket and thinking you're going to make it out the goddamn door. New York is full of thieves, full of crime like you would not believe, but fuck me, man, the specialty guns we're looking for are locked up so tight it takes an expert to get to them.

It's a crime, I know it, but I'm learning from the best. Cain can break into anything. That man knows his shit.

"It's about time," Cain barks out.

I lift my chin at him. "Yeah, what the fuck ever, dude. I felt your bike when I walked by it. It's nice and warm. Besides, I know you, there is no way in hell you left your daughter with anyone while the girls visited Anna." His eyes light up at the mere mention of the word daughter.

128

He's pulled into the happy baby daddy syndrome as much as I am.

"Fuck off. Get over here so we can get this done. Seems like your little punk of a brother slipped past our guy. We've lost him." I start speeding toward them, disbelieving what I'm hearing. There is no way. This guy is a weasel. Smacks around women. How in the hell could he have slithered his slimy self out from under our guys?

Anna and Grace told us everything. It was Junior who showed up and slapped Grace around. He deserves the same treatment he instilled on them, only a lot worse. We all intended to deliver it. That is, until now.

"Calm down, Aidan." Salvatore places his hand on my chest as soon as I get to them. "I'm going to kill someone," I seethe.

"Good. You can borrow my gun," Cain retorts.

"Listen. After the bullshit that went down with Royal, I do not allow second chances anymore. You fuck up once with me and you're done. You know this," Salvatore looks to all three of us.

"I know this won't lead us to finding Junior. However, the men who lost him have been taken care of. We will find him." He then stares me in the eye. This man is a leader. True to his word. I believe him. Does not mean I like it one damn bit nonetheless.

"And my mother?" I question.

"That bitch doesn't know shit. She was on a plane to the Caribbean the day after she left your place," Roan answers.

I know I shouldn't be relieved, but I am. You would also think I would know all this. These guys have had my back the last week, taking care of most of the details in my absence.

"Any idea where he could be?" John strolls in. I respect the hell out of this man. He's a legend in a league of his own. To sum it up in one word, he was the BEST. Still is, but when it comes to his wife Cecily, his daughter Calla, and his cute little granddaughter, or any woman for that matter, he'll come out of retirement, pull his trigger, and blow anyone's head off.

129

"Like I've said before, it's been years since I talked to him. Even then, I only spoke to him when I had to. His entire life he's been groomed to take over his father's shady car dealerships. Those morons who lost him said he went to work every day. Even his phone calls were monitored. So basically, no, I have no idea where he could be." And I don't. The only answer any of us can come up with the entire time we stay at the warehouse is that somehow, we have a mole. Another goddamn traitor, who told the little shit what the hell is going on. And more than likely, he knows exactly where Anna and her mother are.

CHAPTER FOURTEEN

DEIDRE

"Be home soon. Stopping to get more clothes." Yours truly has re-read this text at least one hundred times. Especially the 'be home soon part.' The instant I received this text from Aidan, I all but kicked my parents out the door. Now, here I lie in the middle of the bed, on top of my plum-colored comforter, pillow, and sheets, the smoothness from the cotton doing nothing to help cool my heated skin.

I gaze down at the sexy little number I purchased today. It's stunning. Chemise and satin in the deepest emerald green. The peek-a-boo lace down the sides makes it even sexier. The kicker, the part I really love, is the way the shiny satin stretches across my breasts and ass. It's curve-hugging and tight-fitting, and I want my man to love it.

Us girls made Dilan take a detour on the way home today to Calla's favorite lingerie shop. The guy didn't put up a fuss about it either. He stayed in the Suburban while we shopped. Which reminds me, I need to tell Aidan that I think Dilan has some sort of attraction towards Anna. He couldn't keep his eyes off of her the entire time we were there.

I love her, all of us do. Grace too. They fit right in. Anyone in their right mind would never want to hurt those two. They've been hurt enough. I haven't pried, even though I really want to, to find out about the relationship between them and Ryan Drexler Senior. If Grace knew he had a family in Pennsylvania or not? Surely, she had to have. I'm not one to judge. That's all between them, but my god, for someone to want to kill them over it. It's despicable, really.

My theory breaks when I look up to the man I'm easily falling for standing in the doorway to my room with an even larger duffle bag in his hands than before. His eyes are roving up and down my half-naked body slowly. Seductively.

"My god, Deidre. I'm not sure if my legs can move. You are absolutely every wish come true. I've never seen anything more remarkably beautiful. Can I just stand here and look at you?" His voice is low, deeply husky. It ignites me, sends a surging, undulating vitality of excitement that rips and roars throughout every live part of my body.

He's still standing there, staring at me like he cannot believe I'm real. My mind wanders, wondering precisely what the hell he's doing.

"I would much rather you came closer if you have the need to keep looking at me." My mouth may have spoken those words, but my hands skim down the middle of my body. The silky texture of the material feels lovely. But I know for a fact that Aidan's touch feels so much better.

I watch him close the door silently before he whips around, flinging his t-shirt over his head. I've seen his bare chest many times, and I still go stark raving mad and out of control whenever I see it. He simply takes my breath away.

"I've had so many dreams about seeing you in bed waiting for me. Not once did I think they would come true. In a week's time, you've changed me, made me want to be the man you deserve. The dad that little boy looks up to." This man is showing me his sweet side, although his eyes are screaming something else. I've never seen them this dark. This challenging. I love the tough man he is, but I adore the sweet side of him just as much. This dirty side of him though, I may worship.

"For a man who says he doesn't do romance, I would call you a liar if I didn't know you like I do. You are that man, Aidan, and so much more. Don't change the person you are. Not for me or for anyone. Be you. As far as Diesel goes, he already looks up to you. You're the perfect dad. The perfect everything," I whisper. He needs to know that all sides of him are remarkable. He's everything. Our foundation.

One of his knees hits the bed, then the other. He crawls up my body, his eyes shooting sparks straight into mine. He stops moving, straddling me on his hands and knees, strong arms encasing my head as he begins to run his fingers through my long hair.

"You deserve romance, sweet-tart." Those stunning orbs seek out mine. I gulp.

"I deserve you." I skim my fingertips up his arms, slowly. They move on their own. Like every other part of me, they want to touch him, to be consumed by him. To taste his skin.

"I had very naughty plans for you tonight, but seeing you like this makes me want to make love to you instead of what I had planned." My god, it's true when people say your eyes tell the truth. His are right now. I'm lost in them. I meant what I said about him not needing to change. Obviously, this silly man needs a reminder. My curiosity is strumming away inside me, too, prying away, wanting to know how dirty he wants to get. If it's what I think it is, he has no idea how much I want him that way, too.

"Aidan. I bought this for you. Not because I want romance. I did it because I want you. *You*, Aidan." Drawing my hands behind his neck, I tug him down to me. He falls on top of me, his large body completely covering mine, his thick cock resting above the spot where I want him the most.

"I love this," he says, skimming his hands across the crests of my breasts. His lips crash down on mine. Hard, passionate, and dominating. Every single time he kisses me, my brain zooms into outer space. It doesn't matter if he's in control, or if the kiss is soft and endearing, or if it's one like this, where he alternates his demeanor like

133

he's flipping a light switch on and off. People's moods change all time. If he wants me hard and rough, or soft and delicate, I simply do not care. All I want is him.

He's a master at kissing. I moan deep in the confines of the back of my throat when he swipes his tongue against mine, demanding and taking what is already his. Strong, sensuous, and sensational.

"I want your ass," he blurts out into my mouth. I knew this already. Therefore, I smile smugly inside.

"Take it." His head pops up. There he is. My naughty Aidan, the man who says whatever is on his mind.

"You're sure? Because once I start, I won't be able to stop." Again those eyes of his search mine. I want this too. My eyes are sparkling with mischief. I know the minute my answer registers with him. He plops himself up, scoops me into his arms, and flips me over onto my stomach. His need takes over, those large hands palming my silk-covered ass. I'm nervous and excited. And soaking wet. I shiver with arousal.

He has no clue what power he has over me. It's not the sex or the divine reign his simple touch have over my body. It's everything about him. He's the entire package. I want it all with him.

"You have no clue what this ass does to me. It's so goddamn enticing. So fucking tempting. Every time I look at it, it drives me mad. I want to drive my cock into your plump, tight ass, fill you, please you the way you do me." Oh, god almighty. If he doesn't stop mixing his own kind of sweet with his own kind of tart, I may flip that light switch my own damn self.

I wiggle my ass, enticing him to continue, lustful intentions nagging in the forefront of my very coherent mind.

I squeal when those hands shove the silk up my back, exposing my bare ass. His grip is firm on my backside. The magnitude of my arousal is striking to my won senses.

"I need you to touch me," I ring out like a damn musical instrument waiting to be plucked and pounded on.

The bed shuffles just so, my bottom left wanting when he moves. I hear his zipper, then the soft thud of his jeans hitting the floor.

"Let me remove these barbells." My eyes widen. Shit, I forgot about those. *I can see why you would forget, seeing that your noggin is lodged somewhere in outer space between Mars and Uranus.* My inner whore-bag did not just say that? Oh, my freaking god.

"Touch you." He murmurs in my ear when his flesh presses up against my back. "Anywhere," I moan. My head is dipping back. Those dreamlike fingers touch my most sensitive spot, pressing, circling, and sending embers of awareness heightening my need for him. My inner whore-bag is gone with those two words 'Touch you.' Although she isn't in outer space. She's clapping her hands, spreading her legs, and slapping my ass.

"Jesus, baby. I love it when you're ready for me." I can't speak. I'm lost in his fingers. They've taken me deep into the world of Aidan Hughes. He plays me like the expert he is. Fingers thrusting in then out, then circling my puckered little hole. I'm anxious. Delirious even. I don't think I could construe a sentence even if he begged me to.

Somehow I manage to make a sound, or more like an eager grunt, when his hand pulls my hair back and his mouth travels up the side of my neck.

"You drive me fucking crazy." Then he fills my ass with a finger. He pulls my hair even harder, and I let loose a slur of non-ladylike fucks from my mouth. "Fuck, yes, Aidan." I swear to god I've not once felt this way in my life. I've never had the desire to be fucked in my ass. Not until now. Not until he pumps viscously in and out of me while lubricating me with my own excitement.

I lose his fingers in my ass and in my hair and whimper like a baby. I jerk my head around and the sight before me has me coming. I mean, I come hard. I feel it soar through me. As if he knows it, he releases his grip on his cock where he was coating himself, those dark, very hooded eyes crackling. I could let loose again. He swipes his fingers through my pussy, plowing through my juices, then returning them back to his cock.

"You drive me crazy," I repeat his words.

"That's the plan, baby. Now, arch that back and let me make us crazy together."

Like a submissive taking orders from her Dom, I arch my back. I succumb my ass and inhale deeply when that cock made just for me presses up against my hole. Slowly and steadily, he pushes in, hissing as he does so, my once relaxed body fighting him the further he goes.

"You okay?" God the way he asks me if I'm doing okay, punches straight to my heart. Soft and gentle are his words. I shiver.

"Yes." I pinch my eyes closed, the burning sensitivity almost too much to handle. I want this though. God, how I want this. My fists clench the comforter, and my back curves upward as far as it will go the further he pushes into me.

"Fucking hell. I'm drenched in heaven, surrounded by beauty and... Christ, Deidre." I can hardly hear him. I'm in the same place he is.

He begins to move slowly once his cock is burrowed into my ass. Indescribable is the way I feel. I begin to relax, to enjoy the more he presses and moves inside of me. My eyes are closed, but they spring open when I feel the pad of his thumb press my clit. The rhythm of my body moves with his. He pumps faster. Swears louder. Presses harder, and within seconds of all of that combined, I'm coming again. I muffle my release by planting my head face first into the bed. I give him everything I can, and he takes it. He's satisfying me more than I ever thought possible. It's almost too much. I can't help whatever noises seem to be escaping from my mouth. It's like I'm flying, soaring even.

"I'm going to come, Deidre." He releases his thumb from my clit, grips firmly to my hips, and slams into me, sending shockwaves of nothing but delightful pleasure straight to my pussy.

"Fuck!" He screams so loud, I know he will wake the baby. I feel warm, slick, and wet desire and every blessed inch of my man when he comes hard.

"You good?" he asks when he starts to pull out of me. I know I shouldn't be a smartass right now. Not after what we just did, not after all the sweet things he has said to me, but I can't help it. I am who I am.

"I may walk tomorrow like I've been fucked in my ass by my baby daddy, but to answer your question, I'm more than good, Aidan. I've just been thoroughly fucked."

He chuckles. "See, things like that are the reason why I call you my sweet-tart." I pout when he gets off the bed and plop my exhausted frame down onto my stomach, watching his sculpted ass as he goes.

I lie motionless, eyes glued to the baby monitor, waiting for Diesel to stir. When I hear nothing, I sigh heavenly into my bed until I hear the bath running.

What is he doing? I don't want to move. I do, though. Forcing myself out of the bed, I tiptoe to the bathroom and am once again struck speechless. He's running a bath. Aidan does not take a bath. Ever.

"I know you're standing there. Get in here," he orders, not taking his eyes off of the tub.

No way does he have to tell me twice. I kick it into high gear. I haven't had a bath in I don't know how long.

"Here." Pushing himself up from the side of the tub, he lifts both of my arms and guides my sexy little number over my head, flinging it over his shoulder. He then surprises me more by holding out his hand. I stall when he glides his rough fingers over the ugly scars on my back, sucking in a breath when he kisses each one tenderly. "Hop in." He guides me in. I sink low. It feels so good.

"Thank you," I say, submerging my skin further into the bubbles, lavender scent in my nose.

"Where are you going?" He stops at the doorway, turns around, and contemplates answering my question.

"Can't you hear Jim Beam calling my name from the kitchen?" He's speaking, but right now I'm not listening. He's naked. Gloriously naked. I'm a woman with a very sexy man in front of me. For that reason alone, I'd be a fool not to gawk at what I've claimed to be mine.

"You're staring." He's throwing my words from earlier today back in my face. We could play cat and mouse games for the rest of our lives, tossing each other's phrases back and forth, and still, I would never be able to figure out which one of us is the cat and which is the mouse.

I take my eyes away from his growing cock to look up into his penetrating gaze. He's so damn beautiful. God, I think I'm falling. Hopelessly. Deeply. Crazily in love.

"Would I be an asshole if I said I wanted to tell you about the things I've learned today?" Unable to speak, I shake my head attentively. I watch him leave the room, my eyes trained to his ass. Once he's no longer in my sight, I immerse every part of my body under the water. The woman part of me wants to drown in him, bring him back here, and ride him until he forgets about the crap they've sucked him into.

Oh hell. Will the two of us ever be normal? Probably not.

CHAPTER FIFTEEN

AIDAN

My phone alerts me of an incoming text right before I step into the shower. Ignoring it, I lean my head back, letting the hot spray pound on my back. Unfortunately, it doesn't do a damn thing to relieve the tension surging through my veins.

You would think I would be able to substitute the hold Deidre has on me, the deep sensations pulsing my once unattainable heart that only she seems to be able to capture.

Our relationship can only be described as untraditional. And yet, it works. She crawled under my skin the minute I met her. Left her mark. And fuck me if she didn't leave it there permanently, especially after last night.

I'm not talking about the incredible sex we had. The way her tight ass felt around my cock. The way she took me in her mouth in the bath after I told her everything I learned yesterday. I'm talking about her. Just her.

When she told me we would get through this together, I damn near told her I loved her right then. How in the hell can a woman who has been through what she has endured come back stronger than before? I'm sure part of it is her therapy. The biggest part of it is, though, I know she cares for me as much as I do for her. I can see it in her eyes. I can feel it bleeding out of her whenever she looks at me. Whenever she touches me, kisses me. It's in everything she does.

We talked until the water became too cold for us to sit in anymore. My long legs were so damn cramped. I didn't care, because I had my woman in my arms, who listened, who helped me derive a plan to find that leech of a human, Ryan.

She helped me release the guilt I felt for taking a week off to get to know our son. Guilt that has been clawing away at me ever since I saw what that motherfucker did to Grace. I should have gone the moment they asked me to kill her. Then he would have never hurt her. He'll be sorry when I find him. I'll show him what it feels like to have your ass fucking beat. To be scared. Fucking pitiful excuse for a man.

Deep down, I know this shit isn't my fault. I had strict orders from Salvatore to take time off, to let him handle it. And I did. I didn't fight him on it, and I should have. If I had gone looking for Anna and Grace the minute I found out about them, then that fuckhead would have never laid his hands on her. Any man who puts a fist to a woman deserves the same goddamn thing, only worse.

Now, a week later, I want to kill him. To fuck him up so bad he's begging me to take his coward life.

"Fuck," I sneer when I hear my phone ding again. I hustle and clean myself up, shut off the water, dry off, and wrap the towel around my waist.

Glancing down at my phone, I shrug, blowing it off, knowing damn well it's either Cain or Roan wanting to know if I will meet to work out. I've skipped meeting them for the past week for our workouts. But I decide right then and there that hitting the gym is exactly what I need. I bust my ass to finish getting ready, throw on a pair of workout shorts and a t-shirt, and grab my clothes for the day, stuffing them in a duffle bag. Then I sit on the edge of the bed to put on my shoes.

"Hold your goddamn horses," I yell at my phone when it goes off again.

I snatch it from the bed and unlock the screen. "Who the fuck is this?" I say when I start to scroll through several texts from an unknown number.

You think you've won? You low life piece of fucking shit.

Let me tell you something, you bastard, that's right, you are

a bastard. I know it and you know it and so does our mom.

You fucked with the wrong guy, motherfucker.

"Fucking Ryan."

I scroll down to the next text. My hands are shaking, but not out of fear. I want to kill him.

Where the fuck are they?

If you think I'm scared of you or the scum you associate with,

then you're more fucked up in the head than I thought.

I will find them.

I run my hands through my hair. The urge to throw my phone across the room, to pound into Ryan's flesh over and over, takes every goddamn nerve in my body. I jolt when the phone vibrates in my hand again.

One more thing.

Stay the fuck out of my business,

Unless you want me to come after your son and his whore of a mother!

Fear claws into my throat. My fucking heart is pounding. The enormity of how serious this irrational son of a bitch is strikes me right in the center of my chest. Who in the fuck would threaten a baby and a woman? A sick fucker, that's who! He wants to bring my family into this, wants to pressure me to back off over a goddamn text. He has no idea what kind of monster he has now created in me. I will kill for both of them. They're mine.

He's leaving me with only one thing to do. Two actually. The first one is to call Salvatore and give him the go ahead to find this piece of shit and call for the hit to kill him.

The second is to call my cunt of a mother, to feel her ass out, make sure she really doesn't know what her son is doing while she's off with god knows who on a damn vacation. For once in her pitiful life, she better step the fuck up and be my mother. If she doesn't, I may turn into that cold-hearted bastard she's called me my entire life.

I'm done protecting her from her own threat.

"Mother. Fucker."

"Aidan, what is it?" Deidre's worried voice echoes down the hall.

Goddamn it. This is the last thing she needs to know about. She may be strong, but this, it would send her back to a place I know she never wants to be again. She can never know that somehow Ryan knows about our son. No fucking way.

"Nothing for you to worry your pretty little head about," I lie. I turn around to see her and my boy standing there. Her face is showing her worry. She still steals my breath with her beauty, her vitality to prove to herself how good of a mother she is. The irony of it all is that, right here in this very moment, I know I'm in love with her. God, I fucking love her. But I'm nowhere in the right state of mind to tell her that. She deserves my undivided attention when I do. She deserves every part of me she believes in. All of the self-worth she's pulled out of me just by her very existence.

"You sure?" she questions.

"I'm sure, baby. Bullshit from work. Now, let me have him so you can shower and get ready for your day with Alina." I reach out and pluck my son from her arms.

"Okay," she retorts tensely. I know her too well. She's not buying it. But I'm not giving her any more than that. Her feisty little attitude along with her need to protect will rear its head. I move around her and walk out of the room. The minute I hear the bathroom door close and the shower turn on, I call Jackson. I need him here now.

Then I text words I've wanted to say to him in person. My fingers are moving furiously across the screen, adding all capital letters. The little prick.

142

YOU'RE GOING TO DIE, JUST LIKE YOUR FRIEND. ONLY A PUSSY WOULD SEND SOMEONE TO DO HIS WORK. BUT THEN AGAIN, YOU'VE ALWAYS BEEN ONE.

When Deirde is ready, I kiss the two of them goodbye, thankful Deidre is spending the day with Alina, then grab my bag and make my way out the door. Deidre didn't mention her concern again, but I saw it in her face, heard it in her shaky voice, felt it in the way she clung to me a little longer than she normally does. It's not like her to keep her mouth shut. No one knows this better than I do. I can only hope she believed me. "Goddamn it," I curse under my breath. This is splitting me apart, keeping this from her. She would really break down if she knew Diesel was being threatened. She's come so far, all for the sake of our son. For her to lose it now would take her away from him and from me. I won't allow it to happen.

Pinching the bridge of my nose when I enter the elevator, I realize now that reality is facing me dead on. I stand and watch the floors decrease until I hit the lobby. Like a mad man on a mission, I haul ass through the lobby and hit the door for the underground parking garage. I find my bike, strap my bag down, and straddle the bad bitch. My hands move over the handlebars, the muscles in my entire body clenching to feel the rumble of this bike.

Once she purrs to life, the adrenaline shoots through me like a rocket. I flip my visor down on my helmet, shoot out of the parking lot, and make my way to the apartment building we all live in.

Free, that's how I usually feel when I'm on my bike. Not today. Today I feel like someone is following me, watching my every move. My eyes flit continuously between the road and the rearview mirror. Fuck all if I know if someone is on my ass or not. This traffic sucks. I weave around cars, horns honking at me left and right. Fuck them all. The only thing I care about right now is making him pay. Making him pay for threatening my son.

"Jesus Mother Fucking Christ," Cain screeches from across the gym as I lay into the punching bag like it's Ryan's fucking face. How I wish to god it were. "Brother, what the hell?" Roan stops the bag mid-punch.

My arms burn, my fists sting, and I want more. I want so much more.

I made the call to Salvatore to take the little prick out once they find him. My gut wrenches like a bolt twisted too tight. For the first time in my life, I feel sick, and now there's fuck all I can do about it. Let it ride out. Let him fucking rot right next to his father who made him into the spineless fucker he is today.

"Fuck." Untying the gloves from my hands, I yank them off and toss them to the ground.

My hands go to my hair, pulling tightly. I begin to pace. Turning toward my friends, I let it all out. I tell them everything about the text messages, pleading with my eyes for them to give me an answer on whether I jumped the gun or made the right decision. My heart is telling me I did the right thing, while my head is calling me out. Berating me. Taunting me.

When I look Roan in the eye, my head listens before he even speaks. It's right there in the man's expression. He knows. He gets it. Hell, he lived it.

"This is the life we choose to lead, man. I get it. It sucks. Family isn't about blood. Even though in both of our cases, it is or it was. The bottom line is, we protect those we love, those who return our love. I would have done the same thing. Hell, I almost killed my own brother. Any man who threatens an innocent child doesn't deserve to live. He deserves to rot in fucking hell. That's your family you're protecting. As long as you remember that, then that's all that should matter here."

"You're a better man than I am," Cain clasps my shoulder. "If someone were to threaten my daughter or my wife, I'd kill them myself."

"What about your mom?" My head jerks toward Roan at the mention of her. I haven't called her yet. I needed to beat this guilt out of my system first.

"I'm hoping what your dad told me is correct, that she doesn't know a damn thing." I move and sit down on the floor, bracing my knees in front of me, and my throbbing hands on the floor.

"My dad's thorough, Aidan, he doesn't fuck shit up. You know this. If he said she doesn't know, then she doesn't." His words are clipped and tight. Straight to the point. Neither one of these men have steered me wrong in all the years I've known them. Why I am now having a hard time believing anything anyone tells me beats the hell out of me.

"We're your family, Aidan. Including Salvatore. Children are a no go and you know it. I mean, shit, look at the chick who lead us to Royal last year. Both Salvatore and Ivan could have had her killed. They didn't. And do you know why?" Cain probes then turns around and answers his own question.

"Because she didn't know shit. She was an addict. Got caught up with the wrong person. Now that young girl is clean, going to school to become a counselor for drug addicts. He would never lie to you. I know your mom is a conniving bitch. But something else is going on here, brother. You need to find out, no, I take that back, *we* need to find out what the hell it is."

He's fucking right. Both of them are right. It's hard to imagine my mother would have anything to do with this at all. I still can't wrap my head around the fact she even showed up at my place and asked me to kill two women. Unless she was forced to. Cain's words light a spark under my ass. I hop onto my feet rapidly and head straight for my phone, ignoring my two friends yelling at me like I'm going insane.

"I'm good." I spin around with my phone in my hand, confronting them.

"I need to make a call." Silently, I thank them for being the brothers I need. For always having my back, seeking both of their eyes out individually. They simply nod in return. There's nothing more to be said. We all know how much we care about each other.

I hesitate and collect my thoughts before hitting her number, praying she still has the same one from all those years ago. Standing outside the gym, I brace myself for whatever names she's going to throw at me this time. I stopped caring a long time ago about the shit she says about me. Just like I stopped caring about her.

"Hello." Christ. Her pitch is so high, fake, and sugary sweet I'm about to go deaf.

"Hello, Alexis." God, how I despise this woman. If she has one tiny morsel of love in her bogus, phony body, she will step up now. Prove that she isn't the female version of Lucifer himself. Hateful, bitter bitch.

"Aidan. What are you calling me for? Did something happen?" Her voice becomes low, soft-spoken, and unsteady, as if she's on the verge of breaking, crying even.

"Not necessarily. For everyone's sake, especially your grandson's, you better pray to god nothing does happen." She gasps loudly into the phone.

"Are you telling me you have a son?" I recognize the struggle in her voice right away. One I have rarely heard. I haven't lived with this woman for years. Alexis Drexler has many sides to her. The bitchy and insincere, deceptive one has always been the one that rears its ugly head the most. This side of her, though, I've never heard. She sounds pained. A part of me wants to pour acid inside of her pain. Watch her unravel right before me, the way she destroyed any kind of happiness I should have had while growing up in her household. None of that shit matters anymore. The need to find Ryan outweighs anything from my past or anything she has to say. I want answers so I can move on to build a sturdy, stable home where my child knows he's one of the only reasons why I fucking breathe.

"Are you telling me you don't know I have a son, Alexis?" Then I hear it, for the first time in my life, I actually hear this woman, who gave birth to me then threw me out like the piece of shit human she always claimed me to be, cry. I'm struck stupid. I've not once seen or heard her cry. Always hiding behind her mask of perfection. Living and breathing the money, the power that she has shoved up her ass.

Bracing my free hand on the brick wall in front of me, I lower my head to the ground while keeping the phone to my ear. This could be another trick of hers. One to try and make me think she has nothing to do with the threats against my son. I let her have her fit. My concern for her no longer matters. She hesitates in between her sobs, incoherent noises coming out of her mouth.

Finally, she stops. I hear her sigh deeply before she begins to speak. I'm this close to telling her to hurry the fuck up when what she says leaves me weak in the goddamn knees. Makes my chest tighten to the point I have to catch my breath in order to even hear her.

"I was never good enough for you to call me your mother. I won't ever be. I can apologize until the day I die for the way I treated you. The repulsive things I said, the despicable way I treated you. It's time you know the truth, Aidan. The truth about everything. I'll come home. But can you answer one question for me, please?" I hear the shakiness in her tone, the terror rolling through the phone line.

"What?" I'm not giving her any more than that one simple word. She's right. She doesn't deserve me. I'm the one who's deserving. My child deserves it. I owe this bitch nothing. I owe everything to the woman I love, her very existence in my life over the past few weeks of showing me she cares. Of making me believe I deserve to be loved without her even trying. Without her even telling me I do.

"Are you happy, Aidan?" What the fuck? I don't know what I thought she was going to ask me, but that sure as hell wasn't it. She wants to know if I'm happy?

"I didn't call you to talk about my happiness, Alexis. My life is none of your business. I haven't been your concern for a long time. You're right. You will never be my mother. I called you because your son has threatened the lives of my son and the woman I love. The one who could never do wrong in your eyes. The perfect prodigy of the piece of

147

shit you married. So you answer this. Did you have anything to do with that?" Her breathing becomes winded. I hear her gasping for air. She's outright balling now.

"No, Aidan, I swear to you I know nothing about that. Just… let me come to you. I promise I will explain everything." I close my eyes. Fuck. I want to believe her. I teeter back and forth, choosing my last words wisely before I hang up on her. "All right, Alexis. Come to me. You text me when and where to pick you up. One more thing, you have no idea who you've fucked with here. Unlike you, I'll kill anyone who tries to hurt my child, which includes you. "

CHAPTER SIXTEEN

DEIDRE

I cannot count the times I've hit pause then repeat in my mind all night long about Ryan going missing. It's like listening to my favorite song, only this isn't a song. It's much worse, really. It's beyond unfathomable. Beyond reality. To be frank, I'm sick of it. Sick of these people in this world who think they can control you for their own sick pleasure of pure evil.

What started to be a cozy, relaxing bath turned into a nightmare. Aidan told me everything last night. Not this morning, though. I know he's hiding something from me. I knew it the moment he told me it was nothing. I'm sure it was to protect me, to not make me worry. But how can I not, when another man has disappeared, only to resurface when he thinks it's the right time to strike? This time, I refuse to let a sick man out for revenge prey on innocent people, to get the best of me or those I care about.

My fingers fiddle across my phone, texting Alina to tell her to hurry her ass up, while my eyes repeatedly dart back at Jackson, who's paying no attention to me at all. His eyes are glued to the computer screen in front of him. Investigating, I'm sure. I toss my phone down and clear my throat, which gets me his eyes over the top of the computer.

"You're quiet over there. Are you building a resume for a dating site?" My mannerism is joking.

"And why would I do that? You know damn well I'm not single." No, he's not. Jackson is head over heels for the woman he's dating. I have yet to meet her. Everyone else seems to love her. She's a nurse at the hospital where Alina works, that's about all I know.

"I'm messing with you, Jackson. Lighten up, for god's sake." I stand and make my way toward him. The minute I'm within a foot of him, he snaps the lid to his laptop shut. Damn it.

"Nice try." He bends and tosses the contraption on the ottoman.

"It's not nice to keep secrets, you ass." I tilt my head and place my hands on my hips.

"Look. I get it. You're going out of your mind wondering what the hell is going on. You need to trust him, trust all of us that we will handle it." I scoff at his words. I'm not pointing any fingers at anyone, but look where trusting people got us the last time this happened.

"I hate this. The not knowing, the feeling like I'm being left in the dark. Come on, tell me something."

"At this point, there's nothing to tell. We're looking for him, that's all I know." I roll my eyes, knowing this conversation is a dead end. I reach for my phone and put in my password, which I never changed. I'm not going to, neither will I change my background photo. I smile when I look at the photo I snuck the other day of Aidan cradling Diesel in his arms while rocking him to sleep. Reaching up, I swipe the single tear escaping. These should be the happiest times of our lives. Watching our son grow and change every day. Being able to enjoy every single moment. I hate this.

I stare at the picture until I reach the baby's room, check on him, and continue on into mine. Curling up onto my bed, I adjust my phone, swipe the screen again, and hit the FaceTime icon next to my dad's number.

"Well, hey there." Dad's big, meaty head comes into focus, right along with his loud booming voice echoing through the small speaker.

I laugh.

"Hi." I try to sound cheerful, but this man can read me like a book. I know he has me pegged right away when big frown lines crease across his forehead.

"Talk to me, my girl." I shake my head, not knowing where to start. He knows everything. Both of my parents do. Well, up until the news Aidan told me last night anyway.

"Have you talked to anyone today?" I ask, trying to feel him out, to see if he already knows.

"I've talked to Calla." His answer is cryptic.

"This is such bullshit, dad," I blurt out. Like I said, I don't hide things from my parents. Not even my dirty mouth. They accept me for who I am, which is more than I can say for Aidan's mom. She has no idea what kind of man she is missing out on in her life. Instead, she has her head up the ass of a deceitful woman beater.

"I know, baby. You holding up okay?" I know what he means. He wants to know if I'm losing it again. If I'm breaking down. I'm not. I'm much stronger than I used to be. Part of it has to do with him. Not once did he coddle me when I was going through the toughest part of my life. He stood by my side, held my hand, but he let me do the walking, talking, and placing my trust in myself that I could get better. And I am.

"I'm fine, dad. Well as fine as I can be. I'm worried, but I'm not going to lose it. I won't become a victim to some sick, sinister asshole who's out for revenge again. Not when I have a son to protect." I watch my dad's face change from concern to appraisal in a flash.

"That's my girl." He beams. And I swear to god I can feel his pride. His love for me zaps me through this phone screen.

"I love you, dad."

"I love you, Deidre." Dad and I spend another half hour or so talking, and laughing, and carrying on about anything and everything. It feels good to talk to him. To see his face light up whenever I mention something about the baby. I also tell him about wanting to go back to work, at least part time when this scandal is over. He agrees. After we hang up, I call my mom. She hates FaceTime, so I kick back on my bed and chat away with her, telling her the same things I've told my dad, which gets her going on about being the babysitter. My response is basically a "Duh. Who else would I leave my boy with?"

"I love you, mom," I say right before I hang up. My mind isn't at ease. It won't be until Ryan is found, but at least my parents can comfort the burden squeezing my throat like it's closing up, making it impossible to breathe.

"I love you, sweetheart. Everything will be fine."

"I hope so, mom." I hang up and toss my phone onto my bed. The bed where I gave myself over completely to Aidan last night. I lie all the way down on the bed and splay my hands out to the side. "Why can't life be normal?"

"I ask myself that very same question daily." I jump up. Shocked, I might add. Alina is standing in the doorway. "You scared me." I smile at her. Then I cock my head to the side. "You look different." She does too. I look her over, scan her up and down, then my eyeballs plunge out of my sockets at the huge rock on her left hand glistening from the sun shining through the windows.

"Oh, my fucking god." I bolt off of my bed, stomping toward her.

"It's exquisite, Alina." I lift her hand so I can get a better look. I seize it, lurching her forward in the process, both of us giggling as I do.

"It's called a blue moon diamond. Roan says it's one of the rarest stones you can find." I give her a wonky smile, letting her know I get the true meaning behind the word 'rare.' Alina is rare, genuine, and the best friend I could ask for. Then I turn my gaze back down to the round cut single diamond adorning her finger. "I'm happy for you." I slide her hand out of mine and pull her into my arms to hug her close. Resting my head against her shoulder, my gaze drifting to the floor, I begin to lose control, unable to shake the urge to cry.

"Hey." She drags herself back from me. My sweet friend's hands glide up and down my bare arms.

"What's wrong?" Tears begin to sting my eyes. Tears I've held in for way too long, trying to be strong for not only myself, but for Aidan. I need this, to break down and cry. I feel like crap, raining down on her happiness. But I cannot help it.

Crying doesn't make you weak. It's made for the strong. I cry, sob, and spill my guts out after dropping down to the floor in the middle of my bedroom. I continue to cry even when I hear Diesel wake up, only for Jackson to holler that he's got him. Then I cry some more. Crying is respectable. Talking is moral. Listening to a crying woman on a day that should be one of the happiest days of your life outshines them all.

Best friends make the hard times calmer, the great times memorable, and the in between times better than the ones before. I have that in my selfless best friend, who carries the weight of so many burdens herself. She's overcome them. Made herself stronger, independent, and successful. Yes. Crying is good. It's very good.

Alina stayed the remainder of the day. We baked, laughed, and managed somehow to get Jackson in on our now little adventure.

Now here we are, sitting at the table. I'm getting ready to place Diesel in his new chair. Alina's idea I might add. She was right when she said we should get this. The perfect dig to Aidan. One that is bound to make me laugh.

It was delivered a little over an hour ago. It's amazing how when you offer the store a hell of a lot more money than you paid for the chair they have it couriered right over to you.

"What the hell?" Aidan's eyes are overspun with hatred as he stares at the chair.

It's meant to be a joke, to liven the tension. Only Aidan does not find it funny.

"I told you so," Jackson scolded.

"Whatever." I swat him away with my hand.

"You'll think whatever. Alina, get my son out of that goddamn chair." My back goes rigid.

"Quit it. He's my son, too. And we do live in New York, not Detroit." Seems everyone finds this situation funny except him.

Man, this guy may love his Tigers more than I love the Yankees. I'm beginning to realize it now. Even Roan starts laughing his ass off from behind my big, tall, brow-beating man the minute he sidesteps him and gets a look at the chair.

"I don't care where we live. No kid of mine is going to have anything to do with the Yankees. Now, give me that thing." He enters the room with a predatory gaze, a snarly growl leaking from his lush lips. An angry Aidan is a sexy Aidan. He actually lifts me up, removes my kid from my arms, somehow manages to flip me over his shoulder in one big ole swoosh of air, and kicks the chair into the corner. The plastic and wooden chair goes tumbling to the floor.

"I think that's our cue to leave, baby," I hear Roan say.

"Not so fast, mister." I'm hanging upside down, talking to a very nice, firm ass. I'll stay right here and say what I have to say, while staring.

"Congrats, Roan," I say. He laughs. They all laugh, except Aidan, who whips around forcefully. "Um. Hello. Jolly Green Giant, can you put me down?" My heart is shuttering fiercely.

"Congrats, Alina. Can you all let yourselves out? My woman here continues to test my patience with this Yankee shit. I need to teach her a lesson." Aidan's obnoxiously loud performance rebounds off the walls down the hallway. All I hear is thunderous laughter from our friends, who he rudely left behind.

"Aidan. Put my down." I start smacking his ass, while he continues to ignore me. Then out of nowhere, I'm flying through the air, swallowing my scream when I see through my mussed-up hair my baby boy's eyes go saucer wide when I land in the middle of the bed with a giant plonk.

"Stay," Aidan barks out to me as if I were a dog. I lift my hand,

154

shoving my hair out of my face. I'm damn near panting like a dog, too. I'm blistering mad. I may have even started whining. What has gotten into him? He's freaking gone crazy. Just when I'm ready to go out there and chew him a new asshole on that sexy ass of his, the two of them come back in. My mouth falls open, and I damn near cry at the sight before me.

How Aidan manages to still be holding the baby and carrying a big, pink-wrapped box in his hands beats the shit out of me, but he does. He looks so damn sexy, irresistible. There's no doubt he's irreplaceable. He's proven that since day one.

"Go see mommy, buddy." He kisses the top of his head, hovering over the bed for me to take him. I settle myself in, my back against the headboard, my son in my lap, my eyes trained on the man I love.

"I've said before I'm not much of a romantic, hell, you may even have some of the things in this box. I just... I don't know. Feel like an ass for interrupting your life, asking you to stay here until we find Ryan when I know how badly you want to do something as simple as taking him outside. Hell, we haven't even been on a date. I care about you, Deidre, not because we have a child together, because you make me feel worthy of being his dad, of being your lover and friend without even trying. You've shown me the one thing no one has shown me before."

He pauses and sets the box down on the foot of the bed. And when those penetrating eyes of his catch mine, I damn near come undone. He loves me. I can see it.

No, Aidan isn't a romantic. I'm a woman who doesn't need it. I'm a woman who only wants the man. Not any man, this man. The one standing before me, seeking out whatever it is he wants to say.

"Aidan," I whisper.

"Let me finish, baby." He bends and lifts the lid off the box.

"I love you, Deidre. I do. I love you for so many reasons. To me, you are the perfect mother, you're self-sacrificing, you're beautiful, and you're sweet, tart, and your mine. Most of all though, baby, you listen to me. From day one when you barged into my apartment, you knew before we even spoke a word to each other that a shit storm had blown into my life and here you are. Standing strong by my side. Facing it head on, with me. Besides Cain and Roan and the family I have in the organization, the only other person who has stuck up for me before was my grandfather. Until you. This gift isn't much, but I want you to know it came from here." I watch him with tear-filled eyes as he places his hand over his chest. There are so many things I want to say to him, to show him.

I swipe those tears away and turn Diesel around in my lap so he's facing his dad. The boy has no clue what's going on here. He's in his own little world with his fist shoved in his mouth.

"I love you too, Aidan. We may not have fallen in the traditional way. I doubt anything about us will ever be traditional. There are too many reasons why I love you, but there's one that sticks out and shines above all the rest. I love you because even though you weren't there when I broke down and lost it, with every breath I took, I felt you here." I reach up and place my hand over my heart, mirroring where he still has his. In this very moment, I can feel his love beating inside of my chest. Its warmth radiates throughout me. He may think he's not romantic, but he is. I will never forget those sweet words he said to me.

"Here." He walks to the side of the bed, places the box beside me, and tucks his hands into the front pockets of his jeans. I really want to laugh through the tears ready to burst from my eyes. The mere sight of Aidan nervously looking down at me when we both know he's far from shy has my heart dancing a jig inside my chest.

I open it slowly. My heart clenches without my hand over it when I see what's inside. My vision blurs from the happy tears freely flowing down my face.

"You bought these for me? Oh, Aidan." I peal the tissue the rest of the way aside to pull out my favorite cupcake pans along with three different sizes of round cake pans.

"Very romantic gift, yeah?" He shrugs.

"To me they are." My voice is barely above a whisper. He really has no clue what this means to me.

"Romance isn't all about wining and dining. You already have me, Aidan. Those things mean nothing to me. These," I purposely run my fingers over the glossy metallic texture of the pans. "Are my favorite. Not because you bought them from The Pantry Store down the street from my uncle's bakery," I wink at him, letting him know I know where he got them. "It's because you have so much going on right now, but you still went out of your way to buy these for me."

I swallow. God, how I could go on and tell this man how much this really means to me. How ironic it is that he brought these home on the very same day I talked to both my dad and Alina about going back to work. I'm done talking. I want to show him.

I place the pans back in the box then lift the baby so he's centered in between us, his arms flinging out to his dad. Aidan gladly takes him by pulling his hands out of his pockets and curling Diesel close to his body, which gives me the freedom to touch him. God, how I want to touch him.

"I love you, Aidan Michael Hughes." I touch the spot over his heart tenderly and bring my mouth as close to his as I can without fusing us together. I slide my other hand around our miracle baby, who tugs at my hair. I wince slightly from the sting, but I don't care. I watch my man roam my face with certainty of the power of love they provoke in this crazy dance we call our lives. Our breath is mingling, opening up an intimacy all our own.

I have to give him a gift, too. One he will never forget. I'm slightly angry with myself for not remembering to do this before, but maybe it was meant for me to do it now, after we told each other how we truly feel. I don't know, but what I do know is I know this is going to mean everything to him.

"I love you, too." He smirks. I shiver.

"I have something for you," I say on a whisper. My parents are the only other people who know about this. Throughout my entire pregnancy, I never had a doubt what I was going to write on Diesel's birth certificate. When my dad assured me I could name my child anything I wanted to, I talked to my little boy inside of me, told him no matter what, I wouldn't deny him his rightful name.

I scamper off the bed after releasing my hold on the two of them and open my top dresser drawer, folding out the neatly creased legal document. With shaky hands, I then hand it to Aidan.

He glances at it, then back to me, then back to the paper.

"Shit, baby." His eyes light up. Yeah, best gift ever.

"Crazy, huh? We've talked about everything else but that." I point to the paper.

"You gave him my middle name and my last name?" he says more like a question.

"Uh, yeah. I told you from the beginning I was never going to keep you from him. He's a Hughes. Has been since the day he was conceived." For the second time tonight, he amazes me with words that will once again stay with me forever.

"God, I love you. Not because of this or him or for anything. I simply love you, Deidre. You may have given me these two reasons why I should, but I don't need a reason to love you when I simply fucking just do."

My man is a fool if he thinks he isn't a romantic. Gifts come from the heart; however, words come straight from a person's soul. No matter what he may think, I vow right here that I will take my last breath reminding my man he has the biggest soul of us all.

CHAPTER SEVENTEEN

AIDAN

I do believe I've created a monster, or a woman on a damn mission. What my girl wants, she will get. Thank Christ for deliveries. The entire kitchen and living room are full of all kinds of baking supplies, and it's only noon.

She had this all planned out before we crashed last night. Her idea of asking Anna and Grace to help her was brilliant. I know the both of them are going crazy as well. Although Anna seems to be taken with Dilan as much as he's with her. The moment they showed here about an hour ago, I decided once again that shit is none of my business. The guy may look rough on the outside with his entire body covered in tattoos, but hell, he's a damn good man.

I look from the living room where Dilan is on his computer to my woman on the phone. For the first time in my life, I told a woman I loved her. And I fucking do. More than anything.

Last night meant everything to me. Not only did we tell each other how we felt, but my god, she named my son after me. It's right there in black and white on his birth certificate. I already knew she was an exceptional mother, but this, this shows me how she put him before anyone else. Hell, I could have denied him. Made her take a paternity test. She had no clue what my reaction was going to be, and yet she did this for him.

Again, we talked for hours last night after dinner and putting the baby to bed. We made love for the first time. Slowly. I may love to savor her body, take my time with every inch of her, but god, when you look down at a woman whose eyes shine brightly with love for only you, it's a beautiful feeling.

She knows I'm meeting my dear old mother today. Deidre doesn't want her here or anywhere near our son. I made it perfectly clear to her that I don't either. Once I find out whatever the hell Alexis thinks is so important for me to know, then I hope I never see her again. I'll make damn sure she knows it too. I failed to mention the text messages I received from Ryan. I feel like shit for keeping it from her, but how in the hell am I supposed to tell her that our son has been threatened? No damn way am I going to give her any more reason to worry. Not when she's happy about being able to work from home. Little did I know the gift I gave her would spark a flame under her sexy ass. God, I fucking love her.

Our talks are becoming more important to me every day. I may sound like a pussy-whipped motherfucker, but who gives a shit. What happens between her and I in the privacy of our home is between us. And yes, *our* home. Wherever these two are, I will be.

Over the course of these past few weeks, I can now say we know more about each other than I realized. Every day we both learn a little more, and I fucking love it.

She's been on the phone all damn day with her uncle, discussing her brilliant idea of baking at home. I have one more gift for her. He knows what it is. He better keep his promise and not tell her. She's rambling on about having her baked goods getting picked up and delivered to his bakery, while her mom, Anna, and Grace unload all this stuff she purchased this morning to start baking. Thank fuck she has another spare room here we can use for storage. This is her thing. She's damn good at it. I just need to remind her before I take off to pick up my darling mother from the airport to save some of the left over batter.

I'm hard as a goddamn brick wall thinking about dripping her sweet mixture down her sexy as sin body, then taking my time licking it off.

"I'm proud of you." I speak the truth. I couldn't be more pleased with her. Not once has she shown a sign of weakness. She's been strong through this. That's why I'll only tell her what I feel she needs to know.

"Thank you," she mouths.

"I'm going to take off," I convey to her the minute she hangs up with her uncle. She turns around, eyes gleaming with happiness. Shit, I'll do anything to be able to keep that look on her face. Deidre is stunning. Deidre with a genuine smile on her face is priceless.

"Okay. I wish I could tell you to give her my love, but you can tell her to go fuck off and to never call you again." I stand and stalk her way while adjusting my cock. Her eyes flit down to my hand, then back up to my face. Her sweet smile turns naughty, tempting, and reaches all the way up to her eyes.

"Oh," she squeals when I take her in my arms and she feels how hard   I   am.
"I'll have you saying more than 'oh' later. In fact I'll have you screaming it. Especially if you make those raspberry filled cupcakes." I press my erection into her even more.

"You're greedy." *Yeah, whatever.* He eyes are half-lidded. Who the hell is she trying to fool?

"When it comes to you, I'm everything, sweet-tart." I take her delectable mouth in mine, kissing the living shit out of her. My tongue is tasting her sweet mouth, exploring every part of it. Fuck. I will never get tired of kissing her. Or making love and then fucking her. She's mine. I'm hers.

"I'm making something better." Now she's piqued my curiosity. With my arms still wrapped around her tightly, I lift a brow. This has to be good, because there is nothing better than those cupcakes or her chicken, and well, there is one thing, but fuck, this apartment is filled with people, not to mention I have to go.

"Look what Anna found?" She reaches behind me then thrusts a piece of paper in my chest. I snatch it just as quickly out of her hand, take a step back, and damn near choke down my laughter.

"You're shitting me?" Chuckling, I hand it back to her.

"Nope. Anna thought it was hilarious. I'm thinking it's going to be my specialty cake." Beaming with pride, she tosses the paper on the counter. I shake my head. "Tease away, woman. You'll always be my sweet-tart, and Anna is always going to be a pixie." I then nod toward the light green frosted cake printed on the piece of paper called Sweet-tart and Pixie Stick Cake.

"Love you," she whispers. God, if I could inhale those words, I fucking would. I will never get tired of hearing her say it.

"Love you too. Got to go, babe. Be a good girl and give Dilan a cupcake, yeah? Save some of that cake batter for later." I wink then let go of her. She simply nods. That nod has me flashing back to last night when her head was bobbing up and down while she had my cock in her mouth. Fuck, I love her.

"See you later," I say to Beth, who's feeding Diesel on the couch. I bend and kiss him on the top of the head. He looks up to me, smiling. My heart clenches.

Yeah, I need to find out what the hell my mother has to tell me, so I can make sure my family is safe. Unlike her, I'll do whatever it takes to make sure my child is safe, happy, and loved.

"Later, man." I nudge Dilan in the knee when I pass him. He growls and mumbles a slew of swear words, only to be scolded by Beth. I suppose she's right. Deidre and I should probably watch our mouths around him, too.

I arrive outside of Northern Airlines at JFK Airport thirty minutes after Alexis' plane landed, thanks to the New York traffic that can suck my ass. And there she is, nice and tan with about five suitcases by her side, looking bored and impatient as usual.

I throw my truck into park and hop out, clambering onto the sidewalk in front of her.

"Alexis," I say roughly.

"Would it hurt you to call me mother for once?" Her words sound strained. Tough shit.

"Yes, it would hurt me to call you mother," I bite out. I don't care if it hurts her or not. "Are these all yours?" I ask before grabbing the cherry red suitcases scattered all around her feet. I could be a bastard and make her do it, but the need to get the hell out of here outweighs anything else. I want this done.

"Yes." She gasps loudly when I pick them up one by one and toss them in the back of my truck. I ignore her, and with a sweep of my hand, I indicate for her to get in. She gasps again. I continue to ignore her until she finally gives up and opens the door herself, then lazily hoists herself up into my truck.

"Are we going to your place? I'd really like to meet my grandson." If I weren't driving my truck out of this overly crowded airport, I might freeze momentarily in my spot. I'm not sure what kind of game she's playing with me, but fuck all if I'm buying any of it.

"We will not be going to my place and you will never meet my son. I have no idea what kind of game you're trying to play here, but it's a little late in my life to be playing games, don't you think? I mean, you never played with me when I was a child, so why start now, Alexis?" I glance her way. Her lips begin to quiver. She must sense me watching her because she turns her head and stares out the window.

The only sound in the cab of my truck as we drive to the place I set this meeting up at, in case this ploy of her wanting to see me is a trap, is her trying to silently hold back her sobs. A part of me feels like shit for making her cry. Maybe it's the part of me who always wanted a mother, someone to take care of me when I cried. Hell, I don't know. All I know is by the time we get across town and I park in the lot adjacent to Calla's law offices, I'm ready to crawl out of my skin.

"A law office." She looks perplexed, and I must say I love it.

"Yup. Everything you say will be documented, Alexis. I told you, I'm not playing games. Now, let's go." I tug my keys out of the ignition, climb out, and wait for her. Once she's out, I hit the fob to lock the truck and walk in front of her, giving her no other choice but to follow me.

"You really do hate me, don't you?" Now she sounds desperate, sorry even. I say nothing when we walk through the corridor of the building, the sound of her heels clicking rapidly as she tries to keep up. "Aidan Hughes for Calla Bexley," I tell the gray-haired receptionist named Pamela when I approach her desk.

"Go on up, she's expecting you."

"Thanks, Pamela." I wink and shove away from her desk, heading straight for the elevators.

"Aidan. I'm sorry." I spin around on this viscous bitch, my nostrils flaring.

"Get in the goddamn elevator, Alexis." I point to the now open doors. Her eyes go wide, but at least she fucking gets in the elevator and shuts her mouth.

"Hey, Aidan," Calla greets us as we step off the elevator. "Calla. I appreciate this on such short notice." She waves me off like it's no big deal.

"Hello. I'm Calla. You must be Alexis." Calla gracefully sticks out her hand to shake. With a sigh, Alexis takes it, and we follow Calla down to her office. I'm happy as hell when we walk in and Stefano is seated in one of the three chairs opposite of where Calla sits behind her desk.

Very few people know about this meeting. I made it my mission the other day to fill Stefano in on everything that's been going on. He agreed with me that we shouldn't tell Deidre a damn thing. Not until we absolutely have to. Just like me, he lost his shit. By the way he's killing Alexis with his eyes, I would say he hasn't calmed down one bit.

"Alexis. I would like you to meet Stefano La Russo. He's Deidre's father. You do remember Deidre, right? The mother of my son, my fiancée." She looks flustered. I've tossed her into a damn snake pit. I'm an asshole, and once again, I don't give a fuck.

"Hello," she says nervously. I almost laugh when I see sweat form on her perfectly plucked brows.

"I would love to be able to say it's my pleasure to meet you, Alexis. However, it's not. You see, I don't take kindly to people making threats against my daughter or my grandson. Frankly, it pisses me the hell off. And trust me, if you don't tell the goddamn truth today, well," Stefano shrugs. "I'll see to it that you don't walk again." Heck yes, Stefano. I know he's one badass in the courtroom, but shit, the guise on his face even scares the hell out of me. He is fucking pissed.

"I... Aidan. I would never do anything like that. My god, you really do hate me, don't you?" Jesus. How many times is she going to ask me? I jerk my head back. Does she not realize the shit she's done to me my entire life? I'm not here to hash out how I feel about her. The quicker she realizes this, the faster I can get back home to my family.

I lean into her, my eyes searing straight to her black heart. "We're not here to talk about me and you, there never has been a mother and son relationship between us. Now, fucking talk. Where the hell is he?"

"I don't know," she whispers. Tears well up in her eyes. Her temperament turns from astonished to that of a woman who's scared.

"Jesus Christ. He threatened you, didn't he? What's he got on you, Alexis?" I tunnel into her tainted world more.

"He has nothing on me. I have something on him," she cries out.

This is even better. I wonder what the little worthless wonder has done to her. Something that has her shaking, that's for sure.

"Alexis," Calla interrupts. "You need to tell us everything. I'm here as Aidan's friend. Stefano is here because... well, he's already told you why he's here." Calla shoots a daggered expression in his direction. "Please continue."

Alexis sighs. This time when she does cry, I know her tears are real.

"When we came to you a few weeks ago, I told you Ryan was dead. You never asked me how he died. He was murdered." She clutches her purse against her chest and lowers her head to her chest. Her body shakes, and fuck, I may despise this woman who gave me life, but my god, if what I have running through my mind right now is true, then she could be next.

I reach for her. Take hold of one of her hands. Her head lifts. Her eyes are rimmed red. Her makeup is smeared. She squeezes my hand. A slight smile curves her lips.

"Junior killed him, didn't he?" I ask, knowing damn well what the answer will be.

"Yes," she states.

"How do you know this, Alexis?" Stefano presses.

"I saw it. He shot him, right in his office at the dealership. You know the one on Kings Highway, Aidan. That one. I walked in on them fighting over money, over Junior taking over the business and," she pauses. "Over getting my dad's land." I tug my hand away from her and run my hands through my hair, then down my face. People are fucked up, man. I knew that guy was nothing but a little weasel. But this, this sheds light on everything. Fuck. My woman. My son. If that fucker killed his own father, he won't hesitate to take away the only two people I love.

"He'll never get the land, Alexis. Not even if he kills me. It's land, for fuck's sake. My grandfather's land. Not his. Never his, " I shout at her. She fiddles with her purse more. Her hands are shaking.

"Ryan told him that. Well, not the killing part. Ryan told him to let it go. They bickered back and forth about it, and the next thing I knew, Junior pulled out a gun and shot him right in the head. I screamed. There was blood everywhere. I couldn't move, and when he turned around and saw me standing there, I thought he was going to kill me, too. Instead, he told me to keep my mouth shut, that it was an accident. Then he struck me with the gun. When I came to, I was in the

166

back of an ambulance. He made me come to you after we read Ryan's will. He left a quarter of a million dollars to his daughter. A daughter I knew nothing about. But Aidan, I'm begging you, please. I would never do anything to hurt someone like that."

"Oh, my god." This comes from Calla.

"Jesus Christ," comes from Stefano.

"That rotten piece of shit," I bark out. It all makes sense now. All of it.

"He covered it all up, made it look like Ryan had been robbed." She continues to cry.

"Why didn't you tell the police?" Alexis scoffs at Calla's question.

"Because," she lifts her eyes to mine, stands up, and for the first time as far back as I can remember, Alexis Drexler shows me she's my mother.

"Right before he struck me with the gun, he said he would kill you, Aidan. He left me with no choice. I haven't had a choice since I married Ryan." She holds my indecisive stare. Cautiously.

I let what she said sear into my chest as well as my head. All of it. "What exactly are you saying?" I instruct her to go on.

"I'm saying my husband wanted that land to turn it into his fancy condos or whatever new plan he would develop in his twisted mind. He hated you because my father made it perfectly clear to him it would never be touched because it was yours. He forced my hand when it came to you." She breaks at this particular moment. Slumps back down in her chair, defeated.

"Are you telling me that my life was in danger even as a kid?" This is unbelievable.

"Yes. My dead husband was an evil man. I'm glad he's dead. His death meant nothing to me. But you. I've loved you since the moment you were put into my arms. I have to live the rest of my life knowing my own son hates me. But I will die knowing I saved your life from that man. There isn't anything I can do or say to change the way I've treated you. I see your hatred for me even now." The grief splattered across her face is there in spades. And she's right. It is too late, at least for now.

I'm done with this conversation. I pull my perceptiveness away from her to the astonished expression of sorrow and anger to both Stefano and Calla. I then express to them the second reason I wanted them in this meeting.

"Do you have the papers I asked you to draw up?"

"I do. They're right there." Calla slides a folder in my direction. Without even looking at them, I sign where the little sticky notes tell me to sign.

"Tell your dad thank you for me." She may or may not know what I'm referring to. John will and that's all that matters to me right now. With that, I stand and leave without even looking back at Alexis Drexler. She has no idea that she's going to stay with John and Cecily. Looks like the roles are now reversed. I've more than likely just saved her life.

CHAPTER EIGHTEEN

DEIDRE

I cannot help but laugh as I glance around my kitchen. It's a mess; a clutter that has my mood lighter, my thoughts determined, and my passion overflowing delightfully. This is food euphoria right here.

It also has me thinking of the possibility that I need to move if this plan is going to work. I love my apartment, but shit on a shingle, there is no way I can do everything I want to do with one stove and one refrigerator, not to mention the counter space and everything else.

Most of the day was spent organizing and putting things away. I'm exhausted.

I'm also worried about Aidan. It's been hours and not a damn word as to how his meeting went with his cunt of a mother. I've texted him three times, called twice, and nothing.

"You need to quit worrying about him. He's fine. If he weren't, I would know." Dilan saddles up beside me at the kitchen table.

"It's one of those easier said than done things, Dilan." I sound like a bitch, but I can't help it. I feel as if I'm being left in the dark about something, and quite frankly, it's starting to piss me off.

"I hear you. But hell, woman, this is the life we live. You knew this. You need to suck this shit up and figure out a way to deal with it. Simple as that." My mouth flies open then snaps shut at his brass but very truthful comment.

"Look, this isn't about the mafia life. This is personal to him, and I'm worried. What's crawled up your ass and left an asshole bomb that detonated?" Rising up from my chair, I make my way over to the cake I made. The one Anna found and helped me make. She has a knack for this as well, so does her mother.

"Hey, I'm sorry. I was out of line. Trust me. He's fine." Dilan's voice is tense. Ah, and there she is, the reason why the bomb exploded up his ass. The beautiful Anna. He watches her from behind as she walks past without even seeing him across the kitchen floor.

"God. I needed to get away from my mother. Twice in one day she's looked at me with these little, sad eyes and then says, "You need to start dating, Annabelle Drexler. I'm ready for one of these." I'm like seriously, mom, do you not know what our lives are like right now? It's not like I can go out on a date. Besides, the man I would love to take me out on one just happens to be our bodyguard." She lowers her voice a little when she expresses that little bit of news.

I risk a peep out of the corner of my eye at Dilan, who happens to still be gaping at Anna. I think his ears may be flapping like he cannot believe he heard her correctly.

"So, Dilan, huh? He's a great guy. And I know what you mean about not being able to go out on a proper date. Hopefully, this gets taken care of soon. Wait a second. Does this mean, are you two thinking of staying here?" Oh yes, Dilan's ears are flapping like elephants' do when they're trying to cool down the heated blood flowing through them.

"We are. I cannot believe how nice all of you have been to mom and me. Besides, with dad gone now, it would be a good time for a fresh start." Oh, yeah. He's flapping now. He may get up and fly. I listen with rapt attention as Anna carries on about their plans to move here. She even tells me a little bit about her relationship with her father, too, which I tuck away to tell Aidan about whenever her gets his ass home.

"Do you know much about Dilan?" I look at her with a questioning stare. How stupid I must look when she's the one asking the question.

I blink. Oh, how I could have fun with this, especially with him sitting in the chair not moving at all. Maybe all of his cells have left his body and he's no longer a living thing. Ha! Well, Anna sure does know how to take a lady's mind off of her worries, doesn't she?

"What do you want to know?" I play dumb and start to clean up the counter. Anna makes herself right at home by propping a hip against the counter with her back still facing Dilan.

"Well, I know he's a bodyguard, a thief, and a member of the mafia," she rattles off.

"Yup. Does any of that bother you?" I ask jokingly.

"Not at all. I mean, I may not have a lot of experience with men, but after the shady shit my dad did before he died, I have no room to judge. Besides, I'm not a judgmental person anyway."

God. I want to shift my eyes in Dilan's direction. I don't though. I love Anna and even though this is cracking me up inside, I would never do anything to purposely embarrass her. Now, Dilan on the other hand... I'm high fiving myself right now.

"I think Dilan is a wonderful man. He has a nice ass too, and don't even get me started on those tattoos of his." I fan myself.

"Oh, God. I know. We were working out together the other day, and I shit you not, my panties were completely soaked when he took off his shirt and the tattoo across his back flexed with every pull-up he did." When I look her way, I notice her eyes are closed as if she's in deep thought or remembering the way he looked. I shoo him with my hand. I've never seen a man move as fast as he does. Just in time, too. Because what she hits me with next would have definitely gotten him spotted. He would have crumbled to the fucking floor.

"When I said I didn't have much experience with men, I really should have said none at all. I'm a virgin, right down to I've never even been kissed."

"Oh, Anna. I think that's wonderful." I mean what am I supposed to say?

171

"I just feel like I'm, I don't know, a tom boy or something. I mean, all through high school, sports were my life. Then I went to Hygienist School. Guys were never in the picture," she says rather sheepishly. She reminds me of what it would be like if I had a younger sister to share these kind of stories with. Kind of like the relationship Alina and I have, where you can tell your girlfriend anything, and they will never judge you.

I dry my hands off on a dishtowel and pull her into my arms. "You're not a tom boy, that's for damn sure. You're beautiful, Anna, and any man, including Dilan, would want you. I'm not talking strictly sexually, either. You don't have to prove yourself to anyone. As long as you continue to be you, then the right man will come along and sweep you away. You will have fallen before you even realize it." I glance over her shoulder because I feel like someone is watching us. And shit. Dilan is right there. Oh, shit. He heard her. He knows everything.

***

"All right, goddamn it. I'm not waiting for his ass to get here any longer. I want some of my daughter's cake." My dad showed up about a half hour ago, looking mighty worn. I know he met with Aidan and Calla earlier today. He claims he hasn't seen him since. That his mother went to stay with John and Cecily for her own protection, and that was all he would tell me. Now, he's sitting here trying to butter me up with his comment about indulging in my cake.

"We need ice cream," Grace pipes in.

"I'm sorry. I don't have any. I could go get some," I say, knowing damn well I will not be leaving.

"We can go get some," Anna says while observing Dilan.

"Sure. Let's go." He gives me a weary smile, and even though I feel like I want to pull my hair out of my head and I've killed everyone in this room at least twenty times, I'm panicking, freaking the hell out. And I want Aidan home.

172

"You need a drink, honey." Mom hands me a glass of wine.

"Thanks." I take a sip of the crisp sweet Riesling and let it flow through my system. I stare at the door Anna and Dilan just walked through. My mom's bodyguard is still perched outside like a fucking tool. God, why me? I want to scream. Throw a pissy ass fit and ask everyone to leave.

"He's fine, sweetheart. I promise." Dad hovers over me.

"You don't know that." I swallow back my tears.

"I do know, Deidre. The man I saw today was anxious to get the hell out of that office and back to the two of you." My dad's tone seems very convincing, but I will not settle down until he walks through that door.

"I'm going to go cut the cake." Even though I don't want to cut the goddamn cake. I ease up out of my chair, snag my glass of wine, and lean up against the wall in the kitchen. My hands start to shake, leaving me no choice but to set my glass on the table. My chest feels impossibly tight. I close my eyes, taking deep breaths and letting them out. I have no idea how long I stand this way until my eyelids flutter open from the hot breath I feel against them, the warm body I feel pressed up against mine.

Those anger reflexes inside of me diminish with every breath of his I inhale. I'm still shaking, but somehow I manage to look deeply into big, blue eyes. They sparkle with mischief, while I'm sure mine are wet with the tears I feel streaming down my face.

"Baby. No. Why are you crying?" His voice is low and matter-of-factly. He knows why.

"I've been worried about you." I may sound a little taut when I speak.

"I'm sorry. I know I told you I would text or call. I promise I have a very good reason." He acquires my attention rather quickly. Although, the way he's seeking me out with his gaze, I'd say he's either done or bought me something again. He wears the same expression as he did

173

last night when he gave me my sweet gift. Sheepish.

"What have you done, Aidan Hughes?"

"Not so fast, beautiful. Kiss me first." I look intently at Aidan as he gazes back at me, burning holes into my already heated skin. A rush of heat explodes in my chest. His lips twitch when he leans forward slowly, teasingly.

Then his hands are tangled in my hair, his lips are on mine, and thank you, god, my man is home. We devour each other with our lips, tongue, and mouths, expressing our love without speaking. My hands twist roughly in his hair. He bites my lower lip and grinds his hips into mine. And I soften even more. My desire for him increases with every circle of his tongue. It's maddening in a thunderously arousing way. This crazy love we have for one another works for us.

My heart is splayed wide open for this man, and no matter how worried I become, this one particular person who I have tumbled into the abyss of love with will always come home to our son and me. This is what I'm getting out of this passionate kiss from him. He's letting me know we're everything to him.

He pulls himself away from me way too quickly, leaving us both gasping for air. "Please tell me you saved some frosting?" he asks, which gets a laugh out of me. Moments like these are why I call our love crazy, but we fit. One minute we can be serious, the next playful, and I wouldn't wish for it to be any other way.

"I did. It's in the fridge. More than likely very hard right now." His brows shoot up, while my eyes look down. Again, why is everyone still here? Christ, that is a gloriously looking hard-on straining through those jeans. Fuck me. I hate to have to waste it. As if he can read what's running through my head, he swipes a finger down my cheek, cupping my jaw between his hands. "Just one look at you makes me hard, sweet-tart. Trust me, the minute the last person walks out the door, he'll be back." He smirks at me and shakes his head.

"Come on." Reaching for my hand, he pulls me behind him into the living room where we now have two more people joining in.

"Uncle Sal. Aunt Corrina!" I squee like a little girl.

"Look at you, little mama." My uncle walks toward me with his arms stretched wide. I enter them happily. Even though we've chatted on the phone, it's been a month or so since I've seen him. And my aunt. I haven't seen her since Diesel was born. Last I heard, she was visiting my cousin in Italy as she had a baby a few weeks after I did. I turn from his arms and stroll right into hers.

"Where's that handsome little boy?" she asks.

"He's sleeping, it's been a long day, even for him." I look over to Aidan. I'm surprised he didn't run into the baby's room first thing.

Silence abides the room. I pull back from my aunt, my fix remaining on Aiden.

"You are all up to something. What did you do? Read my mind today and buy me a house with two kitchens?" I verbalize teasingly. Although, secretively I wish they did. Or I wish I could anyway. My savings have all dried up by keeping the rent up-to-date on the apartment while I was away. That's one of the reasons I need to start working again. This is something I haven't conveyed to Aidan or to my parents, even though I'm sure they know.

"Not exactly a house." Dad steps forward.

Reaching out, my dad takes hold of my hand, holding it palm up into the air, then my uncle steps forward, a peak of silver leaves his hand as he places a key onto my palm before he clenches my hand closed while leaving his over the top of mine. I'm baffled to say the least. My head is spinning as I look at the faces of my family. Tears are escaping my mother's eyes, joy whispering across my aunt's face. And pride fleeing my dad.

Strong arms wrap around me from behind, holding me close. "What's this?" I lift the key for them all to see.

"That, my sweet niece, is the key to the bakery. *Your* bakery." My head shakes in a stultified manner. "My what?" I then look to my dad.

Aidan's grip on me tightens.

"We're retiring, honey. I'm not about to sell my bakery to someone I don't know. I want a person who has the same passion as I do. I want my legacy to go on. My legacy is you." Oh, my god. I don't know what to say.

"So, this is where you were today? Did you buy this for me?" I spin around to study Aidan's reaction.

"It's where I was today. And yes, I bought it." I take a long, slow breath, reigning in my anger. He cannot go out and buy me a bakery. Jesus. This is too much.

"Why?" I simply ask.

"Why not?" Is his response. "Well, for starters, you do not buy a business for someone who you just started dating. That's preposterous." He tilts his head a little. A wide smartass smile spreads across his face.

"I can if it only cost me one dollar."

"One dollar?" Right then the room starts to spin. I literally feel dizzy, wrapped up in all of this confusion, driving my brain to overload.

"And we didn't even want to take the damn dollar." I believe that's my aunt talking now. I really do feel dizzy. Taking the few steps needed to reach my couch, I fall backwards, still clutching firmly to the key. The key to my bakery that cost a dollar.

"I'm grateful. I'm a little ruffled, really. Your bakery is worth—"

"Knowing my niece is going to take good care of it. To your aunt and I, that's worth more than any amount of money, Deidre." Oh, my god. I have a bakery. My own business. A place I've worked at for years. A familiar atmosphere with people I love. Now, I am going to cry.

"Thank you so much." I hug Aidan hard. "I love you," I say then turn and hug everyone else. This is perfect. I can work and have my child with me. I can leave when I want to. Go in when I want to. And I can bake!

"Where the hell are Dilan and Anna? They've been gone for an

176

hour." I'm still clutching my key in my hand. I cannot seem to let it go. The reality of it still hasn't sunk in, even though I keep repeating it in my head over and over that it's mine. It really is mine.

Ten minutes after my jagged, short-lived, happy little breakdown, my aunt and uncle left. My parents and Beth are still here, and now my mom's bodyguard is inside. The atmosphere is filled with tension. Something is wrong. I can feel it. I think we all can.

"He's still not answering his phone." Aidan runs his hands through his hair.

"Neither is Anna." Beth declares.

"I'm going to look for them."

"I'll come with you," Dad tells Aidan as dread begins to fill my chest. I drop the key on the table by the door. My eyes flit to Aidan's. We silently exchange the same worried contemplation.

"Like I said, they didn't say where they were going. I assumed they were going to Hitchcock's, which is two blocks over." Aidan's fingers wrap gently around my wrist. His troublesome eyes shift from me to Grace. "Call Roan," he mouths silently. I nod. I stand there for all of five seconds after the two of them leave. Memories slice through my aching head. Too many memories. Ones I've healed from. Ones that if they reach the surface again, I don't know what will happen.

CHAPTER NINETEEN

AIDAN

Dread owns me right now. It has my stomach locked up tight. I can't stop it or slow it the fuck down. I can feel the knives sharpening, my feet heavy like the concrete on this sidewalk that Stefano and I are walking on.

"The cocksucker has them," I grit out. I fucking know he does. There is no goddamn way Dilan would take this long to get ice cream. Not with all the shit that's going down.

If Junior has them, then he's not alone. It's whoever we think is working for us and for him. A fucking mole, a rat-bastard motherfucker, who is going to die once I get my hands on him. I hate fucking traitors who lie to your face. Who cheat and weasel their way into your world only to betray you.

"If you're sure, Aidan, then we need to call Salvatore. Especially if you still think there is someone working on the inside." My hands clench around the smooth steal of my glock, itching to pull the trigger and get rid of the piece of shit who wants me dead. I'm going to fucking kill him. Kill him for all the wrong he has done to me and to Alexis. Kill him for his already dead father, who took my mother away from me. Who forced her to act like I never even existed, then passed his hateful desires down to his cowardly son. I will blow him the fuck away. Put as many bullets into his slimy body as I can.

"He knows there's a rat. Call him. Inform him about this," I spit out. I have my eyes trained in every direction. There are people still milling about. There always are in this damn city that never fucking sleeps.

I vaguely hear Stefano's short-clipped, to the point words slipping out of his mouth. In that particular moment I hear a groan from the alley we just stumbled upon.

Both of us stop, our necks craning in the direction of the dimly lit alley. "Fuck." I run toward the faint sound . The closer I approach the slumbered form lying on the cement, the more acute his groans become. Deep, heavy, gasping-for-air breaths.

"Mother. Fucker. Dilan. Jesus Christ. Call an ambulance, Stefano," I yell. You would think with all these people walking around, someone would have heard him back here. Fuck me.

"Son of a bitch. It hurts," Dilan spittles out. "Where are you hit, man?" He starts rambling shit I cannot understand. I grab my phone, switching on the flashlight. "Jesus Christ, Dilan." There's blood everywhere. "Fucking hell," Stefano says, then adds more light with his phone. "They're on their way." His eyes meet mine, both of unsure what the hell to do. The blood is pooling around our legs.

"Apply pressure to the wound on his stomach. I got the shoulder." I address the wound with my hand. Dilan's entire body jerks off the goddamn ground when I apply more pressure. The warm blood is flowing through my fingers. "Take off your shirt. It will soak up some of the blood." No matter how hard I try after removing my shirt, the blood keeps coming. His breathing becomes less audible. "Come on, man. Hang in there." Out of nowhere, I hear another gunshot. My head whips up and I watch in slow motion as Stefano's body lurches backward onto the cold, damp ground. "Stefano!" I yell. His body is lying lifeless several feet away. I shrink down, my eyes scanning for the shooter and somewhere to hide. Except there isn't anywhere for me to go. I'm trapped. He's behind me. If I run to try and save my own life, I know damn well he'll shoot me in the back. That's not even an option.

No way would I leave my two friends here to die.

The sound of people screaming, telling others to run for cover, call the cops, all that shit someone should have done for my friend, who is dying literally in the palm of my hands, echoes loudly in my ears, right along with the resounding effects of the bullet that pierced through Stefano.

"Back away from him, motherfucker." My phone clatters to the ground. I look down at the lit-up screen showing my background photo; the one I snuck of Deidre holding Diesel, rocking him to sleep.

Son of a bitch. That voice I've hated since the day the little prick was born strains my ears. Fuck him. I keep applying the pressure to my friend's wound, ignoring his demand once again. "I'll kill you right the fuck here." I feel the butt of the gun at the back of my skull. "Do it, you fucking pussy." The gun clicks. I close my eyes, prepared to die right here. Nothing happens for several seconds. The lighting is vague without my phone. I lift one hand off of Dilan's still body, grab Stefano's phone that lies face down on Dilan's bloody stomach, and shove it into the front of my pants. I then laugh at the coward until I'm yanked up from behind and shoved face first into the side of a brick wall.

My hands are snapped securely with cuffs behind my back before I can even try and fight back. Pain is surging through my wrist and upper arms. I will not let this fucker know I'm in pain.

"Get him in the van. We need to get the hell out of here," Junior snarls at my unknown attacker.

"Where is she, Ryan Drexler?" I yell his name as loud as I can, praying like a motherfucker someone hears me. "Shut him up." I'm dragged like a heavy box toward a dark-colored van behind the building. I resist, making his movements slow down. I hear the faint glitter of a siren in the distance. With every step this asshole takes, I poke and jab my feet forcefully in the opposite direction, doing everything I can to stall, to resist.

The sirens become louder, he pulls harder. "You cocksucker." I twist out of the bastard's hold and face my demented attacker. "You always had a dirty mouth, Aidan. I wonder how dirty it would be if I blew your goddamn brains out?" I spit in his face. "Do it. You'll still never get what you want." He says nothing as he wipes my spit from his nasty face.

I react, head-butting the piece of shit. Bones crunch. Blood spills out of his nose. "Shit. Get him in the goddamn van." Fuck that. I'm not going down as easily as he may think. I kick him in his balls. Ram my head into his chest, knocking him off balance. Shots ring out in the air as he crumbles to the ground.

Reaction is a curious motherfucker. I'm ready to stomp him in his fucked-up face when the lights from the ambulance quickly approach. I'm lifted off of my feet by his crazy man and tossed into the back of the van, the solid steel doors slamming in my face.

"Fuck," I yell. The front doors slam shut. My body is whipping around, slamming into... "Jesus, what have you done to her?" Anna is bound and gagged, beaten nearly half to death.

"Shut your mouth, Aidan," the belittling little asshole barks through his busted-up face. He is going to have to do a hell of a lot more that make idle threats if he wants me to shut up.

"I've always known you were worthless, but hell, man, I never thought you had it in you to kill anyone, let alone your dad. You had me fooled. I mean, Christ, I always thought you had a pussy instead of a dick, you know?" I shrug even though he can't see me.

I'm met with silence. I watch him as he busily does his best to clean himself up. The dashboard lights from the van show off just enough light. He's pissed. Good. I enjoy a good game of antagonizing the prick!

"Aidan," Anna gurgles my name. "Anna. Can you sit up? Let me look at you." I scooch in her direction. "My hands are cuffed." I twist my body around so she can see. If she can see anything at all. Her face is so messed up. God. I will kill him if I have the chance. I swear to god I will beat him to death with my own hands.

"He's crazy. He... he shot Dilan," she whispers. Tears are streaming down her face. "I know. I found him. Stefano called an ambulance. He's going to be fine." Her eyes flutter closed briefly. She exhales deeply, like the woman had been holding her breath the entire time, more concerned about Dilan than herself. She's one tough woman. I'm not about to add any more to her pain by telling her Dilan may die.

She may have the blood of a selfish son of a bitch running through her veins, but she is nothing like him. She's caring. After she gets her dainty little self up, she holds on to the side of her ribs, wincing and trying to clamp in those cries of pain. Her hands are tied in the front, scraped and bleeding. Christ, my gut spins, sticks on autopilot at the sight of her. Guilt claws at my throat. I let out a deep breath. Everything inside of me is struggling within themselves. God, I've failed once again to protect someone. And then there are Dilan and Stefano. Will they make it? If they don't... My mind cannot go there. They fucking have to make it.

Deidre will never survive losing both her dad and me. Or either one of us. And my son. Fuck, I need to find a way to get us out of here. How in the hell can I reach for this phone when my fucking hands are jacked behind my back? All I can do is pray to god that Salvatore has a tracking device on Stefano's phone like he does on all the rest of ours. Not that he doesn't trust us. It's for our own safety. Too much shit has gone down with his family and close friends in the past couple of years. This is his way of protecting us.

The guilt begins to strangle me while we bounce and rattle over these streets. My eyes drift from Anna's marred frame to the view in front of me. I know exactly where we are. Not too far from where we were, to be precise. In fact, if I didn't know better, I would say we're going around the same block over and over.

"Go ahead, little sister, tell him where we're going. Better yet, let's drive for a bit. Have a family reunion. After all, I've never been in the same room, let alone the same vehicle, as my two favorite siblings before. It's a shame, really." He widens his snarl into a grin. Fuckhead.

If possible, his attitude got cockier. He may think he has the upper hand here, but fuck him. I know good and well that Roan, Cain, and Jackson are all well on their way to either the hospital or Deidre's apartment. I'm no religious man. It's a damn shame. *If you are listening to me up there, let them be alive, safe, and soon to be surrounded by family. Let Stefano and Dilan live, so if I die, they can come back and kill this prick.*

"You're not my family. You're nothing but a mooch, a scumbag, and a fucking pervert," Anna strikes out. "Let's not forget a killer," I surge forward with my words before thinking. Shit, she probably doesn't know.

"Way to go, brother. She has no idea. And ouch, Annabelle. That struck me right here." He gives his head a slight nod and places his hand over his heart. His face is busted all to hell. I'd give anything to crack it in half, wipe that smug smile off of his face.

"That's where you're wrong, dickface. I know you killed my dad. I also know why. It was all over money and land that was never rightfully yours in the first place. Your entire life you've been mooching from him, you've never been man enough to do anything on your own. He knew that, too. In fact, he used to tell me all the time how much he wished you were more like Aidan and me. And when he finally told you to give up on getting your hands on Aidan's land, you flipped what little bit of your needle dick brain you have left. You disgusted him, did you know that?" She begins to cough. Her little hands joined together splayed across what has to be hurting her in a bad way right now.

"I see." Junior shifts around more in his seat. His eyes focus on Anna's tiny frame. "You really think you knew him? He was just like me. The old man had you fooled, little girl, but hey, if you want to remember the man as your hero, by all means, remember him that way. At least I don't have a mother who fucked around with a married man, then had a bastard child with him." She gasps loudly at his harsh words. And yet, stands on her own two feet, even though she's sitting

183

down. "Oh, please," she stammers out, her breathing becoming more difficult. "Your mother just fucked anything with two legs. Hell, she's such a whore, it's no wonder he went out and looked for someone else."

"That's enough. Not another word. I don't need you as much as I need him for what I have planned. Don't fucking say another word or I will end you, you little bitch." He's clearly dangerous with his vigorous threats of wanting to kill. Then why the fuck hasn't he done it?

His head stays in the same position, but his seedy, little eyeballs slant to me. I shrug nonchalantly at the idiot.

"I know you're hiding our mother somewhere. I suppose you think you know everything like this cunt thinks, yeah? Let me tell you something you don't know, you little fuckers. I win. It's as simple as that. I will kill you both and anyone who gets in my way of me getting what I want. I couldn't care less about your land anymore. I want the goddamn money he left to her. And to our cunt of a mother!" he screams obsessively while flashing his gun all around.

All I can hear ringing in my head is the word 'cunt.' Flashbacks run like a herd of cattle through my head of the night I called Deidre that name. A night she forgave me for. *I have to get the hell out of here*, I repeat to myself. *I need to get home, to my family.*

"If you're so hell bent on killing us, the why haven't you done it already? A professional pulls the trigger right away, he doesn't drive around in circles while people are out looking for him. Are you sure you've done your homework there, Junior? Because man, the way I see it, if you get caught by my friends, they will make an exception out of you. And fuck, I've seen some of their work, it ain't pretty." I imagine John coming out of retirement to use his expertise on making this no-good-waste-of-air suffer and scream like a pig who finally realizes he's about to be slaughtered. Before that happens, his hands and feet are cut off. He's squirming, shrieking, and begging for them to stop.

"I'm not scared of your mob friends, Aiden. We will be long gone before they even get here. Ah. Here we are. No need to inform him where we're going, sister dear." I try to move to see out the passenger side window.

"What the fuck? You rotten son of a bitch!" I lurch forward, only to be shoved back by whoever the fuck this man is who hasn't said a goddamn word the entire time.

"Aidan, are you all right?" Anna scoots closer to me, the pain etched on her cute little face visible the closer she gets to me.

"Matthew. Bring them all out," he snips sharply into his phone. God, no. Matthew. He's worked for Salvatore for years. He's Beth's bodyguard. How in the fuck did he get messed up with Junior? I feel sick. My entire life is in that building. My eyes stay trained to the doorway leading to the apartment building where Deidre and my son are. Just as I see the shadows of people walking through the corridor, a vibration pulses against my lower abdomen. The phone. Someone is calling. I stay still, barely breathing, pulse pounding, until I see them. Deidre holding my son, her eyes flocking all around, scared, helpless, clinging to him like the protective mother she is. Beth and Grace's hands bound behind their backs. Two guns in the hands of Matthew, pointed directly at each of their heads.

Junior may think his plan will work. There's no sign of Roan or Cain, which leads me to believe Salvatore directed them to the hospital. That means he's called in John. Or one of his other hitmen. I pray like hell it's John. Like I've said before, the man despises people who lay their hands on the innocent. If he gets hold of these men, hell will be a welcome compared to what he will do to them.

"You're going to die slowly, motherfucker." Venom mixed with the truth ejects from my erratic mouth. "No. They are, Aidan. And you're going to watch."

CHAPTER TWENTY

DEIDRE

Something feels off. A nagging feeling creeps into my gut. Aidan and my dad have been gone too long. Anna and Dilan obviously longer. Something outrageous is happening.

I reach for my phone to try and call Aidan and my dad. I look up at Matthew before I do, his expression grim and dark.

Discomfort surges through me by the way he is glaring at me, his eyes bobbing between my face and my hand. My hands move back to my lap. My brain is consumed with thoughts as to how or why his sudden presence creates an uneasiness inside of me I cannot explain.

"I'm really beginning to worry." My mom stands up, her hands fidgeting at her sides.

"So am I. You don't think he has them, do you?" Grace speaks softly, tears of worry developing in her eyes.

"Deidre. Did you call Roan?" Mom asks. Before I can answer her, my phone rings. I reach for it quickly, not even checking to see who it is, before the superior feeling in my gut tells me Matthew is about to do something.

"Hello," I answer with a timorous tone to my voice, hoping that whoever it is will hear the fear.

"Don't say a word, Deidre, just listen," Cain speaks softly. "We have every reason to believe that Matthew is working for Junior. You need to get out of there now. I'm on my way." He hangs up.

I feign my ignorance like he's still there. "No, Alina, they haven't showed up yet. Roan said they were going to go looking."

"They can look all they want, they should all be dead by now anyway." He shrugs as if it's no big deal that he's standing here telling us that the people we love are dead.

He reaches for my mom, grabs her by the back of her neck, shoveling her face first onto the floor. His booted foot hovers just above her shaking body.

"Hang up the phone." Matthew uprights himself and pulls two guns from behind his back, pointing them right at my mom and Grace. My mom lies face down on the floor, her eyes overflowing with tears. Grace begins to uncontrollably scream and cry, while me, I stand there motionless, unable to speak, to think, to grasp hold of the reality this sick man is trying to sway me to believe.

"You're a liar. I would know if he were dead. Unlike you, I have a heart and I would feel it here." I stab myself with my finger in my chest. "Oh, god." This is coming from the listless body lying on the floor. "Mom, he's lying. I know he is. Get up. Don't let him win." He kicks her then, making her figure quaver from the injury conflicted to her side.

"Yes, Beth, get up." Matthew doesn't release the hold he has on Grace. He stuffs one of his guns into the back of his jeans and drags her fragile, little body, which is choking and gasping for air, right down to the hall with him. He lifts my mom by her hair, shoving her forward, forcing me to watch in utter astonishment at the way he carelessly abuses these two women.

All the while my son is crying. He rarely cries. He's always so happy. My heart is breaking as I listen to him wail.

"You. Get in there and make him shut his fucking mouth." I follow, my eyes trained to the gun sticking out of his pants. My hands reach for it, only to be caught in mid-air by his firm grip. "Nice try, bitch." The burn from him twisting my wrist, his callous and rough hands digging into my skin, only angers me more. I hold tight to my son, thankful he is too young to acknowledge any of this as Matthew tugs me hard behind him. Shoving me down into the chair once we hit the living room.

My phone rings, so does my mom's over and over as we sit stoic and wait. Diesel calmed down the minute I brought him into my arms, Thank you, god.

It feels like hours, but I know it's only been minutes when we all jump to the unfamiliar shrieking of a phone ringing, blaring out some dreadful, dooming music.

"You got it," Matthew answers sharply, then commands for us to leave.

One brief tiny second he takes his eyes off from me. That's when I grab the screwdriver sitting on the table next to me, shoving it inside of my pants.

I remember asking Aidan to please take care of it after he put a few toys together for the baby. Now all I want to do is kiss him for leaving it there. I swipe it, then stand as if I'm doing what I was told.

"You won't get away with this. There's security downstairs." Mom juts her chin out. Her backbone is back in place. Thank Christ, because unlike her tough daughter, who no one knows is dead or alive, Grace has completely fallen apart. Her sobs spear through my chest. She needs to get it together. "Grace, you need to be strong. Think about Anna. I know she's alive. They all are." Her eyelids are swollen, her forehead crinkled, her ivory complexion ashen and pale.

"There's no one downstairs. Well, there was, but he's followed Dilan and Anna out the building," Matthew says gruffly and with more confidence than I like.

"No. She's all I have. She has to be all right," Grace cries out. "You would be wise to listen to the crazy lady over here." He juts his thumb in my direction. I stand stone still. He's trying to bait me. To break me and make me weak. Fuck him. He underestimates me. They all will. I

188

will survive this time. My son will survive, and I'll be goddamned if I let them take any of my loved ones away from me.

"It's time to go." The piece of shit manhandles my mom once again by gripping her tightly on her upper arm while training his gun at my son and me. I move onward out the door, my anxious mind tediously wishing there were something I could do to stop him. I can't get to the screwdriver while clinging onto one of the only reasons I'm strong enough to survive this.

"Where are we going?" I have no clue which one of them is talking right now. All I can do is try and cling on to what sanity I have left, to hope someone finds us, saves us before... God, I cannot even let myself thin k about what could happen. Or why. Money is an evil bitch. I hate it. It's unfortunate we all need it to survive. Does someone really need that much? I know damn well Salvatore pays his men above what they're really worth. Especially this fucker, who deserves to die at the hands of John Greer. The cleaner. The sweeper. The man who will silence you once he's finished gutting you like a fish. I can only hope he's been called.

My flip-flop-covered feet slap against the cold tile floor of the passageway into our building. The warm air sweeps across my skin when we exit. We keep moving on, down the few stairs that lead into our apartment building from this side of the building. I see a dark van parked along the curb.

And then I see him. Junior and his snarly, self-assured grin in the passenger's seat. The security guard from my building is in the driver's seat. I ignore them when I'm pushed forward past the van. Don't ask me how I can feel it, or sense it, or whatever the hell you want to call it. But I do. I feel him. I feel Aidan and his strength spill out of the back of that van. He's in there. My perception tells me so. I want to run to him, make sure he's okay. But I keep going, holding one half of my heart in my arms while the other half is just a few feet away from me, yet untouchable. He's hurting in there. Oh god, does my chest ache.

We're all shoved into another van. Unlike the one in front of us, this is a goddamn mini-van. "Nice ride, jack-hole." My flaming mouth gets slapped for that comment. My child is tugged from my arms. I yell, and kick, and draw blood from this fucker who dares to take my son from me. "Give him to me! He's a baby! He's done nothing to you! Give me my son!" I scream. The sting on my face is nothing compared to having my child taken from me.

I remember nothing after that. Not a damn thing. Until I'm startled awake with a kick straight to my stomach.

ANNA

Something inside of me breaks angrily. Snaps off like lead at the end of a pencil. I cannot believe the evil, vindictive creature in front of me is even human. But he is. Humans kill other humans. We may not be classified as animals, but some of us sure the hell are.

He's a despicable man who shot Dilan, who dragged me by my hair into the back of an alley, tied my hands together, and beat me with his fist. Kicked me repeatedly in the ribs, while calling me every name but the one my mom blessed me with. I hate him.

People take pain in so many ways. Me, I can hardly breathe, barely see. I feel pain everywhere. But nothing is worse than feeling the pain radiating off of someone else.

I'm not sure how long we've been cruising along. Long enough to know Aidan has checked out on me. Who can blame the man when his life walked by us and we heard those murderous screams coming from Deidre right before we pulled away? I need to do something, anything to get him to come back to me and fight.

Junior has brought enough pain into my life, and now as I sit here staring at Aidan, who cannot seem to move, through my swollen eyes, my anger turns me into one of those animalistic creatures. I'm going to kill this rat-bastard.

190

I nudge Aidan on the leg when the phone he has shoved somewhere in his pants continues to go off. The sound is faint, but I can hear it. "Aidan," I whisper. He finally concedes to me getting his attention, when the little bit of vision I do have detects him fluctuating his long legs in my direction. "Don't move, and no matter what I do, do not make a sound." He's looking right at me, I can feel it. The closer I get to him, the more I can see he's looking right through me. Oh, god. I have to do something, anything to get him back here to the present. His entire life waltzed right by us. So did mine. My mom is wherever they are, too.

Like me, he's stuck in here going to god knows where. I heard Deidre screaming for them to give her Diesel back, and then all of a sudden, the screaming stopped and the laughing coming from the front of our van began while a gun was shoved inside of Aidan's mouth to get him to shut up and sit down.

And the man driving the van. I'm not sure if Aidan has recognized him or not. I have. He's the security guard of the apartment building they live in.

I may not know much about this mafia life these men live. But I do know these men love with everything they have. They are selfless, righteous, caring, and have the biggest hearts out of anyone I have met. Aidan especially.

Who comes to a woman's home they don't even know, to take her away, to protect her and her mother from the scum of a heartless person who wants to take the life of an innocent person?

They aren't perfect by any means. I've heard about the things they do. I know they commit crimes, steal, and god knows what else. I don't care. They saved me.

Dilan took bullets that were meant for me tonight. I know they were. I don't even know if he's alive. I can only pray and hope he is. My heart is breaking right now. It's time someone stood up to this son of a bitch.

Aidan continues to stare right through me. I scooch over as close to him as I can get once the vibrations begin again. I scope out the two monsters in the front, then quickly force my hands forward, my body straddling his legs, and I shove my hands into the front of his jeans. He flinches but says nothing. My hesitant hands find the phone, thankful it's right there at the top.

"Don't take it out. They'll see the screen light up. Just start pressing buttons," Aidan whispers vaguely. Well, shit, if I had known that all I would have had to do was stick my hands down the pants of a man who surely doesn't want them there, I would have done this several minutes ago. Whatever it takes, Anna. I nod, doing what he asked, slinking back into my corner after doing so. The phone stops. And my plan begins.

"Where are you taking us?" Even though I'm scared to death, I'm able to keep my pitch steady.

Just as Junior turns around, his crazed eyes make me slink back into the corner more. I want him to think I'm afraid of him. I'm not, well, that would be a lie. I'm frightened, not only for me but for all of us. If our loved ones are following us, he obviously plans on killing us all. This is for all of them. I will sacrifice getting beat, killed if it means somehow, someway my friends and family can escape.

"Aidan's sacred place. The place he loves so much. You know where, don't you, Aidan?" What a cocky arrogant asshole. He's taunting Aidan. What a little shit.

Aidan remains passive, although he cranes his neck toward the front. I see every muscle in his face twitch and convulse as if each nerve is trying to fight against the other. He's holding back his anger.

"Do you mean the land in Pennsylvania?" I question peculiarly. This gets me a jerk of the head from both of the men, at least I think it does. My eyelids seem to be growing heavier by the second. They're begging me to let them close, but I refuse.

A chuckle comes from the condescending man who thinks he holds all of the cards here. Oh, no. My heart starts beating wildly in my chest, my thoughts going crazy like a caged bird drumming his frenzied little wings.

"You are an evil man. Pathetic and insane. I feel sorry for you. A man who has never been loved by anyone. A man who is jealous of this man here," I lift my scraped up arms, aiming them in the direction of my true brother. "That's really what this is all about, isn't it, you pig. You've been sloping slowly downhill in the shadows of a real man your entire life, and you can't take it anymore. So you're going to take him and his family and show him you're the man, aren't you? Well, let me tell you something. You're no man. You're nothing." I've identified him perfectly. I feel his self-esteem deflate just as I feel his glare bleed me dry.

"For those remarks right there, you little bitch, you'll be the first one to die."

CHAPTER TWENTY-ONE

AIDAN

All hope of happiness have been sucked out of my world. My future has been stolen. And in its place is an abandoned vastness of nothingness. I sit here, stunned, wishing I could have done anything to not have heard the aching screams come from the love of my life. I know she's alive, I know my son is as well. I can feel it in what little bit of my heart is still hanging loosely in my chest.

I cannot begin to imagine what kind of numbness, vacantness, or other emotions Deidre is experiencing right now. Matthew must have stripped our son right out of her arms by the way she was screaming for him to give him back to her. And then there was silence. The only things I heard were doors being slammed shut, an engine being cranked on, and then we took off.

I can honestly say I thought I hated Junior before, but that wasn't hate. It was more like shame, pity for even having to associate myself with him at all. Hate isn't even strong enough for what I feel for him right now. Only the love I have for Deidre and Diesel outweighs the hate I encompass for this man.

Hate lies at the destructive end of the spectrum while love lies at the positive side. My love is more powerful, more meaningful, and this low life, who both hates and loves himself, has tipped that scale in the right direction for me and the wrong one for him.

I know exactly where he's taking us. I've traveled this road before. He's taking us to my land. The land he will never get. I made damn sure he would never get it if anything were to happen to me. Those papers I signed at Calla's office were papers signing this land over to Roan. Junior may have said he didn't want it, but he's a damn liar. He's bringing us here to set about whatever fucked-up plans he has in his head to try and destroy me. Only, I have plans of my own. I may take my last breath in a few hours, who the hell knows, but it sure as hell won't be without making sure he swallows his right along with me.

"Aidan." I feel Anna nudge me, move her body closer to mine. The phone wedged in my pants keeps going off, vibrating against my skin. I can't get to it.

When she tells me not to move no matter what she does, and her tiny little, cold hands meet my sweaty skin, I know exactly what she is trying to do. Although she cannot pull this phone out. I tell her so. Feel her pressing her fingers against the screen until it finally stops moving.

I hold my breath, hoping like hell she hit the right button and whoever has been trying to call can hear the words that escape from her mouth. She's brilliant. In control. Which is more than I can say for myself right now. This beaten woman is smart, intelligent, and if I could pull my head out of my ass and get my hands out of these motherfucking cuffs, I would hug her right the fuck now, help her in the same way she is trying to do me.

I listen to her try and get him to tell us where we are going. My mouth is glued shut to let her finish whatever plan she has mustered up. It doesn't take a genius to figure out she is egging him on by lashing out at him. She's trying to put more attention on herself. Only I know Junior. He may despise her, think she has stolen money that he believes rightfully belongs to him, but his plan is to basically kill her. However, the blueprint he has sketched out is to make me watch, to see me suffer as he snuffs out the lives of the people I care about.

On the inside, I laugh as Anna insults him over and over, his egotistical self-love for himself being placed into a meat grinder, mixed and finely chopped until there's nothing left but tiny morsels of crumbs.

The instant he says he will kill her first, I am pulled back to reality, paying attention to the brave woman, who is burying her fear inside of her. Her entire body trembles from the notion of his slaying words. It doesn't make her shut up though. She eggs him on more.

"That's where you're wrong, you pussy ass. You will be the first one to die. Then your lost little puppies following your orders will die. You're a stupid man by following this piece of shit around." Her gaze drifts to our driver. I follow her gaze. Struck dumb as fuck when I finally recognize who he is. Jesus. He's been working the night shift since the first day I met Deidre. Fucking idiot. Junior will dispose of him. Stupid fucking greedy people who have no reason even to live. They have no idea how precious life is. Who gives a fuck if he dies? I sure the hell don't.

"You don't have a lot of room to talk right now, little lady. I'm the one behind this wheel. While you're the one trying to piss me off by running your mouth. You don't see my hands tied up. Keep talking all you want, I'm finding you quite entertaining." He cranks the wheel, which takes us down the road to my land. I catch his eyes in the rearview mirror. He may not be able to see me, but I hope like hell he can feel me. I'm sending the fucker a warning. Letting him know that these plans they may have calculated out will not go as easily as they think they will.

"I'm not afraid to die. Are you, Junior?" Anna doesn't even wait for his reply. She twists the screw on the grinder into his back even more. "I think you are. I think you're probably even shitting yourself right now. Stinking up your self-righteous little ass even more." I may not be saying a word right now, but I have my reasons for it. I want this fucker to think he's broken me. The minute I have the opportunity to strike at him, I'm taking it.

"Stop the vehicle," Junior demands. His voice is thick with reassurance. *Big mistake, Junior. I know every part of this land. Open this back door, I'm begging you to.*

"I don't need this cunt anymore. Kill her. Then tell Matthew to back his vehicle up. I'm going to run over her dead body back and forth until she is pummeled into the motherfucking ground."

"Oh, no." I block out Anna's frantic words, her trembling body, and her ragged gasp for breath as I wait for them to exit. We have no time to waste. One door slams, then the other.

"Listen to me. Get the phone out now." It takes her more time than I like for her to get her shit together. When she does, she darts out of her corner and takes the phone out of my pants, her hands shaking uncontrollably.

"Wh… what are you going to do?" she stutters.

"I have no goddamn clue. Whatever I do, you take that phone and you run, Anna. You don't stop running no matter what you hear back here. Do you understand me?"

"But what about all of you? My mom…" She's starting to break.

"Goddamn it, Anna, fucking run. Hide. Then pray the phone's battery isn't dead, hit a damn button, and tell whoever you talk to we're two miles east of Cheery Wood Lodge." There's no more time to say anything else. The doors swing open, the lights from the other vehicle damn near blinding me.

I strike, making my move the instant whatever the hell his name is reaches for Anna. I lift a booted foot, connecting right with the middle of his throat. He stumbles backwards, coughing, out of breath as he wheezes for air.

"Run, Anna," I scream as I jump out of the vehicle, staggering as I try to land on my feet. I have no clue what the fuck I'm doing or if she's even taken off. I do know Junior seems a bit stunned, then those icy orbs of his locate me and his gun aims in my direction. "Not fast enough, fucker." I swipe his feet right from underneath him. He falls to the ground. I get one good kick into the side of his face before a gun is shoved against my temple by none other than Matthew.

"You're going to die slowly for that. Goddamn it." Junior stands up, the side of his face plastered with pieces of gravel.

"Fuck you," I spit at him again. This gets me a bitch slap to the face, my head flinging to the side.

That's when I see Beth and Grace in the other vehicle. There is no sign of Deidre or my son.

"You fuckers. Where is my son?" My eyes never leave Beth's for one minute. She's pointing to the back of the van, screaming. "She's back here! She's back here!" *God, sweet-tart, hold on, hang on, baby. Feel me. My heart is beating inside of your chest.* Those are the words I'm trying to convey to her through my mind.

"Your son is no longer your concern, Aidan. The minute you draw your last breath right along with his slut of a mother, her mother, and if my bullet aimed right where I wanted it, her dad, too. Then it looks like the boy is mine. And since you're going to tell me exactly where our mother is before I kill you, well, the way I see it, I'm his next of kin. Looks like I'll be raising your boy." His cynical words sting. Cut jaggedly through my heart. Well then, fuck it. If he wants to kill me, then bring it the fuck on.

I look at every single one of these fuckers, my head snapping from the man on his hands and knees still trying to regain his composure, to Matthew, the betrayer to Salvatore. Then to the arrogant bastard who put this plan all together. That's when I realize Anna got away. Time for me to stall. And by doing so, I crunch my skull into Matthew's. God that hurt. I feel the pain from my blow to his head for all of five seconds before I feel a heavier blow to the back of my head.

"What about the little bitch? You know she will tell them where the hell we are. I'm telling you now, man, there is no time to fuck around. Salvatore is one mean bastard. You need to finish them all off now." This is coming from Matthew, whose gun is still aimed at me, while he holds his other hand over the gash on his forehead. He should be nervous. They all should be. Then it hits me. Matthew's phone. If he has the one on him that he uses for Salvatore, then they're closer to finding us than I thought.

I allow my ragged form to lapse the rest of the way to the ground as I roll my eyes, listening to Matthew carry on. *You should have thought about the consequences, you fucker, before you committed the ultimate sin to the family.* Death by association and all that shit.

"You're right. I have a plane to catch, but first, I need to know where my whore of a mother is. Stan, pull your dick out of your ass and drag the bitch and her mother out of the van. He can watch them die first." Stan? You're going to die, Stan.

Still, I don't move. I'm not sure if I can. Christ. This cannot be happening. It's me against the three of them. My hands are literally fucking tied. Whoever is coming needs to get here like now, goddamn it.

I squint ever so slightly, the sound of gravel crunching from the other side of the van marking my ears like a dead man walking.

"Drop her right here. Right next to her lover." I smell her before I see her slammed to the ground with more force than she can handle. She shutters. Then he kicks her in her stomach, her frame rolling over to face me as she sputters and coughs, clenching her stomach. Those stunning eyes I fell in love with flutter open, shocked.

"Aidan. Oh, my god." Her voice is hoarse.

"Shh, Baby. It's all right." My strong girl loses it then, she's no longer with me. "No. No, it's not. They... They have him." She bolts up, her long messy, matted hair flying wildly. "Where is he? Where is my baby?" Loud, maddening screams come from within her.

"Jesus Christ. Not this again. Bring out the kid. Just fuck it. Bring them all out. I'm done here." My head is about to explode. The rigorousness from Junior's squeaky, high-pitched voice alone is enough to make me want to light the damn ignition. Jesus.

My skin melts off of me when I sit up, watching as Stan drags a hysterical Grace out of the van, her fingers clawing, grasping at Stan's hands clenched around her throat.

A taste in my mouth so bitter exudes from every fiber I have. "That's enough, you fucking bitch. Does it make you all feel like a man to lay your hands on a woman? Because the way I see it, all three of you are fucking pussies. The only man here you have handcuffed because you all know if you un-cuffed me, I'd fucking kill you," I fume. I honestly see sparks flying out of my mouth, that's how angry I am. How close to the end of my tether I am to help them all.

"The way I see it, we're the smart ones here, fuckface. None of us are about to die. None of us are about to watch those we love die, and none of us can do fuck all about it. Now, sit back and watch." Stan turns his attention back to Grace. He lifts her up by her throat. Her eyeballs bulging, she's choking and sobbing. I cannot sit here and watch him kill her. One of these motherfuckers can shoot me in my back.

"Oh, god. We have to do something. He's going to kill her. Wait," Deidre murmurs as she sticks her hand inside of her shirt, pulling out a screwdriver. "Don't move," she whispers. Fuck, if I could kiss her right now, I would. Fuck that. I'm marrying this woman.

It's comical, really. She has placed my weapon in my hand. A screwdriver. The funny thing about it is, I can tell this handy tool is mine. The worn-down wooden grain of the handle tells me it was a gift from my grandfather. I'm going to pick these cuffs off in record time. "Stay close, baby," I whisper, my eyes trained on the other side of the van where Matthew stands, watching Stan.

Her body trembles more, but she glides her back up against mine. She shakes and shivers, whimpers and cries. I jiggle and finagle, digging deep to try and get the end of this thing inside the hole. It's no use. The hole is too small. But I'm not about to give up. I'm left with no other choice.

"Deidre, baby. You have to take this now and run and stab him in the side of the neck. Don't argue. Don't say a word. DO IT. If you don't, he's going to kill her. Aim for his jugular. Do it now."

I drop the screwdriver into her sweaty palms. I will survive this. We all will. What my woman does next makes me fall for her even more. She sprints forward, her body lunging in the air, and she nails the maniac right in the side of his neck. The world stops for these pieces of scum who think they can control my world. Stan releases his hold, staggering backwards, blood gushing out where my screwdriver is lodged in his neck.

There's screaming, gunshots, and dust flying. "Get up," Junior barks in my ear and places a gun at the back of my head.

"Where is she?"

"Who?" I'm acting like I don't know who he's talking about.

"Our mother, asshole. Where is she?" He presses the gun in farther.

"She's in hell, Junior. I do believe she's been there since the day she had you." My voice has no tone. No care. Nothing.

"All right. You want to play. I have about fifteen minutes to play. Watch, big brother."

"Matthew, tie them all up against those trees." I look to where all three of the women are now huddled together. All I see is her. My brave one. We'll get out of this. I have to believe we will. This is not the time to be thinking about this, and yet I cannot help it. I love her, every part of her. I hope against hope that she is strong enough to handle what she just did. She killed a man. His dead corpse lies ten feet away from her. She's clinging to her mom, and I stand here watching all that hope drain out of her.

"Deidre," I call out. Her head whips in my direction. Our eyes lock for one brief moment before she is pulled out of my view.

"You won't get away with this. Our family will find you. It won't take them years, months, or even days to get you." Deidre looks Junior right into his eyes. Her lips tremble slightly, there's no happiness, no sweet, no tart, just a blank, deadly stare. She's giving up. Her sassy spark I dove right into and fell in love with is gone.

One by one he snatches them up, drags them by their hair, and ties each one of them to a tree with their hands stretched behind them and pieces of material shoved in their mouths.

"You are sick man," I spew when he pushes me forward.

"Maybe so. Bring me the kid." He reels around in front of me. I refuse to look at him. My only concern right now is to watch her reaction, the mother of my child, the woman who taught me the meaning of love.

"I say leave the kid in the van, don't let them see him. Besides, the little punk has obviously slept through this whole thing. And we need to get the fuck out of here." Matthew steps in front of Deidre. My view of her is gone. All I see are her unsteady legs. Wobbly. Unstable.

"I really wanted to make you choose which one of these bitches to kill first. By the look in your eyes, you've made my mind up for me." Junior completely ignores Matthew and squares his shoulders back like he's already won.

That's when it happens. The only perfect explosion of my still beating heart is when I see Matthew slump forward, and before his knees even hit the ground, Junior screams out in pain when he's shot in the shoulder of the arm holding his gun.

I lift my foot, slamming it into his arm, kicking the gun out of his hands as I do so.

"Jesus, John, get these damn cuffs off of me!" I yell. I know it's him. There is no one else I know who can sneak up undetected and shoot two people within a matter of seconds.

"I got him." Roan. Fuck me. I may kiss the motherfucker after I have my family safely tucked close.

"She told you you wouldn't get away with this. You fucked up asshole." Roan punches the piece of shit lying on the ground in the face, while he squirms around like the little bitch he is.

"Do you have a key in these pockets, man? If so, I need it. My brother here has a job to do." He shoves his hands into Junior's pocket.

"Fuck you," he shrieks out in pain.

"No, thanks. Dead stinking pussy ain't my thing." He then stands up and looks me in the eye. No words need to be exchanged right now. He knows this as well as I do. Walking behind me, he takes my hands, and I hear the sweet sound of the cuffs being unhinged. I'm running to the van before they even hit the ground.

I lose it then at the sight of my boy sleeping soundly in a car seat. I need to feel him. To feel his little heart beating against my chest. To inhale his scent. To divulge in this life that's part of me. He whimpers and stretches when I take him out. He wakes the moment I cradle him in my arms. Those big eyes are wide. A sleepy smile spreads across his perfect face.

I turn to bring him to his mom. That's when I notice several members of my family. John, Salvatore, Anna, and Alexis Drexler. My mother.

CHAPTER TWENTY-TWO

DEIDRE

It's dark. Even though it's the middle of summer, I'm shaking as if I'm cold.

It's over. My family is safe. I should feel remorseful, guilty for taking another person's life. I don't.

How can I when my entire world's lives were at stake? When my child was torn from my arms, right along with my heart? Maybe when the reality of what I've done finally hits me, I will. Not right now. Not with Diesel wide awake, chewing on my finger, not with Aiden having one of his big hands running through my hair while his other one caresses the side of our son's cheek.

We're almost to the hospital, where both my dad and Dilan are in surgery. That's all we know. All the information Cain was able to tell Aidan when he called him. My mom is too frantic to call the hospital herself, we all are.

I glance up from the backseat of Roan's truck to the woman driving, swerving through traffic like a racecar driver. My mom. Her only mission right now is to get to the man she loves. The man who holds her heart. My dad. I know he's going to be fine. He has to be. He's a fighter, a father, and a grandfather. I'm honored to be his daughter. Those are the first words I will tell him. The exact words I told him when he stood by my side when I fell apart.

Not this time. I refuse to let the enemy steal any part of my true identity from me, to strip away the love that symbolizes my life.

Everyone is silent, too silent really. But hell, we've been through it tonight and survived. There are so many things I want to say and do. None of it matters, not now. Everyone's lost in their own thoughts.

Anna sits quietly in the passenger seat, her arm around her mother's shoulder. Grace is not moving, either. I've seen her eyes many times, from my own reflection gazing back at me. They're blank, left of the reality surrounding her. She's going to need help. Lots of it. I fear for Grace. I've walked in her shoes, the not knowing, the horror, dread, and distress you're under. You lose all control of rationality, you fear for the one life you have as well as the life of your child.

Anna needs medical attention in the worst way. How she ran through those woods like she did, in the pain she must have been in, shows us all what a person will do when the will to survive is strong enough. You push headfirst, worrying about your battered body last, to help not only yourself but those you love.

And she looks broken but still strong enough to soothe her mother. I know the dread inside of her has to be eating her alive. It's the same way Aidan feels. It's pouring out of him like water from a busted damn. Dilan. I don't know much yet, but what I have overheard is he was barely breathing by the time Aidan stumbled upon him.

After John untied us all, the first thing I did was run to where my heart was, straight into Aidan's arms, the two of us clinging, fusing our souls back together, with our child in between us. Peace. All I felt in that moment was peace. That and the fact he decided to leave with me. No questions asked.

I know he wanted to be the one to kill Junior. As morbid as it sounds, I'm proud of him for allowing John to handle it. Unlike me, he won't have to live with killing someone. Even though the man's life I took was nothing but a piece of shit who deserved to die, it may hit me hard when the power of us surviving hits me. Then again, maybe it won't.

I'd do it all over again if the end results were the same as they are now.

Who I'm really stunned about is Alexis. I knew where she was staying, knew her story and why she treated her son the way she did. So many questions are left unanswered. Aidan honored her with a thank you, and we left. Now, both her and Roan are trailing behind us in his truck.

"Aidan." My mom's anxious voice calls out as we pull into the emergency entrance of the hospital.

As if he can read her mind, he releases his fingers from my hair, removes his hand from Diesel, and climbs out of the truck the minute she puts it in park.

All three of the women in the front step out. Anna, who can barely see, gently guides her mother as they all make their way for the emergency doors.

Aidan hikes up into the truck, glances back at me with a wink, then drives into the visitors' parking. He turns off the ignition, gets himself out, rounds the front of the truck, and he's right back where he was as if he never left my side at all. The door wrenches open with a big, fat yank. Aidan Hughes, eyes flaming with tears in them, is the most beautiful man I will ever have the privilege of looking at.

"I know you want to go in there, and god, this is so selfish of me to ask of you right now. But Christ, woman, if I don't have my mouth on yours..."

"Shut up and kiss me," I insist.

I've never wanted him to kiss me more. To feel his lips wrapped around mine... to feel his tongue licking, taking, and drinking in what is his. Letting me savor what is mine. My chest rises and falls more hastily than it ever has before. When it comes to Aidan, I'm always in a hurry, and he's always slow. Savoring. Despite everything we've been through tonight, our mouths mold to each other's with ferocity. It's sloppy, wet, and the best kiss. And I will cherish it for the rest of my life. Because that's what we have now. The rest of our lives.

"We'll meet you inside." Roan clears his throat and shuts his door, leaving the three of us alone. I glance over to Alexis, who seems to be out of place here. Why is she here anyway? I mean, what does she think she will gain? Does she think Aidan is going to forgive her? This is what I mean about questions.

I tear my gaze from her. I cannot stand the sight of the wicked woman less than twenty feet away from me. She gave birth to an unbelievable man, an individual who would have loved her with everything he had if she had purely done the best job God gave her. To simply love him. Instead, she walked down the path of her own self-righteousness. Calculated with the behemoth of her husband and his prodigy and destroyed the one and only childhood he will have. No, I hate her. She will stay away from him, away from our baby. I don't care what I find out, what she tries to prove, she will always be a part of this pre-meditated plan as far as I'm concerned.

"We need to get in there. They should look you over," I say. He's quite banged up himself.

"Not happening. My healing is right here. In my arms, in that car seat." I drop my forehead to his while he imprisons me with his arms. I wish I could bathe in this moment forever. Bottle it all up and never let him go. His words break me from my little family bubble. "But you, my brave woman, need to get in there and be with your mom. And I want them checking you out."

"And what about you? If you refuse to have them look at you, then I am, too," I say, peering up into his still glassy eyes. My heart is breaking for us all. I watch his facial features morph into a terrified expression. His countenance shows he's recalling, remembering. He lets his tears fall. I take my thumb and brush them away.

"I know Dilan's parents are here. They have to be. I'll find them then come to you. Once we know that both of them are okay, we'll get looked at together. Deal?" His voice is hoarse. "Deal, but I don't want to leave you," I verbalize. "Then we'll find out everything together.

Right now though, lets get him inside, see if they have formula and diapers to take care of our little guy here first." And this is one of the many reasons I intend on keeping him forever. Any man who puts his family first is just that, a man. We embrace each other once more. My eyes are examining his mother still standing there, witnessing us convey how strong our bond is. I want her gone. But I continue to bite my tongue, knowing this isn't the time or place to tell her she can leave anytime she wants.

"I love you," I say softly." "I love you too. So much, Deidre. Now, come. Let's get you to your mom." He helps me out of the truck. Gently. Carefully placing me on the ground. Then he gathers Diesel, pulling him into his arms. I shut the door behind us, while Aidan locks it and stuffs the keys into his pocket. The right side of my stomach stings. I hold back my groan, gritting my teeth from the pain. I won't allow him to see I'm physically hurting as much as I am. He'll make them look at me, and right now, I don't want anyone's hands on me but his.

When we turn around, he slips his hand into mine, grazing his thumb across my wrist. Together, we make our way across the short trek through the parking lot to the entrance. We both look up, noticing Alexis still standing there.

"Alexis," he greets her politely. I say nothing. "I didn't mean to eavesdrop, but I um… I overheard the two of you saying you needed a few things for him." She looks attentively to our son. My instincts immediately want to hide him from her. I don't. "I can ask, get the things he needs, while you two check on your family." I study her while she waits for Aidan to answer. She's wringing her hands. Nervous. Unsure.

"I'd appreciate that," he says somberly. "Okay, then. I'll do that," she speaks quietly, her eyes never leaving Diesel.

Aidan pulls me with him. That's all he gives her as we walk into the hospital, ready but not ready, and terrified to find out what's going on.

I'm instantly assaulted with flashbacks of the last time I was here, even though I don't remember being brought here. I do my best to push the memories aside, focusing on finding my mom. But those horrific images are still haunting me, trying to a great extent to surface, to break me down. I won't allow it. I'm stronger than those memories. Aidan squeezes my hand when we approach the receptionist behind the counter. I know he can hear the foreboding, dark, and ugly trepidation in my voice when I give her my dad's name, explaining I'm his daughter.

She tells us surgery is on the third floor. Aidan then asks her about Dilan. Without hesitation she explains his family is also in the same waiting room.

Diesel starts to fuss as we make our way to the elevator. Aidan releases my hand to soothe him, talking to him and rubbing his hands up and down his back.

"You okay, baby?" he asks when we step into the elevator, concern for my well-being written all over his handsome face.

"Yes," is my reply. He seems to be appeased with my answer. Either that or it's because we've already reached the floor. We step out of the elevator and turn right to where the sign directs us to the waiting room. My chest tightens. My nerves fray, threatening to tip me over the edge the minute I see my mom with her hands over her face. Calla and Cain are standing in the corner, arms wrapped around each other.

A couple I don't recognize are sitting with Cecily, along with Alina and her mother and father, Charlotte and Ivan Solokov. God, what they must all be going through right now. The not knowing, the waiting has got to be slowly killing them all.

"Mom," I say quietly when I near her. "Oh, sweetheart." She stands, her legs shaky. I bring her into my arms, pinning her worrisome body close to mine.

Aidan jerks his head in the direction of the couple across the room. I'm assuming they are Dilan's parents. I nod, watching the two of them disappear.

"Anything?" I ask. The second I do, we both turn around to a deep voice calling the name of Stefano La Russo.

"That's us." Mom lifts her head from my shoulder and grips firmly onto my hand, leading us to him.

"I'm his wife, Beth. This is our daughter, Deidre." Her voice is revealing her worry.

"I'm Doctor McNeal. I've just performed the surgery to remove the bullet from your husband's shoulder. First, let me ease your worried minds. He's going to be fine."

"Thank you, god," Mom expresses, while I exhale the breath I didn't even realize I was holding.

"I've done a meticulous evaluation of the surrounding tissues and joints, as well as his muscles and ligaments surrounding the wounded area. He's going to be in pain when he wakes up, but I can assure you there will be no permanent damage. Your husband, your father, is going to recover." I lose it then. All this built-up tension. The entire situation unfolding in front of me. I begin to cry. Hysterically. Uncontrollably.

Once again when I wake, I'm back in a hospital bed. Only this time when I crack my eyes open, it's to a tired but very handsome face with a smile written all over it.

"Why are you smiling?" I say groggily. He just stares at me, eyes unblinking, emotions unreadable.

"I'll tell you in a minute or two." I try and sit up. My stomach is aching and my head is killing me. I reach around to the spot that's hurting, only to discover a knot the size of a golf ball on the back of my skull. I wonder if that's the same spot Matthew hit me in. I don't know anything anymore. This entire night has been noting shy of a traumatic nightmare.

"You smacked your head hard when you passed out. Scared the hell out of all of us."

"I'm sorry," I state. My sincere apology brings an even a bigger smile to his face. What game is he trying to play? The jerk. I'm not in the mood. I glance around the room. It's not a normal hospital room. I'm confused.

"Where are we?" I utter, annoyed.

"In the emergency room. They brought you down here. Drew some blood. You're fine, Deidre. You've only been out for an hour or so. You're exhausted. The stress form the day took you under," he declares.

"And my dad and Dilan? Are they both fine?" I remember the doctor telling us about my dad. I know nothing about Dilan. Surely, they must know something by now. Then before he can answer me, I search the small confinement we're in. The curtains are drawn on both sides. There is no sign of my baby anywhere.

I sit up, not caring that dizziness or the fact I feel like throwing up makes it hard to force my words out of my mouth. I do though. Angrily. "Where's Diesel?"

Aidan tries to gently press me back down. I don't budge. "He's not with her, is he?" His brows scrunch. "If you mean Alexis, no, baby. He's not with her. He's with Alina. She took him to check him out. And before you start to freak, he's fine. Passed out in her arms, right outside in the waiting room." I rub my hands up and down my face, laying my head back down, grateful and relieved he's with Alina

"Did something happen? Why did she have to check him out?" Suddenly, I feel nauseous. I need to calm down. If he says he's fine, then I believe him.

"Precaution, I guess. He's a baby." Here comes that smile again from him.

"All right, damn you. Why are you smiling? This has been a horrible day. If I'm fine, then I want out of here. I need to see my dad. So tell me, asshole." I'm not up for this, whatever has happened he finds quite comical. He freaking starts to laugh. Like one of those throw your head back, deep, chuckling laughs.

"Sweet-tart. You're pregnant."

What in the hell did he just say?

EPILOGUE

SIX MONTHS LATER

My cock slides in and out of Deidre's tight pussy. My hands are palming her breasts. Her tight ass is rocking back, taking me balls deep with every thrust I make. To say she's starved to have me inside of her every chance she can get would be like me not feeding her when she says she's hungry.

And I love it.

"Oh, god. You feel so good," she moans. Not near as good as she does. I flick her nipples, which drives her out of her mind. The farther along she gets in her pregnancy, the more sensitive they become. I can't keep my hands off of her.

"Harder," she request. One thing about her, she is one horny woman while she's pregnant, and I have no problem driving my cock into her harder. My girl loves it rough. Hell, she loves it period.

"How hard do you want it, baby?" I let go of her breasts, spread my hands around her growing stomach, and slam into her. She cries out, and god, does she undo me.

Especially now. She's seven months along. Her bump is the sexiest thing I have ever seen. I've adjusted my cock more times throughout the day whenever I think about her carrying my child. Christ, there is no way I can control the blood flow to my cock when it comes to her and her beauty.

I grip her long hair with one of my hands, yanking her head back. She lets out a small yelp. Like I said, she loves it rough. She loves it gentle, too. It all depends on what mood my sweet-tart is in.

One day she's wacked out, forgetting shit, leaving the damn front door open. Forgetting Diesel's diaper bag. Then she cries. That's Make-Love-Night Deidre. Then the next day, she's all up in my face because she thinks she's gaining too much weight, and it's my fault once again. That's Fuck-Me-Hard-Night Deidre.

At first, I was like, "What in the ever-loving hell is wrong with you?" I had no idea pregnancy can send a woman's hormones up in the air, and they reach up every damn day and pluck out what type of day it's going to be. Crying or happy. Crazy or crazier. I just keep my damn mouth shut. No way am I sticking my own foot so far down my throat it becomes permanently stuck there.

Again, I love it.

She can't blame me this time for getting her pregnant. Well, she can. She doesn't, though. She's the one that missed a day of taking her pill, not me. And she wasn't complaining the night we conceived either. In fact, she never complained about being pregnant again so soon. She just passed out once again in the Emergency Room after I told her we were expecting.

I drive into her once more. Fucking hell. She squeezes, and my dick explodes inside of her. God, I love her. Every damn part.

"I love you, honey. Thank you for being you. For putting up with me and for having such a huge dick and knowing how to use it," she pants. I pull out of her slowly, rise up off the bed, and walk into the bathroom to turn on the shower. Chuckling all the way at some of the things she says.

I know damn well she's going to be half asleep when I peek out there. Sure as shit, she is. I stare at all the beauty that is my woman. She's feisty, yet perfect.

She's buried under the covers, her left hand draped around her belly. The ring I put on her finger last weekend on our date glistening. I didn't get down on one knee, that shit isn't me, nor is it her. However, I did try and make it as special as I could for her. I slipped it inside the small diaper bag she carries with us when we go out. The look on her face when she saw that aqua-colored box inside is a look saved for me. That's mine. One I will never forget. I shrugged. She cried. Then I proceeded to tell her I figured my sons had my last name that their baby momma should, too. That got her laughing, right along with Diesel who had no idea what he was laughing at. It's not an ordinary wedding ring. There is nothing about the crazy longing we have for each other that's ordinary. We love each other, that's all that matters. It's what they call an Emerald cut diamond. What makes it stand out from all the others is that the stone sits sideways instead of the traditional way. Or so the sales lady told me. All I knew is that when I spotted it in the display case, I had to have it.

Our dates, like every other one we go on, consist of walks in the park. Right now, it's the dead of winter. Still doesn't stop the three of us from bundling up and going outside. Even if it's only for a few minutes. This is what she wants to do. No matter if our son will remember it or not. She says *we* will. And we will. The memories we're building together as a family will last a lifetime.

The one time the two of us did leave the state was to go see my land. We left Diesel with her mom for the day. I wanted her to see the beauty of it that I do. It was fucking phenomenal to witness her expression as she took in all the trees and the river that winds down the back side of the property.

And Christ, the look on her face when she saw me standing by the river with my shirt off and my hands tucked into the front of an old pair of cargo pants, thinking about the times I came out there with my grandfather. Fuck. If she hadn't already been pregnant, she definitely would have been that afternoon.

"Get your hands out of your pants!" she screamed like she was

215

dying. I choked on her phrase, stuck my hand down farther just to antagonize her more. By the time she had marched her sweet little ass up alongside me, I had my cock harder than the damn rocks sticking out of the river. She dropped to her knees, shoving my hands out of her way. She gripped and tugged my pants down until they lay pooled around my feet. Then she took me deep in her mouth in the middle of the day, sun blazing, her pitch-black hair shining from that hot sun. She had me kneeling down beside her in minutes, ripping her panties clean off of her, and fucking the hell out of her. Twice.

And the holiday season. I've never had a Christmas like the one we had, nor will I forget the look on her face when she opened up her gifts. I bought her every Detroit Tiger item I could find. She was pissed. Until she saw the only item in her stocking. Then I was forgiven. Even though I can't see it right now, I know she has it on. Adorning her delicate neck. It's not much, but to her, it was everything. Call me a romantic, because my ass actually stepped inside a jewelry store. I knew exactly what I wanted when I walked inside Tiffany's. They had them. Two interlocking hearts. Until I met her, mine wasn't even beating. Now, it thrives every damn day to get home to her.

Again. I love it. And Christ, I love her and the life we're building.

We also do dinner with all of our friends. Anywhere we can take Diesel with us, we go. Being with her is the best thing that's happened to me. Right now, though, I need to quit day- dreaming and wake her fucking ass up. I've got a lifetime with my family to make good memories.

"Deidre, get your ass up. You only have a few hours to get ready before you have to meet the girls."

"Oh, shit." This comes from her. She flings the covers off of her, those sexy legs fall to the side of the bed, and god, my dick gets hard again when she scrambles my way. Her belly as well as every part of her takes my breath away.

"You joining me?" she challenges me as she slides her finger up my dick. I'd be a damn fool to say no. I'll join her all right. She may be late to her girl's morning, but fuck it. What she wants, she gets.

Another round of sex later, where this time I held her up against the tiled shower wall and made mad, passionate love to her, I'm bathing Diesel while she's frantically running around, making sure she hasn't forgotten anything. At least she's not swearing.

My mind drifts while I sit on the floor and watch my son play in the tub.

Why after a great morning do I think back to that night from hell? I have no idea. Maybe it's because as I watch my kid play and talk to his toys in the water, I'm thankful to be sitting here watching him.

Junior is dead. His dad is dead. I couldn't give a shit. They're right where they both belong. All I received was a nod from John when he and Salvatore finally made it to the hospital sometime around the crack of dawn, and I knew it was all taken care of. For him to come out of retirement for me shows me the type of man he is when it comes to his family. We all may live the worst kind of sins. I'm a thief and he, well hell, I don't even want my mind wandering to the shit I'm sure he has done. Not when I have the best of both worlds right here.

I do at times wonder what Alexis is up to these days. I told her the day after all this went down I would do my best to forgive her, but I will never forget. She took it to the extreme, thought that was an open invitation, that we could have a relationship. It's never going to happen. Two days after her trying, she left. I haven't heard from her since. I don't plan on ever hearing from her again. I have everything I need right here. She may have helped save my family's life that night by directing them all to where my land was. I've thanked her. I can't give her more than that. She fucked me over when I needed her the most. When I couldn't take care of myself. So no, she's not welcome in our lives.

Deidre had many more questions for her, too, after she finally came to and grasped onto the reality we were going to have another baby. I tamped that shit down. Told her it was over, that we were not looking back. EVER.

But I had to answer a few of them. She wouldn't let up. I did and then covered her mouth before she could ask any more and kissed her like my life depended on it. And it did. She's my life.

Again. I love it.

Stefano came out of recovery shortly after we left the Emergency Room. Thank god he's fine. The first thing he said when we walked into his room was, "What's wrong, sweetheart?" Deidre smiled. And I stood there like, "What the fuck?" This guy was shot. Had surgery, and the first thing he says when he sees his daughter is what's wrong? If I didn't know before that moment that I wanted to be the best dad I could be to my kids, I knew it then. Life may throw you as many lemons as they want, how you deal with it is up to you. Even when you're down and out, sick or on your deathbed, your kids always come first. I knew it all along, but watching Deidre break down and cry and her dad take her in his good arm made me realize I was damn lucky to have her. She was taught how to love by a good man, a man who still has some aches and pains in his shoulder, but is back to kicking ass in the courtroom. Back to being a grandfather and thrilled another one will be here soon.

And Anna and Grace. Shit. Those two women are family. Grace has been more like a mother to me than mine ever was. She came out unscathed, too. Mentally that is. Deidre was worried sick about her. Hell, we all were, thinking she might fall victim to a breakdown like Deirde did. She didn't. Besides a bruised larynx. The woman is a goddamn saint, along with her daughter. My sister Anna.

Anna struggled at first. Her body was severely broken and battered. Two broken ribs. A broken nose. Bruises everywhere. That woman is tough, courageous, and I owe her more than I can ever repay her for. She's hurting still, and there isn't fuck all I can do to help her.

Her heart, I know, was shattered the most. All of ours were and still are.

Dilan. He survived, barely. He lost so much blood. It took three long days for him to wake up, and once he did, he was in and out of it for at least a week longer. His parents never left his side, until they no longer had a choice.

He took off once he was released from the hospital. Not like Deidre did last year. He told us where he was going. He needed to get away. That night destroyed him like it did me. He needed a clean break and all that shit. I understand needing time, but he's a liar and a coward. You cannot fool another fool and all that shit.

Where he needed the escape, I stayed around my family. I know there's more to it than guilt eating away at him though. Something was spoken between him and Anna on that walk, I know it. Something that made him want to take off. Dilan, like all the rest of us, is a family man. So whatever was spoken must have been too much for him to handle.

Deidre told me the conversation she had with Anna earlier in the evening before hell swept in and tried to take us all into the depths of eternal fire. Dilan heard Anna talking about him. She doesn't buy it, either. Anna refuses to talk about it with anyone. When Dilan calls, he doesn't call me. He calls Roan or his parents. Never me.

Again, none of my business. But we all hate this for Anna. The woman had it bad for him, or I should say has. Even though nothing happened between the two of them, I get it when you feel a connection so strong towards another person that it eats away at you until you feel like there's nothing left to hold on to. No give. She tried to date, not sure what happened there. Well, if you call a couple of dates dating. Some doctor who works with Alina. Total opposite of Dilan. Needless to say, we all think she's still hoping he'll come back. He may come back, but I know damn well he's been up to no good. I also know Salvatore. There is no way he doesn't have someone on Dilan's tail. Watching his every move. Especially when he spent a few years in prison. That's a whole sordid fucked-up mess of a story.

Both she and Grace work at The Bakery. Live in my old apartment.

And the money she inherited from her father? She donated it to the hospital. The children's wing. She's a saint. A warrior. And my family. Dilan needs his ass beat as far as I'm concerned. Idiot.

"Enough of this bullshit, buddy. We need to get ready." Yup, I still swear a lot. Mostly in my head. Every once in a while, the shit spews out. It's the way I am. If Diesel wants to swear, then let him. I'll teach him the when and the where he can say it. The words he can and can't say.

"Dadada," he shakes his head, but raises his arms to me anyway.

"Love you, buddy." In return, I get one of his sloppy kisses planted on the side of my face.

Again. I love it.

***

"If I walk funny down the aisle today, its all your fault," Deidre rasps out, pressing her finger into my chest. "Whatever. Get out of here. Have fun. Diesel and I will see the two of you at the church." I then kiss her, breathlessly, I might add. Then bend down and kiss my son, who's still baking away inside his mother's womb. We found out it was a boy a little over a month ago. I've given her shit about it ever since. Told her I may start up a second professional Detroit baseball team.

That shit didn't go over well. We ended up compromising finally on this baseball feud right after that. She caved, like I knew she would. Took a little longer for her stubborn ass to give in, but she did. Diesel has a Yankee bedroom now. I loved the Harley room, told her we could keep it. But she wouldn't listen, she made our feud over baseball into a feud I know will surely start with our boys. Wicked woman that she is. Her response when I told her that was. "Maybe will be living in Pennsylvania by then. Our kids will have to love the Pittsburgh Pirates. They can't go to school wearing Yankees and Tigers." God, I love her.

Our soon to be born son Harley will have the Detroit Tigers room. Little does she know once we get around to decorating his room, there will be a television on the wall. Right along with three chairs for me and my boys. Hell, I may even put one of those No Girls Allowed stickers on his door just to rile her ass.

Again. I love it.

Which leads me to now. I watch her walk out the door and head straight to her car in the driveway of our new home. No more apartment-living for my family. My kids need a yard, a place where I can toss the ball around with them. Where they can run around, do whatever they want. Be kids. And know without a shadow of a doubt that both of their parents love them and will make their childhood one they will happily remember.

I shut the door to my new home. My son is lying in the middle of the kitchen floor, his head across the back of our dog, Princess. I roll my eyes at the name. We adopted her a few months ago. She's a two-year-old yellow lab, and Diesel's best friend. He'll forget about everyone else, including me, whenever she's by him. Not today, though. I need to get us both ready. But first, I need to make a phone call.

"Come on, Princess," I call out to her after I pick Diesel up off the floor. He grunts. Says his famous word, "Damnit." Then his arms are out, his body twisting at whatever angle he can get to make sure Princess is following behind us.

Of course she is. I lay him down on the floor. He crawls right to her and plops himself back on her body the minute she lies down. She licks him, and his sweet joyous giggles have me smiling.

"Hey, man. How you holding up?" I tease Roan the minute he answers. "Ready to make her my wife," he boosts. "Any word?" I hate to bring this up on his wedding day, but hell, we've all been worried about Dilan since he left. He calls whenever he wants to, is living life on the road, in Colorado somewhere.

"Nothing." I hear the disappointment in his voice. Dilan promised he would show up for this wedding. I will personally kick his ass if he doesn't.

221

"Sorry, man. I'll be at the church soon." I hang up, shaking my head at the damn fool Dilan is becoming in my mind. He needs to pull his head out of his ass and be here for his cousin's wedding. It's a small wedding. Family and close friends only. Deidre and Cain are standing up for the two of them, along with Deidre's college friend Joelle and myself.

Gathering my big boy off the floor and his dog, I make my way out to my truck as I nod at my neighbor, who's loading his three kids into a goddamn minivan. Fucking vans. I ought to blow that bitch up.

Once he's all buckled in, I strap myself in the front seat, crank on the engine, and crank up the stereo. "Ready to jam, buddy?" I place my hand on the passenger seat, twisting my head to look at him and back out of the drive.

And we jam to The Black Moods, some AC/DC, and my boy's new favorite Michigan native Kid Rock. It's a wonderful motherfucking day.

"Let's go find mommy." I tell Diesel, tugging all of his winter garb off of him the minute we step into the church. I stop. My eyes scan her from head to toe. Mine is the only word I can think of.

"Let me take him." I stride to her. He goes into her arms for all of ten seconds before her mom and dad load up next to us and steal him away.

"You're beautiful, baby." My god. She's radiant. And all mine. Her dark green dress clings to her belly. Her breasts have my mouth watering. But it's her face that has me captivated the most. Those eyes are sparkling. She's glowing.

"I love you, Aidan Hughes," she whispers, leans up, and presses a kiss to my mouth.

"I love you, too." I wink then take my place at the altar, alongside my brothers.

The music starts, and it's in that moment I look around at the people sitting in the pews. Everyone is dressed impeccably.

All but one. The man sitting in the far corner with the over-grown hair, and the dark sunglasses on. Dilan. And that son of a bitch is not alone. Fuck, no, he's not. He's with Jazmin Maria Carlos. The daughter of the Mexican Mafia. The worst enemy of the Diamonds and the Solokovs. What in the fuck?

ACKNOWLEDGEMENTS

There are so many people to thank for this book.

First of all always and forever to my husband Tony. The man I am honored to share my life with. To me you are the perfect example of a man, a father and a husband. You stand beside me with outstretched arms waiting to embrace me every day. After all these years together, I'm still so incredibly in love with you.

My children. You've grown up. How I wish that time would stand still, even for one day just so I could hug you and tell you all how incredibly proud I am of you. Someday soon we will all be together, until that day comes. I live for your phone calls, your text messages showing me your lives. You inspire me to live my dream because you are all living yours.

To my editor Julia Goda. You came to me at the right time. You put up with my ADD quirks. You take the ball and run with it woman. AND YOU SCORE!

To CP Smith. My formatter. Thank god for you. You my love are a life-savor.

To Sommer Stein. Words don't do your work justice. Again I have a brilliant cover. You amaze me with the talent you have.

To my blog girls. Oh lord. We could spend days going on about the four of us. But let's just say my life is complete now that I have you.

To My BETA readers. Lord only knows what I would be doing if it wasn't for you. You ladies catch the tiniest detail, the simplest mistake and the whoopers. You push me to be better and not one of you are afraid to tell me like it is. That's love right there. That's trust and a friendship that will be carried for the rest of my life.

Hilary Storm. God, where do I even begin with you? This past year we have grown so close. I feel like I have a younger sister. One I can confide in. Bitch to and listen to in return. This is our year woman. We are going to rock this shit out.

Eric Battershell and Burton Hughes. My photographer and cover model. OH MY FLIPPING GOD. Truth is in the eyes and the minute mine dropped on this photo all I could think of was good lord he did it again and with Burton. A man who captured my Aidan perfectly.

To all my girls who are constantly posting and pimping my name everywhere. How can I even begin to thank you? You ladies put so much time and effort into what you do and expect nothing in return. You're selfless and it show every day. I would be nothing and nowhere without you.

To every reader, blogger out there. Sweet baby Jesus, you have all welcomed me. Helped me become what I've always wanted to be. You read my stories, you message me with thanks when in reality it should be me thanking you. For without you, where would any of us who write be? Lost, empty and not living a dream. Not doing what we love to do and that is bringing the best stories into your world. Thank you for embracing my work. For the reviews. For the sweet gestures. I adore you.

And lastly. To my sanity, my helper, my friend Helena Rizzuto. I'd have my head buried in the snow by now if it wasn't for you. The ideas you toss my way. The way you jump and have something done before I even ask you about it. The way you've come into my life and pulled those reins tight and took control. I adore you Helena. You are the greatest thing to have stalked me. HA!

Please leave a review for Aidan and Deidre when you are done. Those reviews help Authors more than you will know.

Until next time,

Kathy.

Other Books by Kathy Coopmans

The Shelter Me Series

Shelter Me

Rescue Me

Keep Me

The Contrite Duet

Contrite

Reprisal

The Syndicate Series

The Warth of Cain

The Redeption of Roan

The Absolution of Aidan

Late winter of 2016

The Deliverance of Dilan

Spring of 2016

45488615R00130

Printed in Poland
by Amazon Fulfillment
Poland Sp. z o.o., Wrocław